BURN ZONE

Burn ZONE

JAMES O. BORN

G. P. PUTNAM'S SONS

New York

G. P. PUTNAM'S SONS

Publishers Since 1838

Published by the Penguin Group

Penguin Group (USA) Inc., 375 Hudson Street, New York, New York 10014, USA • Penguin Group (Canada), 90 Eglinton Avenue East, Suite 700, Toronto, Ontario M4P 2Y3, Canada (a division of Pearson Penguin Canada Inc.) • Penguin Books Ltd, 80 Strand, London WC2R 0RL, England • Penguin Ireland, 25 St Stephen's Green, Dublin 2, Ireland (a division of Penguin Books Ltd) • Penguin Group (Australia), 250 Camberwell Road, Camberwell, Victoria 3124, Australia (a division of Pearson Australia Group Pty Ltd) • Penguin Books India Pvt Ltd, 11 Community Centre, Panchsheel Park, New Delhi–110 017, India • Penguin Group (NZ), 67 Apollo Drive, Rosedale, North Shore 0632, New Zealand (a division of Pearson New Zealand Ltd) • Penguin Books (South Africa) (Pty) Ltd, 24 Sturdee Avenue, Rosebank, Johannesburg 2196, South Africa

Penguin Books Ltd, Registered Offices:
80 Strand, London WC2R 0RL, England

Library of Congress Cataloging-in-Publication Data

Born, James O.
  Burn zone / James O. Born.
      p.   cm.
  ISBN-13: 978-0-399-15454-6
  I. Title.
  PS3602. O76B87   2008   2007029271
  813'.6—dc22

Printed in the United States of America
10   9   8   7   6   5   4   3   2   1

BOOK DESIGN BY MEIGHAN CAVANAUGH

To my friends

    the Butterworths.

        You guys rock!

ACKNOWLEDGMENTS

I would like to thank my friends with expertise in diverse areas:

Meg Ruley, a great agent who took a chance on me and believed in this book from the beginning.

George Jackson, retired ATF agent and former member of NEST, for his insights on nuclear weapons.

Lieutenant Colonel Ray Hinst, USAFR (Ret.), for his help on information about bases in Panama and other military details.

To the PBA for its support. John Kazanjian is a champ.

My very good friends at the Federal Bureau of Alcohol, Tobacco, Firearms and Explosives, West Palm Beach Field Office, for their support and inspiration. ATF is a great outfit, and I hope my books reflect this.

Karen Martin, FDLE forensic scientist, for her info on DNA and lab work.

x   ACKNOWLEDGMENTS

Nevin Smith, FDLE port security chief, for his info on ports and for making me attend training that really helped.

Neil Nyren, a great editor who always has time for his writers.

Brendan Duffy, who has made me believe that Colgate is one great school.

Michael Barson, not only for his PR abilities for Putnam but for his support from the very first novel.

Caroline Sun, another Colgate grad, for her upbeat take on everything related to Putnam books.

1

"YOU EVER THINK WE SHOULD WRITE SOME OF THIS BULLSHIT down and put it in a book?"

Alex Duarte didn't even cut his eyes to his partner. Chuck had stupid ideas like that all the time. It was better not to encourage him.

The parking lot of the Publix shopping center was too crowded for things to go right. Duarte could see that as soon as they set up surveillance. The drug enforcement guys were used to these kinds of deals, so he figured they knew what they were doing, but he didn't like the bystanders. He made a quick check of the SIG-Sauer P229 on his right hip under the loose, unbuttoned shirt. He had left his Glock at home and switched to the ATF-issued handgun.

Chuck Stoddard, his partner, slumped in the driver's seat of the immense Ford Expedition, munching on Cheetos and breathing through his mouth. Duarte thought about lecturing him about his health again, but the gigantic man would only nod in agreement and continue to eat anything that had once been an animal, mineral or vegetable. The Glock on his hip looked like a popgun in comparison to his gut.

Duarte kept the radio on low to discourage conversation. He also liked the comfort of the radio show he listened to most mornings, the conversation between the hosts and their producer. He had to admit reluctantly that he knew more about them than about most people.

During a commercial, Chuck said, "You know the DEA invited us along just so we could lay paper on the suspect."

Duarte mumbled, "Uh-hum."

"Doesn't that ever bother you? They get all the fun and we get to do is write up additional charges for the guns the dealers have on them."

"You know, Chuck, we *do* work for the ATF. Last I checked, guns were our main jurisdiction."

"I know, but I'm just saying, why can't they come on *our* deals sometimes?"

"Because if a guy is selling illegal guns, he doesn't have any cocaine or pot. If he did, he'd be selling the drugs instead. Much greater profit margin."

"DEA has got a lot more guys than us, too. Ever notice how they bring out ten guys on a deal like this?"

Duarte shrugged, keeping his eye on the lot. He had heard enough of Chuck's whining for the day. Now he just wanted to be involved in some police work. He liked being out of the office on a simple case: if the guy showed up and sold dope to the DEA undercover agent, then he'd be arrested; if he didn't, then he probably wasn't a serious dope dealer in the first place. Simple. After his last case he didn't need anything complex.

The parking lot was alive with activity: people pushing shopping carts, kids tagging along, couples talking. Most people never noticed, but on surveillance, when you were pulled out of the daily rat race and had a chance to watch, it could be pretty interesting to observe a place as simple as this. Like it was another universe but not quite parallel to the outside world.

Duarte was glad his friend at the U.S. Drug Enforcement Administration, Félix Baez, had called him in on this deal. The target was a local shlub named B. L. Gastlin, who was believed to be hooked into some Panamanian named Ortíz who traded guns illegally and imported marijuana by the truckload. That was why Duarte had jumped on the case so quickly: the possibility of working the investigation up the ladder to someone really important. He felt satisfaction when an insignificant dope dealer got an extra five years because of one of his "Armed Trafficking" charges, but to really make an impact he wanted to nail a big importer or exporter. That would also help him get a promotion. He'd passed up an opportunity for one a few months earlier, but now he wanted to try again.

Duarte checked the lot. He could see the various DEA cars, all Chevys and Fords parked near the entrances and exits. He knew that once the target drove in, they would contain him. No federal agency wanted to get involved in any kind of car chase; it was against policy and bad for the vehicles. At the end of the lot he noticed a Florida Power & Light truck with an extendable bucket parked next to a pole, a man standing in the bucket. That'd be a great surveillance ploy, he thought. No one would notice you, and you'd have a great view of the area. He still looked at situations like this from a military perspective, searching for optimum terrain and hazards once the action started. Unlike his time in Bosnia, though, there wasn't a lot of action in these kinds of deals. . . .

A blue Jaguar convertible cruised east on Southern Boulevard, and by the way the driver slowed and looked carefully toward the lot, Duarte believed this might be their man. At almost the same time, he heard someone on the radio say, "The target is in a blue Jaguar and just drove past on Southern. Stand by."

Félix, who was leaning on his car, a nice Corvette they had seized from a cocaine smuggler last year, straightened up, gave a quick nod to the two DEA cars closest to him and adjusted his shirt. Duarte was pretty sure he was checking the gun in his waistband.

Duarte had done very little undercover work and appreciated Félix's ability to remain calm and cheerful doing something so unnatural, but that was just his personality. Félix liked to talk to people—one of the differences between him and Duarte.

The radio crackled, "The target is in the east end of the lot, slowly weaving in and out. He's checking for us."

This was the hard part. Making sure you didn't look too much like a cop when a suspect conducted countersurveillance. The cars were spread out, though, and the DEA guys were smart enough to look like they belonged. The other thing in their favor was that suspects always thought they were smarter than the cops. He had never met a drug or gun dealer who didn't think he could outwit them all, bless their hearts. Arrogance was their downfall.

The Jaguar slowed to a stop near Félix and his Corvette. Although he couldn't hear anything, he knew that Félix had a transmitter somewhere on his body and that someone was listening to a receiver. His trouble signal was, "This don't look good."

Chuck wheezed and said, "Looks like it's showtime."

The man from the Jaguar, Gastlin, stepped out of the low car, his eyes still scanning the parking lot. Dressed in shorts and a loud, untucked shirt with a photo of Jimmy Buffet covering his wide stomach, he looked like a bowling pin compared to Félix's lean body. He leaned casually against the Jag, chatting.

The two men were about four rows away and ten spots back. When the arrest signal came, Duarte and Chuck would close the distance in the yacht-sized Expedition, then spring out with five or six DEA agents to secure the target and make sure Félix was safe.

Chuck said, "I know the DEA wants that Jag. You watch, they'll treat that car like a crystal egg. No matter what happens they won't hurt that car."

Duarte nodded, concentrating. Once Félix gave the arrest signal, Duarte knew he expected to have the cavalry rush in right that minute. Cops always claim the slowest time in the world is between when you give the arrest signal and when your buddies rush in. Your heart pounds, and adrenaline courses through your body.

The visual arrest signal was when Félix opened his trunk. That was the sign that he had seen the pot.

The DEA supervisor came over the radio and said, "Looks like it's going smooth. Don't move until I call it over the radio. And don't ding the Jaguar."

Chuck perked up. "See, I told you, I told you."

Duarte nodded silently, involuntarily checking his pistol. He preferred to use his hands or feet in a fight, but only an idiot tried to punch someone with a gun. He watched as the two men continued to talk, then walk to the side of the Jaguar. The target leaned in and motioned for Félix to look, too.

Then Duarte saw Félix jump. It looked like a whole body twitch, then the DEA man jumped away from the car and shouted at Gastlin. The pot dealer looked like he was trying to explain something when Félix shoved him.

Duarte sat up in the Expedition. "Chuck, something's up. Get ready."

The radio crackled on. "Let's move in. I can't tell what happened. Go, go, go."

All at once, four cars started to move.

Duarte felt his pulse increase; this was the stuff he loved about his job. Keeping his right hand on his hip, he reached across to the door handle with his left. What had happened to cause the arrest to go early? He saw Gastlin look up and notice the vehicles as they closed on him, notice, too, that, like any good undercover agent, Félix had stepped away so the arrest team had free access.

Duarte saw the target reach into the Jaguar and thought he might be going for a gun, but before the big Expedition could come to a stop, the target sprinted away across the lot with a satchel in his hand. He had grabbed the pot sample. For a chubby guy, he could really move.

The man had timed his run perfectly as the front vehicles stopped and the drivers were getting out of the cars. They also blocked the other approaching cars. The man darted toward Southern Boulevard just as Duarte jumped from the ATF Expedition and started sprinting after him. He knew big, lumbering Chuck would be behind him somewhere.

The pot dealer was obviously panicked, his head swiveling, looking for an escape, and then he saw the Florida Power & Light bucket truck in front of him and bounded up to the cab.

Duarte yelled, "Stop, police," and drawing his Sig, he raised it in the direction of the fleeing man, the DEA agents closing in from the other side.

The truck had had the engine running to provide power to the bucket, and now it lurched forward as the dealer tried to drive it away, the supports for the extended bucket scraping on the asphalt as the truck started to move. The man in the bucket shouted something, then hung on as the truck picked up speed, passing the DEA agents.

Duarte heard a car horn and turned to see Chuck in the Expedition right next to him. This was a pleasant surprise. Duarte yanked the door open and leaped into the seat. Chuck hit the gas, and they were in the chase. Alone for the moment.

The FPL truck sped up as the dope dealer apparently figured out how to raise the supports, while the man in the bucket worked the controls to lower the extended workstation as quickly as possible. The truck tilted to one side, then the other, as the pot dealer tried to negotiate the parking lot, and then suddenly the man in the bucket leaped into the low branches of a black olive tree planted in the swale.

Chuck said, "Did you see that?"

Duarte looked out over his shoulder and saw the man clinging to the tree branches. "Now he can speed up. Catch him, catch him."

The truck turned onto the side street heading south and continued to accelerate as a DEA vehicle fell in with Duarte and Chuck's Expedition. The street was empty of traffic in both directions. Thank God, thought Duarte.

Chuck brought the big Ford SUV up behind the lumbering bucket truck in a matter of blocks, then said, "Know what?"

"What?" asked Duarte, still watching the truck.

"If I got next to this thing, you could jump into the back."

Duarte had to look to see if his partner was kidding. He looked serious. "Let's see what happens in the next few minutes."

"If you say so." Chuck didn't have any plan except to follow the big truck.

Two DEA surveillance cars screamed up next to them, obviously in the same dilemma. The truck took a hard left, causing the lowered bucket to swing wide to the right side. At the next corner, the pot dealer tried to take a sharp right, and as he turned, the arm to the bucket, which was sticking out from the truck since the last turn, caught a telephone pole and swung the truck violently in a tight arc until the arm was free from the pole. The truck kept running—only now it was pointed directly at a house's yard. The heavy FPL truck thumped over bushes, glanced off a tree, and then struck the side of the one-story, dark green, old Florida house, the sound of the impact shocking. It reminded him of the explosions he had caused in Bosnia. The effect on the house wasn't all that different from those of his C-4 concoctions. The wall to the house collapsed around the cab of the truck, and the destruction continued in a domino effect because the exterior roof began to sink until the entire peak of the roof dropped into the center.

Duarte sprang from the Expedition before Chuck had even brought it to a complete stop and raced to the front door, thinking about what might have happened to the residents of the house. The front door was unlocked, causing Duarte to fear that the residents were home. He shot through the wrecked house, noticing debris scattered across the furniture, a TV lying smashed by a falling beam, bright sunshine streaming through the wide swath now exposed to the elements.

"Hello, police!" shouted Duarte. "Where are you?" He no longer cared about the arrest, fearing only for the safety of the people who might be in the house.

He heard a voice and froze: "In here." It was faint and female.

He followed the sound and pushed at the only closed door, on the east side of the house where the truck would've struck. He turned the doorknob and tried to open it, but it was hopelessly jammed by something low. He shoved and felt little give. The upper half of the door bent slightly inward.

He yelled, "Stand clear of the door!" Then he stepped back and launched the hardest, highest sidekick of his fifteen-year martial arts career. The door cracked at the site of his foot's impact. He repeated this twice more until the door split in half and he could scurry over the broken lower section. The truck's cab had come all the way inside the wrecked room, but he stole a glance and the cab was empty. A DEA agent was crawling over the wreckage into the house.

Duarte twisted his head, searching for the source of the cry.

He yelled, "Where are you?"

"In here," came the voice, and he noticed one more closed door, which had been blocked by a chunk of wall thrown by the truck.

He leaped over some wreckage, content to let the DEA guys and Chuck find the missing pot dealer. He bent down and lifted the piece of wall which had tipped down and didn't weigh that much. When he pulled the door open, an attractive woman in her early sixties stood in the middle of a large closet, wearing panties and a bra that covered very little of her breasts.

Duarte froze for a moment, staring at her. She didn't seem at all self-conscious. Finally she said, "Are you done?"

Despite his Latin coloring and dark hair, he felt himself blush. "Sorry," he said, looking down. "Are you all right?"

She mumbled something.

"Excuse me?"

She mumbled and then said, "Look at me again."

He slowly raised his eyes, but the woman was still unclothed. Now he noticed her eyes kept shifting to the shelf next to her. Then she cocked her head that way and he realized what she was trying to say. He pushed her out of the closet, then knocked out the shelf's support beam in a smooth motion, heard a yell and saw the tubby shape of B. L. Gastlin, former drug dealer, plop hard onto the ground.

Duarte dropped to his knee and threw a quick elbow into the dealer's face to incapacitate him for a second, then quickly patted him down for weapons. As he was about to call for help, the woman appeared again in the closet doorway.

Still nearly naked, she said, "Look what this asshole did to my house," and delivered a vicious stomp to the dazed man's face. If Duarte hadn't stopped her, she would've done it again.

She stepped back and said, "He shoved me in the closet and then balanced that roof beam so he could come in and let it hit the door behind him. He didn't think you'd check a room that was already blocked in from the outside."

Duarte nodded and pulled the now bloody man to a sitting position.

The woman threw in another kick to the man's ribs.

"Ma'am," Duarte said in a clear loud voice. "You'll have to stop that." He looked up at her and added, "Please tell the others where I am."

She disappeared, and a few seconds later Chuck and a DEA guy appeared at the closet.

Chuck looked down and said, "Man, Rocket, you really fucked that guy up." He looked at the DEA agent next to him and added. "Did you hear what the problem at the deal was?"

Duarte shook his head.

Chuck smiled. "He tried to play with Félix's dick."

Duarte could tell by the way the prisoner moaned it was true.

Chuck laughed and said, "Félix is old-school Cuban. It didn't go over too well."

Duarte shook his head. Some people were too stupid to live.

The DEA guy smiled. "He tell you anything?"

Duarte helped the stunned man to his feet. "Yeah. He said the Jaguar is a rental."

THE HEADQUARTERS FOR THE DEA IN WEST PALM BEACH SAT IN an office building not far from the Publix parking lot. In an interview room that had its own entrance so prisoners wouldn't be brought through the office and see the agents' faces, Alex Duarte sat and listened while Byron Gastlin stared at his cell phone and contemplated his future.

Félix Baez just kept a steady stare on the man. Duarte knew the DEA man had more experience than he did turning guys like Gastlin against their suppliers. It had taken them almost two hours to get him to make the call to Panama in the first place. He had already given up all he knew about the shadowy Panamanian smuggler known as Mr. Ortíz.

When Félix asked him Ortíz's first name, Gastlin had shrugged and said, "I don't know. I just call him 'Mister.'"

Duarte had thought the response might earn the dealer a smack, but Félix was professional. He'd dealt with guys like this a thousand times before.

Now Gastlin looked up. Sweat ran down his face like a waterfall. A pile of damp, wadded-up paper towels covered the table next to his phone.

"Just a call?" said the portly dealer.

Baez nodded. "For now. Prove you can actually talk to someone in Panama."

"And this little thing I stick in my ear will record it?" He jiggled the wire to the tiny microphone, which connected to a small recorder.

Félix nodded silently, keeping his stare on Gastlin.

The drug dealer picked up the phone and flipped the cover. His hands were shaking so badly, Duarte didn't think he'd be able to hit the proper buttons.

Gatlin looked up. "What if I can't reach Ortíz himself?"

"Will someone answer?"

He nodded, jiggling tiny jowls.

"Then talk to them."

"Sometimes I talk to his assistant, Pelly. Sometimes someone else. It depends on how busy they are."

"Would it be odd to ask to speak to Ortíz?"

"Yeah. I never have before."

"Then stick with the plan, and we'll see what shakes out. Now make the call." Félix leaned in to make sure the dealer knew how serious he was.

"Look, I only ran a few loads for the guy. Just business. I don't know how his outfit works or how big it is or nothin'."

Félix and Duarte both remained quiet and kept their eyes on Gastlin.

The man picked up the phone again and this time slowly started to dial.

Pelly wiped the sweat from his broad, rough face and swore. The stubble was only two hours old, but still it scratched his hand. He had long since given up worrying about the hair on his back and shoulders, and just tried to keep his face and neck clear—he even used an electric razor on his eyebrows every night—and still he felt people's eyes on him. The scar on his cheek didn't help either.

He didn't wince at the sound of the whip. His boss was flailing a woman he had tied over a picnic table, Pelly wasn't even sure what her offense was. Here in this village on the west coast of Panama, his boss decided what was right and what was wrong. By the size of the woman's swaying breasts, Pelly guessed it was all merely an excuse for him to terrorize a well-built middle-aged woman. He didn't know why, but he had seen it enough for him to conclude that somewhere in his employer's life he had had a bad experience with a woman who wore a large bra.

The woman let out a yelp as the short leather whip bit into her back. A thin line of blood dribbled out of an earlier lash. Pelly's only concern about these events was that they didn't do anything for their bottom line. He understood pleasure and letting off steam, even if this wasn't exactly his idea of fun, but if his boss was busy beating women he wasn't thinking about sales, shipment and secrecy, the three elements vital to any smuggling operation.

His boss had a decent sweat going from the heat, the effort and the rage which surfaced whenever he had a woman in a similar situation. Pelly had never noticed him show much interest in men, unless he was really torturing them. He seemed to have a fascination with severing parts off them. That, and beating women. Who could figure out such personal issues?

The cell phone sitting on the corner of the picnic table rang with a tone like a European police siren.

He looked at his boss, who froze, set down the whip and looked at the small phone's screen. He quickly looked at Pelly and nodded, then answered.

He started to speak English, so Pelly knew it was a customer from the U.S. His own English was okay, but he didn't have the flair of his boss.

The boss smiled as he said, "Good afternoon, Byron. I was hoping you might call soon."

The woman moaned and turned her drooping head toward Pelly, who put his finger to his mouth to shush her while the boss was on the phone.

"Por favor" was all she said, tugging her arms, which were bound at the wrists to the legs of the table.

Pelly shrugged. Maybe the boss would forget.

As if on cue, the boss started to wander off, engrossed in the call. Pelly drew a heavy Benchmade knife from his front pocket, thumbed open the blade and cut the woman loose. She immediately sprang upright and crossed her arms to cover her breasts. He nodded, and she scampered back into the house, one of several buildings owned and operated by their corporation. She had been in charge of ensuring the workers got enough food and occasional medical attention.

Pelly waited as the boss settled onto a patio chair, still on his cell phone. There were only a few people out behind the buildings. They all worked for the corporation, and most had seen a beating like this. Some of the men seemed to enjoy it.

He knew he had a few free minutes, and there was a book in the car about an Englishman who had become an artist using only his left foot. He was fascinated by stories of people who overcame handicaps. For some reason it seemed like all these people were from England, at least the really interesting ones. His favorite was Robert Merrick, who was called the Elephant Man. He knew what it felt like to be compared to an animal.

Instead of grabbing his book, though, Pelly arched his back, then bent to stretch his legs. After a moment, he started practicing a kata, then threw a few kicks into the air. Most of the men knew he had a black belt in Shotokan karate—he rarely needed it in his job, that's what guns were for—but he had cracked a few heads and knocked out some teeth for inappropriate comments, and these guys knew it.

The boss walked back to him, folding the phone as he approached. He smiled, his Spanish as elegant as his English. "Pelly, my friend, we may have the right man to ship our special load to the U.S."

"Was that Gastlin?"

"It was, and he seemed open to a load of pot. A big one. We can stick our package in the container, and he'll never even know it."

Pelly frowned.

"What's wrong, my friend?"

"Boss, I just don't see the value in shipping this thing to the U.S. It'll make it much harder for us to ship in our drugs."

His employer's face darkened. "You know how important this could be for the country. You know how I feel."

"I do, boss. I just don't know if you're thinking this through."

The boss folded his arms and tried to act calm. He looked at the loose rope across the picnic table.

"Where is Maricella?"

"I thought you were done."

The boss thought about it and said, "I was going to throw a few more on her, but she got the message. I doubt she'll make any more personal calls from the office." He looked off over the open field with the low, brick wall around it. "Pelly, I know you're a little young to understand my hatred. You were up in the mountains when the Americans rolled into the country, crushing any hope of national pride, but this is important. This is why I went into this business. This is the one load that does mean something to us. Can't you see it?"

"I understand what happened. I learned it in history class. But I don't see how antagonizing the U.S. will help anything."

His boss smiled. "If nothing else, it'll help me sleep at night."

"You're risking a fortune to sleep a little better."

"What else do I have to spend my money on?"

William "Ike" Floyd strained under the weight of the two hundred twenty-five pounds he had just bench-pressed for the tenth time. He knew his close-cropped hair, which had been growing out only for the past few weeks, would not cover the bulging vein on his temple, as he grunted then let his spotter take the weight and guide it onto the supports. He liked working on his "beach muscles"—his chest and biceps—even though the nearest beach was over a thousand miles away.

Ike lay still, enjoying the few seconds to look up the shorts of his training partner. The twenty-year-old man knew that Ike stole peeks at his legs occasionally, but he had been careful not to be alone with the larger man. Ike knew it was only a matter of time. But he had to be discreet. A man in his position couldn't be caught with another man. He had learned that lesson in another group and still had a scar under his new hair as a result.

He didn't want people to look at him and know his politics, which was why he had grown his hair out, so he'd look more respectable to the uninformed public. He knew that the things that had been set in motion were too important to risk his being recognized or having the cops follow him around. That was why he had put out the word to the others to keep a low profile, especially here in Omaha. No fights, no protests, nothing at all. It hadn't gone over big with the members, but they knew he was still dedicated, and if he said to keep things cool it was for a good reason.

Ike sat up on the bench, the blood rushing slightly to his head. The wide-open gym was generally slow this time of day, while most poor slobs were off at work. His job at the telemarketing office had him coming in tonight at six. Soon he hoped to not have to bother with a job. He'd either be a hero or dead.

"How you feel, Ike?" asked the younger man.

"Good, Sean, good." He took a couple of deep breaths to clear his head. He liked the way his nickname sounded in the young man's voice.

"You look like you can't concentrate today. Everything all right?"

He hesitated. So far no one knew who he had met through the president of the National Army of White Americans. No one knew of his plans. He was anxious to tell someone, but he knew that operational security was vital. If he blabbed, he might not go down in history. But he looked into Sean's dark eyes, and he just knew the young man was trustworthy. As well as hot.

"Yeah, I got a lot going on," started Ike. "But if I tell you anything, you gotta swear that you'll never breathe a word about it."

"I swear, I swear."

Ike looked at him, feeling the sincerity as well as seeing it in the twenty-year-old's earnest face.

"We have a chance to make one hell of a statement. We just need to focus and keep our heads down."

"What are you gonna do?"

"I met someone through President Jessup. He's a foreign man, a beaner to be exact. From Panama, but this guy can help us more than any good white man ever will. We can get attention to our cause, force the federal government to close the borders and go down in history all in one afternoon."

"How's that?"

William "Ike" Floyd smiled and said, "You know anything about the Ukraine?"

Alex Duarte watched her bound into the gym inside the Palm Beach County Sheriff's Office main building.

Alice Brainard smiled, looking like she'd just come from an Old Navy commercial, then popped onto the treadmill next to Duarte and immediately had it cranked up to seven miles an hour. Without even breathing hard, she said, "In before dark. I'm impressed."

"Busy few days. Needed the break."

"I heard about the crash."

"TV news?"

"Yeah, but the vice guys love it. Any time the DEA or FBI does something like that, they all razz each other. Having the ATF along is just gravy." Her blond ponytail bounced behind her.

Duarte nodded, knowing the police tendency to ridicule. He'd yet to pick up the habit. He thought some stuff was funny, just like anyone else, but he didn't have time to set up the elaborate practical jokes the other cops seemed to pull all the time.

"The case is rolling. We turned the dealer, and he made a call to his supplier in Panama. Looks like there's a gun angle, too. Might get a trip out of it."

She cut her blue eyes toward him. "Not bad there, Alex. Just be careful."

"Because of the crime in Panama?"

"No, because the women there are beautiful. You don't need a pretty Latina to confuse you."

He considered this as he kept up his pace.

Then Alice said, "And now you're supposed to tell me I'm beautiful and that you'd never fall for a Latina while you were away."

"Okay."

"Okay, what?"

"What you said."

She sighed and shook her head.

He ran along in silence, falling into the rhythm of the big treadmill as he pushed the pace from seven-and-a-half-minute to six-minute miles. He noticed Alice speeding up, too. This girl was impressive, beautiful too. A forensic scientist with the sheriff's office lab, she had helped him over his last, brief relationship.

Alice finally said, "So, would you like to go out to dinner after this?"

He looked over at her.

She sighed. "That's what I would expect *you* to say to me at some point." She waited, then added, "Should I just do all the talking for both of us?"

He thought that would be a good idea, but knew it wasn't what she wanted to hear, so he kept his mouth shut. If she were hungry, why didn't she just say, "Let's eat?" He knew he still had a lot to learn about women. His years in the ATF had not been conducive to discovering much about their mysteries.

He cleared his throat and said, "Would you like to have dinner tonight?"

"I would, thank you. Where would you like to eat?"

He thought about the restaurants where he normally ate.

Alice said, "You've said nothing compares to your mom's cooking. We could go by the house."

"That's okay. I'd like to take you out somewhere nice."

"Somewhere without your family?"

"I wasn't gonna invite them, if that's what you mean."

She made a growling sound and slowed her treadmill. "You moron. Just what am I to you, I wonder?"

"Huh?" He didn't slow the machine. Once you hit your stride, you never let up.

"Am I your girlfriend? Workout partner? Buddy from the S.O.? You live at home and eat there most nights, but I still haven't met your family. Am I not good enough?"

"No," he said, meaning that she was good enough. She jumped off the fast-moving treadmill as he said, "I mean, you are certainly good enough; I just didn't realize it was an issue."

She stood in front of his treadmill. "I swear that for a smart guy you can be such a jackass." She spun on her heels, then stopped a few feet away and turned back, "I'll finish on the road. Go eat with your mama." She was out the gym door in seconds, and Duarte had nothing left to do but finish his treadmill workout and head home. Three hours early.

3

THE PANAMANIAN LOOKED AT THE CALLER ID ON HIS CELL phone and smiled. The phone was virtually untraceable, and only five people had the number. He had been waiting for this call. The idiot from Florida would do nicely, but before he agreed to the deal, he'd have to hear how the fat man was going to get the load into the U.S. How tight would customs be? How long would it take? Where would he cross? He couldn't use a go-fast boat. That's why he wanted to make the load of pot too big for a speed boat. He would need a freighter.

This might be the one. He'd waited too long to pay back the Americans. Since Christmas of 1989, he had put up with their arrogance and their rationalizations for why they invaded such a small country. He knew Noriega was a crook and a bastard, but he was *their* bastard. Now, after all these years, the American public would be reminded of their mistake.

Duarte sat at the dinner table with a plate of thin, pressed steak that some people called *palomilla* steak, a pile of sweet plantains and a salad. He hadn't eaten much, but his brother had gobbled down mountains of his mother's cooking.

She looked at him from the same seat from which she had looked at him for nearly thirty years and said almost the same thing. "You're not eating enough. Are you feeling all right?"

"Yes, Ma. Just got a lot going on right now."

His father, César Duarte, looked over and asked his same questions. "Did you do good work today, boys?"

"Yes, Pop," both grown men said at the same time.

Their father looked at Frank, the older by eighteen months. "What did you do?"

"Worked on a brief to have a suit dismissed against the Toyota dealer accused of selling cars that weren't roadworthy."

"The one who was cheating people with the warranty service?"

"Cheating is relative, Pop. I think they were just good businessmen, and people are jealous."

"Is the poor woman who can't feed her kids over on Tamarind Avenue jealous? That dealer is crooked."

Frank smiled that politician smile of his and said, "A crook maybe, but entitled to a lawyer at two hundred bucks an hour, absolutely."

Alex Duarte caught his father trying to contain himself. Plumbers have little use for services that don't help people. He had made it clear he didn't see how lawyers ever helped anyone.

The older man looked at his youngest son. "And Alex, what did you do today?"

"Just follow-up on our arrest."

Frank cut in. "Hey, you think the lady whose house you destroyed has an attorney?"

Both Alex and César ignored him. Alex Duarte had to smile, realizing just how much of his father's attitude he had adopted. "We might be able to work the case up the line to someone big."

César nodded, keeping his glare on Frank to ensure he had no more comments. Then he said, "Excellent. Will this case lead to a promotion?"

"Don't know, Pop. They may not be too happy with me turning down the last one."

His mother said, "But that would've taken you so far away."

Duarte just nodded, though Washington wasn't the reason he hadn't taken it; it was the case he had become involved in. He had allowed a prisoner to escape, and that had led to a series of horrific events, including the death of a young boy, Héctor Tannza, killed by a booby trap. Duarte had pursued the case across the country, all the way into the heart of a conspiracy that made him question whom he could trust. He had had to see the case through—but it had cost him the supervisor's job. He still had no regrets. Now he realized that a promotion would come when it came. He loved his parents, and even his brother, but if he had to move it wouldn't bother him. He had spent almost two years in the Balkans. The only one he would really miss if he moved was Alice. If she was still speaking to him.

Pelly drove the Cadillac SUV behind the older Dodge pickup truck on the uneven, narrow road that cut over toward the area near Colón on the east coast of Panama. The typical, bumpy, Panamanian mountain path was often called the Cocaine Highway, for obvious reasons.

Pelly said, "You really think that following those men in a separate vehicle is wise?"

His boss smiled as he looked out at the passing tropical foliage. "No, but my days of lifting and moving are over. These two have sat with it in the warehouse for a week. I want to keep the knowledge of the crate's contents as quiet as possible."

"What if Gastlin is working with the authorities? What if they find the package?"

"Pelly, I *hope* he is working with the DEA or customs. That means they'll be looking for drugs and nothing else. If they somehow discover our little present, then we'll be as hard to find as ever. We'll just wait and buy another. I have the feeling it's a buyer's market." He chuckled.

Pelly knew his employer's arrogance could get him killed, but he had proven to be a brilliant businessman in the past. He probably did know how to push things.

"You'll see, Pelly. This will be a great thing for Panama."

Pelly let his head bob to the bounces of the Cadillac. Maybe his boss would take it as a sign of agreement without Pelly actually having to agree with any part of this crazy plan.

His boss said, "I need some lunch. Pull ahead and have them follow us to the cantina near Gamboa."

Pelly heard the second line on his boss's cell phone ring with a distinctive tone. He always answered that one formally.

Alex Duarte liked the fact that the West Palm Beach office of the DEA had a secure room for placing special phone calls. His own ATF office, while in a much nicer building, was still cramped even with about a quarter as many agents. Because of the nature of their work, the DEA agents had to make undercover and overseas phone calls all the time. He sat back in the comfortable swivel chair while his friend, Félix Baez, continued to speak in Spanish on the phone. As Duarte listened, catching about a third of the words, he couldn't help but think of his parents and relatives telling him to learn Spanish. It couldn't hurt.

They were in the small room with the door open because this wasn't an undercover call. Félix was speaking to a police administrator in Panama the DEA office in Panama had set him up with. He was the head of some Panamanian narcotics enforcement unit.

Listening to the call, Duarte realized his mind was drifting to his conversation with Alice Brainard. She had pushed him to define his relationship with her, and he had not been able to answer. Since she had walked away from him at the gym, he had been surprised to realize how much he missed her. This was an entirely new experience for Duarte. He had always been close with his family, even if his brother annoyed him more than encouraged him, but outside of them he had been extremely self-reliant. Between the army and his job, he had not had time for much of a personal life. It wasn't until his relationship with Caren Larsen, the Department of Justice attorney on his last case, that he had realized women could be so distracting. Before the case of the serial bomber, he had laid awake at night, troubled by nightmares about some of his actions in Bosnia. The bomber case had exorcized some of those demons and eased his insomnia, but now he found he lay awake from time to time thinking of Caren. She had left the DOJ and was now in Ohio and dating an old college boyfriend, but he still felt the connection between them. He had been surprised when he had started to sleep better, but he still had restless periods when he'd have to read or even work out in the hours before sunrise. The increased sleep had not seemed to make him feel more rested or alert, but he knew it had to be having an effect. If nothing else, he didn't feel like striking his brother Frank every morning at breakfast when the attorney complained about his life.

Félix hung up the phone. "He was pretty helpful."

Duarte watched him, the dark eyes set in the angular face, the skin pitted with craters from a youth spent with acne.

Félix said, "Rocket? You telepathic? Is that why you never say anything?"

Duarte kept a straight face and just stared at him.

"Funny," said Félix. "I heard you had no sense of humor."

"Most people aren't funny." Duarte cracked a smile mainly to let Félix know he could move on with a summary of the call.

The DEA man looked at his notes. "Our office says we can work with this dude and they'll back us up on anything we need."

"What's his name?"

"Colonel Lázaro Staub."

"That's an odd Latin name."

Félix shrugged. "Who knows where these Central Americans's come from. Panama attracts all kinds."

"Is he aware of this Mr. Ortíz?"

"Oh yeah. He says they've been trying to identify him for years. They think he might be a Colombian. He's bought up a lot of cops and has a bunch of lower-echelon guys who insulate him from everyone."

"So Gastlin may be the only link to him?"

"Looks like."

"And this really is a big deal case?"

"Think so." Félix leaned back in his own chair. "Looks like we got a lot of paperwork to do so we can take a trip to Panama."

Duarte thought about it. "Won't we need someone here to take care of the load if you get it sent to the U.S.?"

Félix nodded. "Yeah, I guess."

"I could do that. I've been to Panama before, for training. I don't mind staying here."

"That could make things a lot easier. Why, you don't wanna leave that fine squeeze you got?"

Duarte didn't answer.

"C'mon, you can admit it."

Duarte said, "I like hanging out with her, that's all. She's funny and smart."

"And hot."

"I know. I know."

"But you can't call her your girlfriend, can you?"

"No. I don't know why."

"Because you're a dude. We avoid labels like that."

Duarte had to smile.

PELLY FINISHED A WHOLE ROASTED CHICKEN WITH SOME VEGE-
tables at an outside table where he and the drivers could keep an eye on
the vehicles. The boss was on the phone to someone in the capital and
seemed preoccupied.

The older of the two drivers said, "Pelly, you ever gonna tell us what's
in the crate?"

Pelly just shook his head. The man had been around long enough to
know that he didn't like to answer the same question twice.

A truck with laborers pulled into the lot next to the cantina and four
men piled out of the back to crowd the window of the smaller, much
cheaper café next door. Three men scooted out of the truck's cab. All the
men were grimy from manual labor under the unrelenting sun of Panama.
The largest of the men, a giant of six-foot-three and well over three hundred pounds, stretched his thick arms, then arched his back. He had a
belly, but not much of one. He glanced over at Pelly and the drivers.

In a booming voice, he slapped one of his companions on the back
and said, "José, look at that guy. He looks like a monkey."

Pelly felt his stomach tighten. Why did a man he didn't even know have to make a comment? Out of the corner of his eye, he saw the two drivers sitting with him slowly creep back. They had seen confrontations like this before.

The giant man yelled to one of the men at the café's window, "Get an extra banana for this boy. He looks hungry." He laughed, then watched Pelly stand to his full five-feet-eight, which made him only laugh some more, the others joining in.

Pelly's head started to spin. He had an H&K MP-5 in the car but didn't see a need for the submachine gun. A firearm was overkill.

The giant looked at him and said, "Hey, Monkey Boy, you forget to comb your face this morning?"

Pelly slowly advanced on the big man. His friends must've thought he didn't need any help against someone so much smaller, but Pelly noted who was laughing.

"Sir," Pelly said slowly, "you like to make fun of people you don't know?"

"Look, it can speak!" The friends' laughter had slowed. They realized this was dangerous country and that taunting the wrong man could result in gunfire.

Pelly thought about explaining hypertrichosis and its genetic origins, but doubted it would enlighten any of these bullies. He gave a good glare to the others and saw that all but two were backing away. He approached the three remaining men slowly, keeping his eyes on the big man in the middle but aware of exactly how the other two were standing. He stopped about three feet from them, just outside the long reach of the big man, looked up into his face and set his left leg back as if he were going to kick him.

Now the man looked a little uneasy, like most bullies when their bluff is called.

Pelly said, "I don't like people making fun of me." He let his eyes slip to the right to check the man there, and then to the left. "I think you owe me . . ." But he didn't finish the sentence. Instead, he launched a vicious front kick with his poised left leg to the man on the left side, connecting directly on his hip girder and feeling the man's leg pop out of its socket. Before the man could collapse to the ground, screaming, Pelly had his left foot planted and his right twisting into a round kick, shattering the other man's ribs. He waited until both men were clearly down and out of the fight and the others had moved back even farther.

Then he stood silently and watched as the giant started to tremble slightly. Pelly balled his fist.

The big man said, "Look, I think you misunderstood me."

"I thought you said I looked like a monkey."

"No, no, that wasn't what I meant."

Pelly didn't answer. Instead he lifted his fist, drawing the man's hands up to block the punch and instead delivered a crushing round kick to the man's knee. He tumbled like a redwood.

As the giant sprawled on the ground, Pelly stomped on the man's outstretched good leg, crushing that kneecap from another angle.

The man started to cry for his friends to help, but no one was anxious to defend the loudmouth.

Pelly stepped around and grabbed the man's hand, then bent it back and fell on his arm so that his elbow snapped. He repeated the action on the other arm.

The hairy young man stood up, looking down at the man whose limbs now all seemed to be pointing in the wrong direction. He glanced around at the others, who shrank back from his stare.

He heard his name and looked toward the Cadillac.

His boss said, "Pelly, let's go."

As Pelly stomped back toward the car, he saw the look on the men's faces in the truck. He knew they'd never make fun of him and neither would all the men they would tell.

Once inside the SUV, his boss said, "That sort of activity draws too much attention to us. We have an important task."

Pelly turned and looked at him. He wanted to ask if his boss thought whipping half-naked women didn't draw attention, too, but decided he liked his job. Maybe one day he'd address these issues with him.

It was almost sundown when Pelly watched the two men settle the crate into the front of a twenty-foot cargo container, secure the false wall and then lug in over fifty bales of compacted pot. The heavy hand truck strained under the stress of some of the bales. As with any imprecise and unregulated industry, the weight of each bale could vary from three to five hundred pounds. They had plenty, so they usually threw in a little extra to avoid complaints. Much of their success was based on staying out of confrontations. Of course, the boss went a long way toward eliminating problems before they arose.

Pelly saw him approach from the parked Cadillac SUV where he'd been on his cell phone.

"This looks better and better, Pelly." He looked at the men working. "How much longer?"

Pelly shrugged, "Two more bales."

"You want to, or should I?"

Pelly frowned. "Is it really necessary, boss? These two are good workers. They have no idea what's in the crate."

"Pelly, you let me worry about the security and just focus on doing what I say. Understood?"

"Yes, sir," he said, watching as the men shoved the big doors to the container closed. Without a word, his boss walked toward them slowly. He had his hand on the grip of a Walther P-38 behind his back.

Pelly shook his head, knowing that there was no real reason to kill these men, but that never stopped the boss from doing it. At least this time he wasn't torturing the men before they were killed. That seemed to be their only reward for being decent, hardworking employees.

The men turned, pleased that the big boss was apparently coming to thank them for their hard work. The first man, a twenty-five-year-old farm boy from Bocas del Toros never knew what was coming before the bullet to his face stopped him cold. The other man, a much older Colombian, had the time and presence of mind to take a step back, but the instinctive movement only seemed to enrage the boss, who, instead of shooting him in the head, put a nine-millimeter round into each of the man's knees.

The terrified worker dropped straight to the ground, his legs unable to support his large torso.

The boss walked up to him and put a bullet in the man's groin.

Pelly shook his head. This did nothing for the business operations—in fact, now Pelly would have to explain to anybody who knew them how the two workers had disappeared. He decided to say they were informers for the national police, and he'd had to make an example of them. Maybe he could salvage some benefit from this senseless behavior.

Pelly could only shake his head again as he watched the boss stand over the screaming, squirming man and slowly pump bullets into other nonfatal parts of his body while the man bled to death.

William "Ike" Floyd answered the pay phone off Forty-second Street on the first ring. It was eleven o'clock on a Wednesday night in Omaha, and he knew who it was.

"Yeah?" He wasn't tentative; he wanted to show this guy he wasn't afraid.

"William?"

"It's me, Mr. Ortíz. And call me Ike." He'd call Ortíz by his first name, too, if he knew it. Besides, this guy was a heavy hitter, even if his beaner accent made him sound very un-American.

The deep voice with the Latin inflection said, "It looks as if everything is in order. You will want to find a contact at the port in New Orleans or perhaps Galveston. That is where I will suggest as a point of entry."

"Think you can just waltz it right though?"

"I'll have some help, but it will still need to be off-loaded."

"I'll get it done."

"Good, good. I will have to set up two days a week to call you."

"Can we make it earlier? I don't like waiting out here by a pay phone this late."

"Surely the leader of a group like yours is not frightened?"

"You ever seen the wild animals that roam the streets in Omaha? Even the cops don't like to fuck with these niggers."

"Regardless, I will need to be able to reach you both Wednesday and Sunday nights. At the same hour." There was a silence on the overseas line, then he added, "Our mission is too important to be threatened by minor inconveniences. Do you not agree?"

"I guess."

"Very well. I will inform you of our progress."

The line went dead, and Ike, pissed off and tired, slammed down the receiver as the dry wind kicked up off the plains. He was close to his apartment on Fortieth Street, well away from any of the neighborhoods he was bitching about, but he didn't want this beaner thinking it was too easy to wait by a pay phone at eleven at night.

He turned and started to walk toward his building, thinking about what they had in mind. This was big. Bigger than anything he'd ever done, and, considering what else he had been involved in, that was saying something. This time no one had anything on him. He wasn't talking to the cops and wasn't facing any charges. This was gonna be straight and decisive. He would be proud to be known as the man who changed America. No matter how many died to save it.

DUARTE LIKED HAVING FÉLIX WORK OUT OF THE ATF OFFICE sometimes because it made him feel as if the two agencies were on a more equal footing. The DEA was so much larger and better funded, though, since the 9/11 attacks, it had become somewhat of a forgotten agency. As the public focused on terrorism, narcotics had taken a backseat. Few people realized the connection between the two crimes, and how much of a vital link the DEA had been in the intelligence machine.

B. L. Gastlin sat at a small table in Duarte's office. They had not handcuffed him, even though he was only temporarily out of jail. They had checked him out earlier in the day to make more undercover phone calls to Ortíz.

Félix gave him one of his ready smiles and said, "You done good, Byron. You got the man hisself on the line, and you set up a deal. Snap! Looks like it'll work out."

Gastlin grunted. "Not for me. You think my life will be worth anything after I do this?"

Félix leaned on a desk and said, "You have my guarantee you'll be safe. Or at the very least we'll find your killer." The DEA man laughed at the old joke, but it didn't seem to amuse the chubby drug dealer, so Félix said, "The judge will go a lot easier on your ass."

"I know it'll go easier on me if I talk, but I'm more worried about what'll happen outside this office. My business associates didn't go to Harvard. These guys are badasses."

Félix answered right back, "And some of the brothers at Marion or Leavenworth aren't dangerous? You look like a big, puffy chance to get rich or get a blow job. Either way, bro, you won't be happy."

"But I'll probably live."

"Look, besides pot we found the Beretta. My boy here," he nodded toward Duarte, "will lay down a simple 'armed trafficking' count, and you'll be one step closer to permanent residence in federal prison. Then there are the state charges for the assault on the old lady."

"Assault? I wrecked the truck."

"Yeah, then you grabbed a half-naked sixty-one-year-old woman and dragged her into a closet. That's not only assault, I think the state's attorney will manage a lewd and lascivious count, too."

Gastlin reached up and touched his swollen eye. "That lady got her revenge. My face and ribs are killin' me."

Félix didn't let up. "Then there's the theft of the truck and the reckless endangerment of the guy up in the bucket."

"I didn't even know he was there."

"Yo, dude, you sayin' your defense is that you *did* steal the truck, but inadvertently almost killed the FPL worker?"

Gastlin looked down at the table, then picked some spilled food off his orange jail shirt.

Duarte could read that signal easily. He was a beaten man. Félix was not only a good undercover, the guy had some interview skills as well.

Félix looked at Duarte, nodded, then with a tilt of his head, tried to get the ATF agent involved in the interview.

Duarte sat across from the despondent prisoner.

"Look, Gastlin." He waited for the man to look up into his eyes. "What do your initials, B. L., stand for again?"

Félix chuckled and said, "Based on my sore dick, I'd say 'butt licker.'"

Gastlin's face flashed red, and he looked down. "Byron Leon." He looked at Félix and said, "I already apologized. I just got the wrong vibe from you. I'm not gay."

Félix snorted, "You could've fooled me."

Duarte interrupted. "It doesn't matter."

Gastlin held firm. "It does. It does to me. I'm not gay."

Félix held up his hands. "Okay, you acted gay." He started to chuckle, and Gastlin sat, silent.

Duarte gave him a few moments to get over the joke at his expense. "We can protect you, and you can save a lot of years behind bars if you just cooperate."

Gastlin nodded slowly, then started to cry.

Duarte waited as the tears started to flow harder. "Wait, wait, don't cry."

The man looked up like he was about to be comforted. Like his day might turn from horrible to merely miserable.

Duarte added, "There's no crying here. You had a loaded pistol and drugs. You're a criminal. An armed trafficker. You don't have the right to cry. You didn't lose a house to a hurricane or have your family swept away by a tsunami. You're just a dimwitted guy who did something stupid. Now we're giving you the chance to make it right. Talk or take it like a man, but stop crying right this second."

Gastlin sniffled, wiped his nose with his hand and looked at Duarte. "You're right. What do you want to know?"

Duarte had to take a second because he had meant what he said; it hadn't been an act. But he was still stunned that it had worked. Now he was part of this case.

After debriefing Gastlin and finding only passing references to Ortíz in a couple of intelligence reports, the two federal agents slowed down.

Félix said, "Yo, Rocket, we need a break. We been at this since ten o'clock."

Duarte glanced at his G-Shock watch. It was almost three now. They had both skipped lunch. That didn't happen much with Chuck. In fact, he knew that Chuck, who had taken Gastlin back to the jail, had probably stopped for lunch over an hour ago.

Duarte turned and stared through the tall window that looked out over Flagler Boulevard and onto the intracoastal waterway. The brilliant sky met the ocean and the colors set off a fresh feeling in him, like when he'd been a teenager and slept the whole night through, and dreamed of building things instead of blowing them up or investigating how they were blown up. He had missed Florida in the service, and once he'd come back he had never taken it for granted. He only wished the window was open so he could smell the fresh air.

He heard the office doorbell and then the buzzer as the secretary let someone in through the outer door. A minute later, the office secretary leaned into his doorway and said, "Rocket, you got a visitor." He didn't ask who. He just cut across his cramped office, looked up at Félix and walked into the entryway. He stopped when he looked though the thick ballistic glass and saw the young woman there, her hair short and pulled back, her glasses resting on a nose that had been broken more than once.

He cracked open the door and said, "May I help you?"

She turned and said, "Are you Alex or Félix?"

"Alex Duarte. What can I do for you?"

She gave a sly smile and said, "I think it's more like what I can do for you." She held out her hand and let her wallet fall open.

All he saw were three initials that stood out: FBI.

As one of the few federal prisoners housed at the Palm Beach County jail, Byron Gastlin didn't feel cramped in his cell with the six other prisoners. But he didn't feel safe either. One of them, a Hispanic guy, was also a DEA victim and Gastlin knew him from the area. They had traded pot and coke a couple of times. Three of the others were being held on criminal tax charges while they waited for a bond hearing, and they were all bitching about a hard-core IRS agent named

Robinson who had figured out their scam—they were no threat either. But a giant, flabby, toothless redneck from The Acreage kept looking at him like he was his next meal. Maybe Gastlin had seen *Deliverance* one too many times, but this guy made him nervous to the point of nausea. He was a failed bank robber, apparently, and kept saying the government was responsible for his problems because they hadn't provided him with help when he'd been fired from his job as a marine mechanic at the Port of Palm Beach after beaning a guy with a wrench. The guy was no Einstein, but that didn't make him any less dangerous.

Gastlin sat on his lower bunk listening to the inmates in the general section make their never-ending racket. It in no way quieted down, even after lights out. If he had known he might end up in a place like this, he never would've sold drugs for a living. But it was just so damn profitable. As a boat salesman, he'd been lucky to make thirty-five grand a year. After allowing someone to use one of his company's boats to run in a load of coke, he'd had the contacts to sell product himself, and in the first three months in the trade he had made a hundred thousand bucks. He took a lot of vacations and didn't work too much, so things had leveled off, but he made a nice living. He shepherded in one load every couple of months and sold mostly pot the rest of the time. But now it didn't seem nearly worth it. He hadn't slept. He hated the baloney sandwiches and Kool-Aid for lunch and he didn't want to wake up to find he was a pillow for the bank robber. He felt his eyes well with tears again. The swollen right one hurt to wipe. In the general population, he might worry about getting a beating for being soft, but here, with the federal prisoners, crying was accepted.

He was surprised he had gotten hold of Mr. Ortíz on the first try from the DEA office. The man was comfortable with him, that was obvious, and also the only reason he had any hope of escaping a lengthy sentence. He hadn't told the good-looking DEA guy, Félix, that he usually met one of Ortíz's employees when he went to Panama. He had only seen Ortíz himself twice and spoken to him in person once. Ortíz was a big-time player; he didn't have time for little fish like Gastlin.

He knew, however, not to downplay his relationship with Ortíz to

Félix or the quiet ATF agent. That guy, he was the one who spooked Gastlin. He had those intense, dark eyes, and he never flinched or turned away. He kept staring until people answered his questions. Gastlin got the idea that he could be a real ballbreaker if he wanted to be.

He stretched out on the bunk, wiping his eyes. As he looked up, a giant shadow passed over him. He saw the bank robber grin at him and quickly looked around the cell to see if he had any support. No one could meet his scared eyes.

6

DUARTE NOTICED THAT FÉLIX'S VOICE HAD AN UNUSUAL HARD edge to it as he addressed the new FBI agent. They were all in the ATF office's conference room, and Félix was leaning forward. She was not unattractive. Duarte noticed her athletic body, but no one would think of her as a model either—unless she was modeling martial arts equipment.

Félix said, "I don't understand how you knew we had a case on someone named Ortíz."

She smiled that arrogant smile that FBI agents learn in the academy and said, "You don't have to understand how, you just need to understand that I was sent here to work on the case with you."

"What was your name again, sweetheart?" Félix smiled, knowing he had pushed some buttons. Duarte just watched his friend sort this out. He had a feeling he knew what would happen.

"My name is Lina. L–I–N–A. Cirillo."

"Hispanic?"

"Italian, why?"

"I was looking for some hope."

She smiled again, this time revealing perfect teeth in a predatory smile under that crooked nose. Nothing on her face lined up correctly. "I'm bringing you hope. We're very interested in this Ortíz character, and we have sources he might know here in the U.S. We might save you a whole lot of heartache on this case." She looked at Duarte. "Agent Duarte doesn't seem to have a problem with me being here."

Duarte looked at her. "Even if I did, I have the feeling you're staying."

"That's the army mentality, isn't it? Adapt and overcome."

"How'd you know I was in the army?"

"Same way I knew Félix was born in Havana. I work for the FBI."

He remained silent. This woman was smart, and she knew more than she was letting on. Besides, she looked like a girl who could back you up in a fight, which he found fascinating, so he didn't mind her staying, at least for a while. He could relate to her determination, and he sensed the ambition in her, too. How else did you have enough clout to show up from Washington in another agency's office and dictate a case?

Félix said, "This is bullshit. We'll see what my bosses have to say about this." He stood up and stormed down the hall toward Duarte's office and a phone.

Lina Cirillo turned her unusual face to Duarte and said, "Are you going to protest, too?"

Duarte shrugged. His universal language. She could interpret it any way she wished.

She reached across the table and patted him on the arm. "I'm not the enemy; I'm here to help."

"I think I've heard that before."

"My concerns are not about a drug kingpin. They're about national security."

"What makes you think I'm not worried about national security?"

She just kept a straight face and looked at him.

After a few minutes, Félix appeared at the door. He had clearly been in a heated conversation on the phone and his face was still red. He said, "Okay, you win. But I won't make this easy for you."

She smiled and said, "It never is."

Duarte checked his watch for the third time at six-fifteen, thinking Alice might have stood him up as a lesson in not taking her for granted. He deserved it and frankly thought it was a pretty good lesson. He got it. He was mad at himself. Why couldn't he commit to something as simple as calling her his girlfriend?

He paced in the open courtyard on the second floor of the City Place Building in front of the popular restaurant and bar. He even had on a sport jacket, one of the few he had worn since a dance at Fort Leonard Wood, which all the recruits had been required to attend. He didn't mind the coat. He always wore a second, button-down shirt to conceal his Glock. This just felt a little warmer.

He heard her voice, Florida with a tinge of Tennessee, before he saw her walk in.

"Rocket."

He smiled and stepped to greet her.

She held off slightly. "So are we buddies, or more?"

"How about both?"

"We'll see how I feel after a few drinks."

She didn't look like his buddy in her short blue dress with a white chemise. She had an athletic build with a muscular back and broad shoulders, but that didn't mean she wasn't feminine. Tonight he thought she looked like an angel.

They found a high-top table near the front window so they could people-watch, and, as usual, he let her do most of the talking. He did have a few things to say and waited his turn patiently.

"I have a better handle on the big case I'm working with DEA."

"Oh yeah? When do you leave?"

"I'm not going to Panama."

"Really?"

"I still have to travel, but only to New Orleans."

"I wasn't serious about you finding a Panamanian beauty. At least not too serious."

"No, Félix Baez is going down with the informant. I'm going to wait for the load at the port in New Orleans."

"By yourself?"

"No, there'll be DEA guys around and . . ." he stopped short. He didn't want to raise any questions. But it was too late.

"And who else?"

"The FBI."

"How'd they get involved?"

"Don't know, but an agent from Washington showed up today."

"That's just what you guys need, some old fart giving unwanted advice."

Duarte just nodded. He didn't want to make her paranoid just as they were starting to get serious. Telling his girlfriend he was going to New Orleans with another woman would raise some flags. Just the mental image of Lina Cirillo caused him concern. Looking at Alice, he realized she was built a little like the FBI agent. Maybe that's what Duarte found attractive about her. Lina didn't have Alice's delicate face and bright smile, but she radiated energy and fitness. Duarte liked that.

Then he thought he was hallucinating. At the front door a woman in a nice business suit stepped inside, her short, straight hair loose on her shoulders. The suit looked like the one Lina had worn earlier. Duarte blinked and realized it *was* Lina. What the hell was she doing there? Then Duarte's surprise moved to astonishment when he saw Félix Baez step inside right behind her and place a gentle hand in the small of her back.

Alice saw his face and said, "What is it?"

He shook his head and said, "It's just, ah, Félix. My friend, Félix."

"Invite him over."

"No. I thought we'd leave for dinner. I haven't told you where we're going yet."

"He can sit with us for a minute. Don't be rude."

"I'm sure he has other plans." He knew the combination of Lina and Alice would disrupt his plans for the evening. His heart rate increased like he was setting a bomb. At least he was trained for that. This was all new to him.

Duarte saw Félix look his way and tap the FBI agent on the arm, then head toward him. His friendly, easy smile did nothing to relax Duarte.

The DEA agent said, "I heard you say you were coming by here tonight, so I thought we'd surprise you." He took the empty seat across from Duarte and offered Lina the one next to him.

Alice cleared her throat and Duarte said, "I'm sorry, Alice, this is Félix and Lina."

They all smiled and nodded. Then a young man spoke into a portable microphone making an announcement about some special event. Both of the women turned in their seats to see and hear him. Duarte leaned into Félix and whispered, "What are you doing? I thought you hated her."

"I hate the FBI. Look at her. Pussy is pussy." He gave one of his little cackles.

Then Duarte was faced with small talk as the announcement ended and the women turned to face them again.

Alice said, "Are you both with the DEA?"

Lina quickly replied, "No, I'm an FBI agent from Washington."

Alice's look at Duarte said it all. His evening was about to end.

SOON AFTERWARD, DUARTE PULLED HIS PERSONAL VEHICLE, A three-year-old Toyota Tacoma pickup truck, next to his brother's new Porsche. Sometimes it seemed crowded here when his ATF Taurus and the other two cars were crammed into the limited space behind his parents' house, but tonight he hardly noticed or cared. He had tried to speak to Alice to explain, but short of grabbing her arm and forcing her to listen to him, he didn't see how he could have stopped her as she muttered some excuse about a previous commitment and left the restaurant.

He slipped out of the truck and looked up at his apartment. All the lights were on, so he figured Frank was working at the kitchen table. Duarte trudged over to his parents' rear kitchen door, already smelling the spices his mother had no doubt worked so carefully into whatever she had made for them. He hoped Frank had eaten already or was too absorbed with his work to come down yet.

As soon as he was in the kitchen, he heard his brother.

"There he is now. For a rocket, you don't seem to move that fast. You're late."

"Sorry," muttered Duarte.

His mother stepped into the kitchen and kissed him on the cheek like she had every single time he had walked in the house since he was a toddler. At fifty-six, his mother was still a beautiful woman, though over the years she had put on a few pounds, mainly as a result of her own skill in the kitchen.

"Where's your guest?" she asked.

"Another commitment. Sorry, Ma. I'll eat enough for both of us."

Frank called from the table, "What happened? Did . . ."

He was cut off by his brother's glare. Even Frank knew not to push Duarte when he gave a look like that.

His mother said, "No matter, your father and I waited for you. Frankie has work to do, so I let him go ahead and eat."

Duarte plopped into the same chair in which he had sat for nearly thirty years. He looked up to see his father's boney hand on the banister as he came down from his study, which had been his and Frank's room before the elder Duarte had converted it, now that they had moved to the garage.

"Hey, Pop," called both brothers in unison.

César Duarte nodded, having felt he knew enough about the world after watching the NBC news and fifteen minutes of the Jim Lehrer report.

He sat at the end of the table, lowering his narrow body into the chair like a king presiding over his court.

Duarte's mother had the table set, and in a flash put a bowl of steaming shredded beef in the center to go with the rice and plantains that were already sitting there. No one dared ask her if they could help. His mother insisted on preparing the food and setting the table herself, even though he had been taught it was rude not to assist—one of the many confusing lessons he had been taught growing up in a household from Paraguay.

They ate in relative silence as Frank explained to everyone how hard he had worked to sue some ill-prepared small businessman and how the judge was likely to commend him in open court for his efforts.

César Duarte waited the proscribed amount of time before he looked at his younger son and asked, "Did you do good work today?"

"Yes, sir."

"What're you working on, Alex?"

Duarte shrugged, his mind elsewhere.

"Nothing new? I thought you and your friend from the DEA were on something big?"

"We are. I'm sorry, Pop. I'm a little distracted."

Frank chimed in with a grin, "Yeah, Pop. He's got women problems."

Duarte knew the idiot would blab sooner or later, and they were no longer kids, so he couldn't just smack him. But he wanted to.

His mother said, "Alex, you can tell us what's wrong?"

"Nothin', Ma, really. I thought I might bring a young lady by for dinner, that's all."

His mother smiled and sucked in air like she had just witnessed a miracle.

Frank said, "C'mon, Ma. It's not like he's gay. He was bound to meet a woman sooner or later."

Duarte said, "I'll bring her by, Ma."

"When?"

"As soon as I can."

She seemed satisfied with that answer.

His father came to the rescue. "What about the case?"

Duarte relaxed a little and said, "Looks good. Félix is going to take the informant down to Panama and meet the main violator. I'm going to go to New Orleans and wait for the load. Should be interesting."

César Duarte smiled and said, "That sounds like a good day's work." His highest compliment.

The Panamanian looked out the bay window of his modest home, enjoying the vista of the mountains in the distance and the winding river that ran behind the house. It was all a sham, of course, so he could stay under everyone's radar. The house was large, but not a mansion. The wide area behind him looked like another parcel but was, in fact, owned by one of his corporations, so he knew no one would ever build a house on the surrounding forty-two acres. The small guesthouse at the front of his property housed security people in case he ever did have problems, but he didn't think he needed to worry. This house, his front, the quiet neighborhood so close to the capital, no one was smart enough ever to put it all together.

His name, for instance: Ortíz. It had no meaning to anyone but him. Unlike with the Americans, who always gave their military operations or government agents code names that gave away the secret. He had taken his new name from a housekeeper his father had employed during his formative years. She had been his only warm, human contact as a child. His father had been consumed with his government position as a trade negotiator, and the only conversations they had shared had focused on his father's anger for the way the United States dealt with her friends to the south. His father had been so busy he had not even attended Ortíz's graduation from the University of Panama.

His mother's death in childbirth had also added to his father's resentment.

As a result, from the age of seven, he'd started to cling to the lovely María Ortíz. She had seen him to school and fed him a snack every afternoon. The broad-shouldered woman with the ample breasts had never talked about her own life growing up, but he had had the sense this was the first time she had not worried about where her next meal was coming from, and she had doted on him.

When he had turned thirteen, he started to notice that the housekeeper was what many would consider a "handsome woman." He started to learn that the changes in his body were often directly related to María. He wanted to ask her what was happening to him, so one evening, while his father was staying overnight in the capital, he asked María questions a young teenager might have. The thirty-eight-year-old woman decided it might be better to demonstrate some of the interactions between men and women rather than explain them.

This class in lovemaking lasted two years without anyone asking questions. Now, instead of a snack after school, María provided something more exciting. He had felt an attachment to the housekeeper that easily eclipsed his feelings for his father.

Then, after a weeklong school trip to visit the ancient Aztec ruins at Chichén Itzá, he'd returned to find to his shock that his father had similar feelings for María. Hoping to surprise her, the boy had slipped into the house and then to her tiny bedroom off the kitchen. Without knocking, he'd burst through the door only to see his father's bald head and wrinkled bare ass between María's thick, smooth thighs.

That day he learned that women were whores, and that employees were not to be trusted.

Now, as Mr. Ortíz from Colombia, he felt confident he had confused the law enforcement authorities in both his home country and the United States. The DEA was always quick to believe that Colombians ran the rest of Latin America like lackeys. Just because Colombians had routed the Cubans in the Miami drug wars of the 1980s, the DEA believed they were tough, vicious kingpins.

He had made a fortune from his import/export business. A fortune for which he had no use. No real vices, no one to share it with, nothing of interest to spend it on. Except revenge. That had crept into his consciousness over the past dozen years as he considered the indignity after indignity suffered by Panama at the hands of the United States. The invasion in 1989 had been only the most obvious blow. He still remembered the news story about Stealth bombers flying over undetected. The F-117A Nighthawk squadron based at Nellis Air Force Base in Nevada had been built with the Soviets in mind. Against a small country without even night-vision equipment, the jets were overkill.

He knew all about the base near Route 6 outside the town of Tonopah, Nevada. He had imagined the pilots laughing at the Panamanians' futile attempts to stop their formidable weapons, and he imagined them laughing still. They didn't realize the war was not yet over.

Now he had the means to strike back at the U.S. in a meaningful and terrible way. And using "Ike" Floyd would heighten the Americans' unease. Since 9/11 they had focused their suspicion on Middle Easterners. Having to shift their attention to one of their own citizens would create an atmosphere of distrust that could cripple the country. At least for a while.

ALEX DUARTE FELT HIS FRUSTRATION RISE AS HE AND FÉLIX attempted to get the assistant U.S. attorney to approve Gastlin's trip to Panama.

The pudgy, dark-skinned man peered over his half-glasses and said, "Last week you guys told me to ask for 'no bond' because of how the guy ran. Now you want me to ask a judge to allow him to leave the country?" The Harvard-bred disdain in his voice never failed to annoy the agents who worked with him.

"You understand perfectly," said Félix, containing a smile.

"I don't see the humor in it."

Duarte said, "Look, Larry, this is a big target. It's gonna take some extra effort on everyone's part to make the case. Otherwise we should give up on anything but the street-level dealers."

The assistant U.S. attorney peered over at Duarte and said, "If you remove all the street dealers, then the problem is solved, because there is no outlet."

Félix stood up. "Are you stupid? No, don't answer that; it was a referential question."

The attorney sighed and said, "Rhetorical."

"What?"

"It's a rhetorical question."

"What is?"

"If I'm stupid."

Félix said, "I'm glad you agree. Look, I know this is a pain and you have to work harder, but this is what needs to be done, brother."

Duarte watched the young attorney shift in his seat. He was obviously not used to being bullied by agents. Duarte tried to ease his anxiety by adding, "I'll testify at the hearing that it was our idea and explain why we needed this extraordinary change in procedure."

The assistant U.S. attorney leaned forward and said, "Didn't you let a prisoner escape a few months ago?"

Duarte felt his face flush. "I did."

"And what happened in that case?"

"He was killed before being recaptured."

"Gentlemen," the attorney said, leaning back in his seat. "I believe you have my answer."

Duarte and Félix met up with Lina for dinner about six. Duarte had been simmering ever since they'd left the attorney's office. But all that was about to change.

Lina, dressed in a simple blouse that showed her lean frame, smiled as she approached the table and handed Félix a sheet of paper. The DEA man looked at it and said, "She got us approval. Too bad we can't bring Gastlin."

Lina said, "What happened?"

Duarte sat back while Félix relayed the whole conversation with the assistant U.S. attorney.

She calmly took out her phone and dialed a number. Duarte could see the first numbers were 202, so he knew it was Washington. She said, "We have a holdup in the U.S. attorney's office on Pale Girl." She paused and said to Félix, "What's the attorney's name?"

"Larry Gandle."

She repeated the name into the phone and said, "Thanks." She put the phone away and looked up at her dinner companions. "That should do it" was all she said, and Duarte knew better than to ask.

William "Ike" Floyd had spent the better part of the day trying to reach the man that Mr. Jessup, the president of the National Army of White Americans, had provided to help at the ports. Ike didn't know the guy's job title, but his area code was 504, which was in Louisiana. He was calling from the pay phone and had to feed quarters into it every time he even left a message, which was to call him at the pay phone off Forty-second Street at eight o'clock. Two nights in a row he had hustled down to wait for the call. He had even missed *American Idol* one night, and now he was starting to doubt the man would ever call him back. Besides, he was sick of phones. It felt like he spent his every waking hour on them. He didn't mind his phone solicitation job; it paid okay, and they didn't expect him to do too much except call people who were too stupid to be on the national do-not-call list. Tomorrow he was calling about some vacation rental places for sale on the west coast of Florida. He liked the weather in Florida, but there were too many niggers for him to be happy. He'd stay in Nebraska a while longer until things got too hot and he had to move.

Then, as he looked down the long, straight, empty street, he heard the phone ring. He picked it up on the second ring. "Yeah, this is Ike."

"Good, good," came a man's gravelly voice. "I like someone who keeps to a schedule. Old Jessup said you'd be calling."

"He say why?"

"Only to help you at the port."

"Can you help?"

"All I need is a ship name and the date of arrival. If it comes into New Orleans, I can handle anything."

"Excellent." Ike considered this new asset.

The man said, "Ike ain't your real name, is it?"

"No. I'd rather not use my real name."

"Just wonderin' because my pa loved Dwight Eisenhower and always called him Ike. Till the day the old general died, my pa called him Ike, like they was old friends or something. That who you're named for?"

"Nah, just a nickname one of my mom's lame friends gave me. Had something to do with a musician in Chicago, I think."

"Good name just the same. Now what will you need me to do at the port?"

"Just unload part of one container. One item I'm told will be under a thousand pounds and about seven feet long."

"I can do that. And you want it quiet, right?"

"Yeah, no one can know."

"No problem."

Ike said, "Is it dangerous?"

"I don't know what's coming in exactly, but, yeah, of course it's dangerous. Financing a revolution is always risky. But it'll be worth it when we're written about in textbooks one day."

"President Jessup didn't give you the details?"

"Just to help. He said there was money and benefit to the Cause in it."

Ike considered this and how it might sound to a cop. "You sure your phone is safe?"

"This is a pay phone, and you're at a pay phone. I'd say it's safe."

"So you can help?"

"To save my country? You bet your sweet ass I can."

For the first time, William "Ike" Floyd thought this might work. He had thought that about other plans to spark a revolution and once he'd even been right. Too bad he hadn't been able to take any credit. Maybe he was better off. He'd either be dead or in jail if he hadn't had that special arrangement with the government. And this time they had much bigger goals than a truck bomb. As he slowly walked back to his apartment, a shiver ran down his back. He had never thought of textbooks before. He hoped they used his real name.

This was gonna be big.

Duarte knocked on the door to the town house north of the airport near West Palm. He felt a little like a fool, standing there at eight o'clock at night with some flowers he had just bought at Publix, but he felt as if he needed to apologize to Alice . . . even though he wasn't sure what he had to apologize for.

He stood, staring at the front door, until finally he heard a voice inside. "Who is it?"

"Alex?"

The door opened quickly. Alice, in a sweatshirt and shorts, immediately smiled. "You're not a jerk, are you?"

"Is that a referential question?" He smiled at his own joke as she ushered him inside.

9

THE DAYS THAT FOLLOWED TAUGHT DUARTE THE MEANING OF government bureaucracy. If it weren't for Lina Cirillo cutting through all the red tape, they might not ever have been able to pursue the case. The most amazing incident occurred when Duarte and Félix went back to the assistant U.S. attorney who had denied their request in the first place. As they walked into his office, he looked over his half-glasses and reached to his desk.

"Here, and I'm sorry if you misunderstood me." He handed them a single court order.

Duarte looked at it, then up at the attorney.

"All charges dropped?"

"For freedom of travel. We can indict him if it doesn't work out. But for now he's a free man."

"I thought you weren't going to budge."

"I didn't know the kind of people that were interested in the case. Now I do."

Duarte started to ask more questions when Félix pulled at his arm. "Let it go."

D uarte and Lina left for New Orleans a few hours after Félix and Gastlin boarded their flight for Panama. Since Gastlin was at least temporarily off the hook on the charges, the DEA didn't need to send a pack of agents to guard him. Like any frugal federal agency, they were content to have Félix and the agents in Panama handle it.

Duarte settled into his seat, with Lina in the seat next to him. Her short hair seemed to know just how to fall behind her ears, and she instantly relaxed. Closing her eyes, she turned her face toward Duarte.

She had a peaceful look, and Duarte found he could study her face for a moment without feeling self-conscious. He realized how pretty she was, even with the nose that had been knocked one way then the other. Her dark Italian features gave her face sharp lines accentuated by her high level of fitness. She looked like a lean, satisfied lioness.

She opened her eyes suddenly, almost startling him. As she smiled, she patted him on his hand and said, "Maybe now that I have you cornered, you'll have to talk to me."

"I've talked to you."

"You shrug and use the occasional word, but you haven't really spoken with me."

Duarte felt vaguely like he'd been trapped in an interrogation. Although he couldn't picture a nicer-smelling interrogator.

"Is this your career case, like Félix says it is for him?" she asked.

"I hope to have a long career."

"You know how the DEA guys talk. They want the big score. Then they can either move up the ladder or coast on it for years."

"I don't see many DEA agents coasting."

She let out a little laugh and said, "Yeah, the agency doesn't seem to have a long memory. I hear a lot of guys say it's 'what have you done today.'"

"They're a tough bunch. I like working with them."

"You don't like the FBI?"

He looked at her and was about to shrug, then said, "I like FBI agents. I'm not sure about the agency. An FBI agent saved my life once."

"You mean Tom Colgan?"

Duarte shifted in his seat so he could look at her face-to-face. "How'd you know that?"

"When one of our agents is killed in the line of duty, we all know about it. You didn't have anything to do with his death." She paused. "I thought you caught the killer."

"He wasn't technically captured." His dark eyes focused on her. "But he was brought to justice."

"Whatever. I'm just saying you have a good reputation. I hope to rehabilitate the bureau in your eyes."

"Why? Who cares what an ATF street agent thinks?"

"I do."

He shrugged and sat back for the takeoff.

Once the flight was on its way and the instructions were finished, Duarte thought of an important question he had wanted to ask, although he thought Félix might know the answer since he seemed to be closer to Lina. He turned his head and said, "How'd you know about our case?"

She hesitated, then said, "I'm not supposed to talk about it, but we have a source."

"A source connected to Ortíz?"

"Can't say, but this source is pretty hot. We call it Pale Girl."

"A hot Pale Girl? Sounds like something you guys would use."

"Pale Girl is just the name of the source. Doesn't mean it's male or female."

Duarte shrugged. This was why he didn't talk to people a lot. They said stupid things.

Lina said, "You should be happy I'm here. If it weren't for me, you and Félix would still be twiddling your thumbs waiting for permission to enter Panama. And you can't tell me the U.S. attorney's office would allow you to take your snitch."

"What'd the bureau say to make the attorney change his mind?"

"It came from higher up. An HBO called."

"HBO?"

"High bureau official."

"I always thought when the FBI said HBO, it meant he'd be 'home by one.'"

"Very funny. I didn't think you made jokes."

"Only about the FBI. But I'd still like to know what you said to the U.S. attorney's office."

"Believe me, when national security is at stake, they don't fool around anymore."

"How is Ortíz a threat to national security?"

"How was Mohammed Atta until after 9/11? We're a lot more proactive now."

Duarte looked at the young woman. He didn't guess she was older than him. Maybe thirty or thirty-one. "How'd you qualify for a counterterrorism slot?"

"You don't qualify in the bureau. You apply, then get trained. I was assigned to Newark out of the academy."

Duarte made a sour face.

"Newark's not a bad assignment. You can't live there, you have to live in an outer suburb, but it's not as expensive as New York, and there's a lot of shit that goes on." She waited for him to comment, then realized to whom she was speaking. "Anyway, I was dating an editor with the *Newark Star-Ledger*. Nice guy, but he lived over in Ocean Grove, and we just didn't see each other very often. After we split up, with the bureau shifting resources because of 9/11, I took a transfer to D.C. and never looked back."

"Where's your family?"

"Connecticut."

"You don't get to see them much then?"

"No big loss." She saw the look on Duarte's face and said, "Why, are you close with your family?"

"You might say that."

"What about your girlfriend, Alice?"

"What about her?"

"She's very pretty."

"I agree."

"And a crime scene tech."

"Forensic scientist."

Lina shrugged. "You guys serious?"

"Don't know."

"What's that mean?"

"I didn't think I'd have to explain 'I don't know.'"

"Just like a man. I'm sure you don't know the meaning of 'commitment' either."

Duarte shrugged and settled back for the rest of the flight.

10

FÉLIX BAEZ BUMPED HIS WAY THROUGH THE BUSTLING TORRIJOS
airport in Panama City, Panama. He felt like he was on a caffeine buzz.
He had dreamed of a major case that might get him some travel since his
first days in the DEA academy. It was a harsh reality to learn that the
agency valued arrests in quantity, not necessarily quality. Because of his
heritage and ability to speak Spanish, Félix had been put on the street
buying a kilo here and a few ounces there. He didn't resent it—in fact, he
enjoyed undercover work—but he knew it was cases like this that made a
difference. If he could bag a guy like Ortíz, people would notice.

He wasn't too worried about Gastlin trying to flee. Even though the
tubby dealer had been to Panama before, Félix had sensed a real willing-
ness to cooperate. It was after he'd been in the county jail a few days. He
just seemed more subdued and helpful. He clearly wanted to have the
charges dropped for good and avoid prison time. Félix hated to admit it,
but Gastlin was starting to grow on him. He just hoped his charm and
good looks didn't push the snitch to make another pass at him. Félix had
been careful to mention how interested he was in Lina Cirillo so Gastlin
would realize he definitely wasn't gay.

In fact, Félix had put some of his best moves on Lina, and although she was friendly, he hadn't even got to kiss her good night when he dropped her at her hotel. He'd thought that by surprising Duarte and his girlfriend for a drink, Lina might feel inclined for companionship, but, boy, had he been wrong. Was she a dyke? No, something about her gave off a strong sexual vibe around men. Well, maybe he'd have a chance to try again.

As he stood among the crowds of people rushing in both directions, a tall man with light hair approached him. He was wearing a loose, un-tucked shirt and baseball cap, and Félix smiled, thinking that even in a foreign country an FBI agent looked like a fucking FBI agent.

"You the DEA guy?"

Félix looked at him and shrugged.

The man looked a little panicked.

Félix started to speak Spanish. *"No sé. No habla inglés."*

The man backed away, eyeing Gastlin as he did. Félix suppressed a smile and started to follow him, this time raising his voice. "Hey, Mr. Undercover. I'm Félix Baez."

The man stopped and said, "I can tell this'll be a fucking peach of an assignment. Good thing the Panamanians are working most of it with you."

"What do you do?"

"I'm your taxi until I can hand you off to them."

Félix nodded to Gastlin, who scurried to catch up, then made the informant carry his single suitcase to the FBI man's beat-up six-year-old Crown Vic.

Félix chuckled. "This your G-ride?"

"Down here, this is a damn Bentley. Get in."

The capital city of Panama sprang up slowly at first as they traveled from the airport, until it seemed like out of nowhere towering apart-ment buildings were crammed onto each block. Félix didn't want to look like a tourist as he watched the people trying to move on the crowded sidewalks. The traffic resembled something out of the worst sections of Miami, with no one appearing to obey any particular rules.

They stopped in front of a relatively small office building in a quieter section of the city. Several blocks of two-story buildings covered the area to the east. On the west was a view of the ocean. The ocean didn't smell like the one off Miami Beach. There was more of an industrial tinge to this odor.

"This your office?" Félix asked the driver.

"Nope, we're in the embassy. This is the off-site narcotics division of the national police. They're gonna be working this shit with you."

"What about you guys?"

"We got other issues."

"I need to speak to the DEA here."

"They're out on something, that's how I got this detail. They'll hook up with you later. The boss here, Staub, has a personal interest in your case. You'll get a lot out of these guys, and they don't have to answer to an attorney general for their actions."

Félix said, "You coming in?"

"Nah, I'm gonna drop your bags at the Holiday Inn and head back to the office." He handed Félix his card. "Call my cell if you need anything."

"On what?"

The FBI man smiled and handed him a cell phone. "So you don't think we're useless. That's our undercover phone. Local number, and you can use it till you leave."

Félix smiled. "Thanks. I still think you're useless, but I appreciate the phone." He slid out of the car, the door creaking as he shut it. Gastlin was right by his side.

The FBI agent nodded and headed off down the street.

Félix approached the front door of the building, with Gastlin locked in step beside him.

Félix turned and stopped, almost causing the informant to run into him. "How'd you ever do business down here if you're this frightened?"

"This is different."

"How?"

"I'm with the cops. Someone might get shot."

Félix shook his head and pushed on through the large glass door.

As he pulled out his ID and told the armed, uniformed man at the counter he needed to see Colonel Staub, the guard kept looking over to

Gastlin. The guard, an odd-looking, younger man with a bristling five o'clock shadow and a name tag that read Pelligrino, picked up the phone and turned away from them to speak. Then he walked away and talked with the second uniformed guard.

Félix felt naked without a gun and started to think he was not going to be allowed in the building.

The second guard spoke to Félix. "Mr. Baez, you may see the colonel, but non–law enforcement personnel are not allowed in the secured area. Your associate will have to wait down here."

Félix shrugged and turned to Gastlin. "He says only cops can go up. Wait here."

"How'd he know I wasn't a cop?"

Félix almost turned to ask the guard, but looking at Gastlin's gut and ratty boat shoes, he decided it was obvious. "He just knows. Now wait here, and I'll be back soon."

He followed a guard to the bank of elevators, and they rode up together six floors. Another security checkpoint outside the elevator slowed them briefly, then Félix was led to an office with a separate sentry.

The guard spoke to the sentry and then opened the double doors wide, and Félix walked in to a panoramic view of the Pacific Ocean.

A tall man with a full mustache rose from behind a giant desk and smiled. Speaking Spanish, he said, "Welcome to Panama. I am Lázaro Staub, and together we'll finally get this bastard Ortíz."

Félix already liked how this guy thought.

Ortíz looked over at his best boat captain and said, "Just agree with what this idiot wants after a little haggling. We need a big load. Make it look good."

"Yes, boss," said the young man with the rough skin.

Pelly, standing to the side, frowned.

"What is it, Pelly?" asked the boss, his tone not hiding any annoyance.

"I thought the whole idea was for us to make money. Even if we have other plans, it wouldn't hurt to get some cash up front."

"Pelly, there is more to life than money."

"Not if you're poor."

"You're not poor now."

"But I remember what it was like."

The boss sighed and said, "But we have to allow the Americans to think they're in charge,"

"But they are."

"Not forever."

Lina Cirillo smiled as she watched Alex Duarte eat a muffuletta in a little deli off Canal Street. She had heard a lot about the young ATF agent when she'd been briefed on the case. They said he was known as the "Rocket" because of his focus and drive—and that one Department of Justice official had learned that at his peril. He'd tried to use Duarte to his advantage only to learn the ATF man was really more of a guided missile, capable of not only zeroing in on a lead but changing direction if necessary.

Lina wouldn't make the same mistake. Although she had been told to keep a low profile and involve only one other FBI agent in the case, she knew that both Duarte and the DEA man had no ulterior motives. The poor, uninformed grunts were trying to make a drug-and-gun case. Lina had other fish to fry.

Byron "B.L." Gastlin sat in the open courtyard of a small restaurant just outside the downtown section of Panama City. A tape recorder was carefully secured under the table, squirreled away by the national police without anyone noticing. Gastlin knew there were DEA guys and at least one FBI agent, besides Félix and several national police all, watching him and waiting to see who showed up. He was scared. Not like when he was as a kid watching *The Wizard of Oz*, but like he was about to go into combat for he first time. "Terrified" didn't even cover how he was feeling. He was so scared he had not even eaten the pastries in front of him.

He had followed the instructions left for him by someone in the Ortíz organization. It was how they had worked in the past. He'd call a number and ask for Ortíz. Usually he got Pelly or one of the other guys. Last night he had been told by someone where to meet at nine in the morning. That was a businessman. Nine in the morning instead of ten at night at some strip bar, which was what happened when he sold the shit in Florida. Everyone wanted a long, expensive night at Rachel's or one of the other high-end strip clubs. He wondered if it was some kind of tax write-off for them.

He used the napkin on the table to wipe the sweat from his forehead and face, then ran it under his arms as well. He lifted his polo shirt and decided he had too much hair on his belly to try and keep dry.

He had been here in Panama five other times to negotiate a deal, usually a load for someone else in Florida, and he'd take his cut. He brought in one hundred kilos of cocaine in a sailboat once, the years of sailing lessons his parents paid for finally put to use. Once he drove a camper loaded with marijuana across the Mexican border into Texas. Twice he had just arranged the loads and had local smugglers from Panama deliver them to him in a fishing boat just off the coast of Key West. He had never come close to being caught and never felt half this scared. He realized he could've been killed in the other deals and that having the cops around him was safer than being alone, but he'd had always had the impression that as long as it was business and he paid his bills, he was in no danger.

He looked up again, surprised his eyes burned from sweat already. He was out of napkins. He glanced around his table and then jerked the cloth that covered two bread rolls in a small basket. The cloth soaked up his facial sweat, but he didn't worry about his arms this time. He didn't have time anyway. He could see a young, fit man, like all the ones that hung out with Mr. Ortíz, walking down the small street toward him. Gastlin's eyes involuntarily darted round checking for the drug agents. He couldn't see any, but realized that meant they were doing their job. He was sorry Mr. Ortíz had not come himself, but relieved he didn't have to look at the tall man's imposing face.

The young man nodded as he entered the gate.

It was showtime.

DUARTE LISTENED TO ALICE'S VOICE ON HIS SMALL NEXTEL CELL
phone. Even on the cheap piece of electronics, she sounded like music
to him. He smiled, despite the fact that he was using his personal line
and she was racking up his prime-time minutes.

After filling him in on a case where she had discovered a fingerprint
which had linked a local veterinarian to the baseball-bat beating and
attempted murder of his estranged wife, she said, almost without a
breath, "So how's New Orleans?"

"Fine."

"Is that the telephonic equivalent of a shrug?"

He smiled as he settled into the chair at the local FBI office, where he
was waiting while Lina briefed the local special agent in charge. He realized Lina would be telling him more about the source they called Pale
Girl but didn't care. It was on a need-to-know basis, and the army had
taught him not to ask about things that were not important to him for an
operation.

As Alice started to tell him about her workout that morning, he heard a beep on his phone, and he said, "I'm sorry, I have a call. It might be about the case."

"I understand."

She started to say something else, but he was already switching lines, hoping he wasn't getting himself into trouble again. He realized he hadn't come as far as he'd thought in dealing with women. "Yes?"

"Rocket, it's Félix."

"How's it going down there?"

"We're all set. We're a go."

Félix sat at a table in a family chicken place not far from the national police headquarters. Gastlin had needed a few minutes to compose himself after the man from Ortíz's organization had left the little café. The dried sweat on Gastlin's shirt was a testament to the trial the meeting had been. Félix spoke to him alone because he knew Gastlin would be more comfortable that way. It also freed up the others to try and follow the man who'd met with him. If they could find a permanent location for the man, they might be able to better identify Ortíz. It was all pretty standard.

Gastlin took a deep breath and then gulped down a glass of water.

Félix said, "You okay?"

Gastlin nodded, panting a little now.

"Sounded like it went well," said Félix. He'd listened to the tape but wanted Gastlin's interpretation of events.

"Real easy." He grabbed Félix's water glass. "Don't even have to front any money."

"That unusual?"

"Not really. If I bring in extra for someone else, they usually let me send the money later or have someone come up and collect. I've never been late."

"How will they deliver the load?"

"They'll get a legitimate shipper to transport the container and deliver it to the port at Colón."

"And the load is only pot?"

"Yeah, but a lot of it. Twenty thousand pounds. That should be enough for you guys. Enough to get me out from under the charges."

Félix smiled. This guy had worked too hard and been under too much stress to let him hang. "Yeah, my guess is they'll let you walk."

Gastlin let out a huge sigh and then had to wipe his eyes.

Félix said, "They'll even deliver it to the port in Colón?"

"Yeah, they always do that. They deliver it to the boat or truck. Once they brought it all the way into Mexico so I could drive it over the border into Texas. That's nothin' new. But doing it tonight. That's fast. Even for these guys."

"You did good, Byron. How's it coming?"

"One container. A twenty-footer. They lift it right off the trailer."

"Shit. So far this whole case has been easy." Félix stood up and said, "I gotta brief the colonel to see if he can trace it from the trucker." He thought about what to do with Gastlin, then said, "Meet me back here in two hours."

Gastlin only nodded while he drank the last of the water in Félix's glass.

Félix was escorted up to the colonel's office immediately by the officer with the thick beard. He liked the view and felt the national police had done a good job on the case. He briefed the colonel on everything Gastlin had told him.

Colonel Lázaro Staub leaned back in his chair. The tall, fit-looking man smoothed out his mustache and said in Spanish, "All is in order. My men and the DEA are still following the man who met with the informant. We are one step closer to finally identifying one of the country's most notorious drug traffickers."

Félix said, "Now we must figure out how to get the cargo to the U.S."

Colonel Staub nodded. "This will not be a problem. We can make all the arrangements with a legitimate shipper. They will not realize we are the police. They will transport anything if the price is right. There are many ships that travel back and forth."

Félix couldn't keep from smiling. The case was flowing right along. "You guys get things done."

Staub smiled. "We are a small country. Those of us that have been in public service tend to know each other. There is little red tape."

"How long have you been in this job?"

"Three years as the head of narcotics. Fifteen years with the national police and ten years with the defense force before that."

"Is that the Panamanian army?"

"Yes, just a small force. We, of course, rely on the U.S. for some level of protection." His left eye twitched slightly. "Are you of Cuban descent?"

Félix nodded. "I was born there and moved to the U.S. when I was six."

"How did you arrive in the U.S.?"

"My father was a coach for the national baseball team. He was able to bring us on an exhibition circuit through South America and defected in Venezuela. We moved to the U.S. the next year."

"Cuba could be so much more if Castro weren't a nut and the U.S. didn't hold a grudge."

"You don't like our policies?"

"You forget, we were on the receiving end of a policy shift. The 1989 invasion taught us that U.S. interests are everyone's interests."

Félix wasn't sure where to go with this conversation, so he changed back to the case. "What do we do now?"

The colonel thought about it and said, "It is now up to Ortíz. When they deliver the container, we can move forward. What's the plan once it arrives?"

Félix knew the plan had to be fluid. "Once we secure it in New Orleans, there are supposed to be three recipients of the extra marijuana. We'll keep everything quiet and see if we can deliver the pot and then arrest whoever accepts delivery. Our customs guys say we'll get the container through the port with no hassles."

"Excellent. I'd get some rest and be ready to move tonight." He came from behind the desk and said, "I'll walk you down." He placed his hand around Félix's shoulder.

The colonel was wearing a casual tan sport coat that covered a P-38-style automatic nine-millimeter in a black flap holster. He looked like an old-time Gestapo plainclothes officer. Félix bet that this guy's name was known to most of the cops in the country and that there wasn't any place he couldn't go. It also seemed likely he knew everything that went on. That was probably why this Ortíz character had gotten under his skin. He hated someone doing something he didn't know about.

Once they arrived in the lobby, Félix sensed the heightened alertness of the security personnel now that the boss was in the room. The door was opened by two men as they crossed into the Panamanian humidity and heat, even more oppressive than Florida's.

A block south of the office building, they stopped next to an alley.

The colonel lit a cigarette he dug from his coat pocket and said, "I need to be getting back, but I think I'll take advantage of the case to make the trip with you back to New Orleans." He looked at Félix and added, "If that would be all right with you, of course."

"We would be happy to have you as our guest. I'll make arrangements with the FBI legate here in Panama right now."

Staub smiled. "I love New Orleans. Besides, it'll be good to practice my English."

"You speak English?"

Staub took a second and switched languages. "I speak the English and the Spanish and the French," he said in a heavy accent. "I have been traveled to Miami and New York." He smiled.

"That's good. I speak English and Spanish, but nothing else."

Still in English, Staub said, "I will enjoy this break in my hobby."

"Hobby?"

"Job?"

Félix nodded.

"Excellent."

Byron Gastlin sat for about ten minutes, then decided that, since there was no way in hell he'd ever come back to this godforsaken place, he'd take a few minutes to explore. Maybe he'd meet Félix at police headquarters instead of here. He walked past several shops that sold what was purported to be native jewelry and handmade blankets. He stopped at one place and thought about buying some dolls for his niece in Sarasota. He was tired all of a sudden. He walked, thinking he was on the right street for the police building, but then saw he was a block off— the top floor of the office building popped over the lower roofs of the businesses and apartments. He picked up the pace, pushing his stubby legs along as fast as he could without exerting himself.

Finally, he found an alley that crossed onto the next street and discovered that his worn topsiders gave him little traction on the slight incline of the alley's bricklike surface. There were doors to apartments along the narrow street and the occasional moped or bicycle, but no cars would dare make it down the roadway. It curved slightly, giving Gastlin a partial view of traffic on the next street: old, beat-up American cars traveling as fast as they could, white, nasty exhaust pouring from their tailpipes.

As Gastlin stepped onto the main street, he paused on the sidewalk to get his bearings, and a man almost bumped into him. It took the American a second to realize who it was.

He fumbled for the words, then finally said, "Hello, sir. I just finished talking with your man."

The taller man smiled, but with no warmth. "That's funny," he said in almost unaccented English. "I thought you just finished talking with a U.S. drug agent."

Gastlin froze. He knew the man was connected, but not this well. Gastlin had to think fast. "No, no. I was speaking to a distributor from the states. He's another smuggler like me. He couldn't be with the DEA."

Mr. Ortíz stared at him and said, "You flew into Panama with him."

Gastlin didn't know how to answer. The DEA had a bad leak in it.

Flustered, Gastlin said, "I, um, did see him on the plane."

"And an FBI agent met you both."

Gastlin stared at him. He finally said, "If you knew all that, why did you have your man meet with me?"

"I had my reasons." He smiled and arched his eyebrows.

It gave Gastlin a chill. He suddenly realized that his business partner might be completely insane.

Gastlin felt his usual sweat kick into high gear, and the cloth below his underarms looked like he had peed in his shirt. His stomach gurgled as he fought the urge to be sick. This was why things had gone so smoothly. Mr. Ortíz really *did* control the cops. He wanted to run, but now regretted all the Twinkies and making fun of runners because he knew he'd never leave this alley.

ALEX DUARTE STOOD ON A BALCONY OF THE ADMINISTRATIVE offices for the Port of New Orleans, looking out over the busy water operations of the Napoleon container terminal as he listened to Félix Baez on his cell phone.

"Are you sure he isn't just out for a while?" asked Duarte. "You know, sightseeing or something."

"C'mon, Rocket. It's been over twenty-four hours. I'm tellin' ya, Gastlin got cold feet. He was afraid the U.S. attorney wasn't gonna give him credit, and he skipped."

"But you got the load?"

"Yeah, they dropped it near Colón over on the east coast. Staub's men got it through the port and on an old tub named *Flame of Panama*. It left late last night."

"When are you coming back?"

"I fly out this afternoon. Colonel Staub is coming with me. He's been a huge help. They been looking for Gastlin, too."

"And you don't think the bad guys got him?"

"I thought about it, but the cops were watching the guy he met when he disappeared. They delivered the pot just like they said, too. If there was a problem, they wouldn't have dropped off the container."

Duarte thought about it and added, "Just seems strange. The guy didn't impress me as a runner. I thought he was too shaky to do something like that."

"Me, too. I got a few more hours to find his fat ass. Maybe he's chasing transvestites over in the central district."

Duarte considered this and remained silent. He knew the DEA man was masking how he really felt. He was quiet so long, Félix said, "You still there?"

Duarte said, "Uh-huh."

"Where's Lina? She missing me?"

"She's here with the FBI guys. I get the feeling they're interested in someone other than Ortíz."

"Who?"

"I'm just listening and learning."

"I'll get her to open up when I fly in."

Duarte remained silent, even though he doubted Félix's ability to loosen up the FBI agent.

Félix said, "I'll call if we round up that tub of lard."

"Good luck."

"See you tonight."

Duarte shut the phone and looked up to see Lina coming toward him on the balcony, the wind whipping her short hair to the side. In jeans and a simple T-shirt, her athletic body stood out. "What's up, Alex?"

"That was Félix. He's flying in tonight. Everything is on schedule."

"That's great. I wanna see who the other distributors for the pot are."

"You think they'll be threats to national security, too?"

She looked at him, trying to decide if he was being sarcastic, then said, "It's our job to find out."

Duarte liked that attitude of taking responsibility and not shying away from duty. But he didn't like not knowing what the story was as his case started to go. He felt like maybe now he had a need to know.

"Why Ortíz and his contacts?"

"Why what?"

"Why are they a threat to security?"

Lina looked at him. Her dark eyes set in that crooked face. He could see the intelligence in them, but also that famous FBI arrogance. She didn't say a word.

Duarte said, "I'm curious . . . You really think I'd let something slip?"

She kept that hard gaze on him. He returned it. A stare not learned from police work or four years in the army, but a natural one that God had given him instead of the ability to relax around people. When other teenagers were going to parties and learning about life, he had decided to learn karate and push himself to the limit in sports, completing the Disney marathon in Orlando at eighteen. Lina Cirillo could try and stare him down now, but she'd be in for a shock if she did.

Finally, after a full minute, longer than Duarte thought she could hold out, she said, "It's not that I don't trust you, but there are some things that I'm not supposed to talk about, and this source is one of them. You should just be happy that we were able to move things along." She leaned back against the rail on the balcony and said, "One way to look at it is that all drugs are a form of terrorism toward the U.S."

Duarte changed his stare. "Marijuana? C'mon, don't treat me like an idiot."

She smiled, her white teeth forming the only symmetrical feature on her face, but the overall effect was attractive. She sighed and said, "One of Ortíz's contacts here has been involved in some pretty serious stuff. We think he's one of the guys getting the pot."

"I assume the FBI doesn't consider dealing pot a threat to national security."

"No, but it's not like this guy. We think he might be using the pot to finance something worse."

"What sort of serious stuff has he been involved in?"

She hesitated and then leveled her gaze on him. "Let's just say, if it weren't for 9/11, this guy would be associated with our worst attack."

Duarte wanted to hear more, but realized he had already gotten more than Lina was authorized to tell him.

The man known as Ortíz looked out of the cracked, grimy window-pane above the Avenida Quarto de Julio. The second-floor apartment was one of several apartments that he and his associates owned throughout the capital city. It was vital that Ortíz not be seen meeting with certain people.

Ortíz felt his left eye twitch; it ocurred whenever he was agitated. Right now it was because, as he looked out on the city, he recalled the battles fought against the Americans in 1989. He often passed the former location of the national police, which the Americans had destroyed early in the conflict. He would let the burn zone left by the bombs fuel his anger. It sustained him.

His position in the elite 2,000th Battalion at the start of hostilities had given him a front-row seat to the rout of the Panamanian Defense Force. The use of the then ultrasecret F-117A Stealth Fighter had been more like a training run for the Americans. Panama had had no defense for such technology. Then an AC-130 Spectre gunship had pounded Fort Cimarron. He was lucky to get out alive. Now he intended to make the U.S. feel the same way: hopeless. And he had the perfect target: military, symbolic and vital to the United States.

A moan turned his attention from the second-story window back to the room.

In the middle of the sparse living room, Byron Gastlin sat with his torso and legs secured to a wooden chair. Pelly, Ortíz's most effective assistant, gave the tubby American a sip of water. They weren't ready for him to die yet. It had only been an hour. They had to make certain of the information.

Ortíz looked at the bloody mark on his left hand where Gastlin had grabbed him, begging for mercy and then scratching him when he removed his hand. Without thinking, Ortíz had snatched a butcher knife from the kitchen and severed the three middle fingers on his right hand. He wouldn't be grabbing anyone else for the time he had left on Earth.

Ortíz had cringed slightly when Pelly had then used the same knife to cut a sandwich in half. He'd wiped it, but then still he'd declined when Pelly offered him half.

Ortíz said, "You're sure no one was following him?"

"Yes, boss. Our men called me to say they were breaking off, and I saw the Americans follow them out of the business district. Héctor called me ten minutes later to confirm that he was alone."

Ortíz looked at Pelly. "And what about you?"

"I came way around and then through the Barrio Chorillo to get here. No way anyone but one of us gets through there without gunfire."

Ortíz looked at Gastlin. "Very good. Let's finish up." He stepped over to the trembling American. "Now, Mr. Gastlin, you are certain no one knows me?"

Gastlin shook his head, his eyes darting down to his mutilated hand every few seconds.

"Did you hear anyone talk of Ortíz?"

"Like in the office?"

"Exactly."

"Yeah, they all wanted to identify Ortíz. No one knew who you were."

Ortíz took out a ballpoint pen and made a few notes on a steno pad sitting on the counter that separated the small kitchen from the living room. He turned back to Gastlin and leaned down. "You're certain?"

Gastlin, panting, said, "Yeah, yeah."

Ortíz set the end of the pen on one of Gastlin's stubs where his index finger had been a few minutes before. He pressed the end of the pen into the open wound.

Gastlin sucked in air and said, "I swear, I swear." He started to wail.

Ortíz let up pressure. He looked at Pelly. "Unzip his pants."

Pelly moved like a cat and had his hairy fingers in Gastlin's lap and the zipper started before the smuggler could even say, "Please, don't."

Then, after catching his breath, the dope dealer said, "I swear I won't say anything if you let me go. I swear to God."

Ortíz smiled. "Mr. Gastlin, I know you won't say anything."

Gastlin's eyes widened. "No. I meant if you let me go."

"I see. I'm sorry you cannot be accommodated. We could have used an individual like you in the U.S."

"Use me, use me."

Ortíz picked up the knife from the inside counter.

Gastlin said, "No. Think about it. You need me for the load."

"The load is already on the way."

"They'll miss me."

He chuckled. "I doubt it. Your friends at the DEA might miss you, but they'll never know what happened."

He held up the eight-inch knife. It was pointy but not sharp.

Pelly said, "Boss, I gotta clean up, would you avoid cutting anything else off? I can throw the fingers in a bag, but anything else might be messy."

Gastlin looked between the two men, obviously terrified to hear anyone discuss him like a cow ready for butchering.

Ortíz said, "You want it clean?"

"If possible."

Ortíz saw his assistant's point, but he didn't like it. This man had plenty of appendages that could be trimmed. Instead, he stepped over into the kitchen, opened a cupboard and pulled out a loop of heavy, coarse twine, the same kind they had used to bind Gastlin.

He pulled the loop until he had enough string to double between his hands. He casually stepped behind Gastlin and placed the rough twine around Gastlin's neck.

The heavyset American started to weep and shift in his seat. He had to know it was coming. What a terrifying idea, imminent death.

Gastlin said, "Wait, wait. Why?" and just babbled on.

As he tightened the string, Ortíz said, "Because we are not a colony of the United States." He rubbed the twine back and forth across the flabby flesh of Gastlin's neck as he tightened. He smiled at the erection he felt as Gastlin gulped for air that was not going to come.

Ike sat up in his bed in the little hotel room in Metairie, outside New Orleans. He had wandered through the town for three days now and felt like he had seen all he wanted to see. The place turned his stomach as far as the people who lived here. There were beggars on every corner. Drunken foreigners staggering around Bourbon Street. It seemed like every chick had some kind of colored boyfriend. But he had kept his mouth shut. It all went back to why the country needed to shut its borders and end immigration. They couldn't depend on the Minutemen to do it all. Those poor guys were wearing themselves out on the border between Arizona and Mexico. Once the country saw the problems with immigration, then maybe they could deal with the lowlifes that were already here. Send back a few Jamaicans and a trainload of Mexicans, and maybe crime would drop. He didn't feel it too much in Omaha, but he knew it was a problem in the rest of the country. They had already lost California. The Mexicans were bragging that they had won it back without a fight. Florida might be a lost cause, too. It wasn't so bad with just Cubans, but now it seemed like every form of beaner had taken up residence in the Sunshine State. Ike didn't even think they had that many Jews anymore.

After dressing and hiding his valuables from the sporadic cleaning crew, he decided he could walk to the library about six blocks from the hotel. The big U-Haul truck attracted too much attention and was difficult to navigate through the narrow Louisiana streets. With summer over, the temperatures were nice, and the sun was out. Sleeping or working during the day had given him a complexion like a vampire. The sun would give him a little color. He needed to look as mainstream as possible. His hair was already there. For the first time in several years, he had had to run a comb through it when he woke up.

Years earlier he had shaved his head so the Hammerskins would look at him more favorably. The working-class party of white people had proven to be an active, solid organization. Too bad they got an idea of some of his interests. Too much beer one night had made him show one of the longtime Hammerskin veterans the wrong website, and, after splitting his lip with a quick right hand, the man had informed him that he should not now or in the future claim membership in the Hammerskins.

Before that he had been in the National Alliance, but they were too concerned with race purity. They were looking for a holy war that Ike knew wouldn't come, and if it did he didn't really want to fight it. He'd be content to stop immigration and have the country take a serious look at people from outside the borders. Besides, the National Alliance expected a lot of work out of its members. He had a job. He didn't need a second one.

He had met up with some members of the Phineas Priesthood, but quickly realized crazy was crazy no matter what race you were. The members of the priesthood were just too extreme and expected everyone who joined to be the same way. They might really do something to make people notice one day, but he knew what it would take to change things.

He entered the small library and looked over to the round table with six computers available for library patron use. He had already used the computer to check for messages three times. The library only required him to use his first name on the log and only then if there was a waiting list. This morning, things looked pretty quiet. The reference librarian just pointed to an empty computer as he walked up. He nodded and smiled at her.

He typed in *Yahoo.com* and then tracked his way to Yahoo mail. He entered his user name and password. His name was a variation of *World-changer,* and the password was *freedom.* He was not the only one in possession of these phrases. Since it had been widely reported that messages passed over the Internet could be monitored, he shared the account with the president, Mr. Jessup, and the beaner, Mr. Ortíz. He would enter the account, then check messages that had been saved but not sent. That way no one ever looked at the messages, and they were absolutely secure. Only the three men knew it. The process was foolproof.

He found one message. It simply said "On the way. Ship—Flame of Panama—O."

Now things would get interesting.

ALEX DUARTE NODDED AS HIS FRIEND FÉLIX WALKED UP THE
hallway to the main administrative office of the Port of New Orleans.
He shook his hand and glanced over his shoulder at the tall, well-built
man behind Félix.

Félix said, "Rocket, this is Colonel Lázaro Staub." He turned to the
colonel and said, "This is Alex Duarte from the U.S. Bureau of Alcohol,
Tobacco and Firearms."

"Mucho gusto, señor Duarte." He bowed slightly. *"Me honra satisfacerlo."*

Duarte looked at the fifty-year-old man and shrugged. He shrugged
so frequently he could put emotion into each shrug. This one was an
apology shrug.

Staub shook his head and said in English, "I sorry. I thought you were
Hispanic."

"I am."

"Where were you born?"

"Florida, but my family is from Paraguay."

"And you speak no Spanish?"

"I'm working on it."

"No matter. I practice the English anyway."

They settled in a conference room, where Félix started by asking about Lina.

Duarte said, "She took off with another FBI agent on some mission here in New Orleans."

"You learn anything about their source? Pale Girl?"

"Nothing." He kept his eyes from darting to Staub. He knew Félix wasn't authorized to hear about Pale Girl. He also knew that a visiting cop from Panama shouldn't even know there was a source of information related to the case.

Félix said, "The Colonel here was a lifesaver. He had men load the container onto the ship and got the ship out right on time. It'll be here by midnight."

"That fast?"

"Yeah, less than two days on the seas. The port in Colón is about eight hundred miles from New Orleans."

Duarte nodded. "What about Gastlin?"

Félix looked down, maybe the first time Duarte had seen him less than energetic. "No sign of him. We got the DEA guys and the Colonel's cops all looking for him."

"How do we find out who the pot in the container goes to without him?"

"We already thought of that. Won't work. We figured we'll hold the load for a day or two to see if he surfaces. If not, the effort isn't a total zero. We still have a direct buy from Ortíz."

"But still no ID?"

Félix shook his head.

Staub spoke up. "We have been trying to identify this Ortíz for two years. He is very difficult. It is not so easy to find wealthy men who wish to remain unknown."

Duarte nodded and for the first time noticed a slight twitch in the colonel's left eye.

Lina returned in the evening. She acted as if she had been gone an hour instead of nearly ten. The introductions were made, and Duarte noticed two things that he might have been too dense to pick up on a few months earlier.

First, Lina's hand lingered in Colonel Staub's handshake, and she gazed directly into his eyes. Second, Duarte realized that Félix wasn't happy about her reaction.

Duarte kept his mouth shut and minded his own business, just like he tried to always do.

Once they were seated at a conference table waiting for the *Flame of Panama* to arrive, Félix looked across at Lina and said, "So where you been all day?"

"Errands."

"Like what?" His tone was sharper than normal.

She didn't answer.

Félix wouldn't let it go. "So your errands are classified, too?"

Lina flashed a glare at him.

Duarte cut in and said, "Let's figure out what to do with the load if Gastlin doesn't turn up."

Staub said, "It is safe at the port, no?"

They all nodded.

"Will your customs officers search it or ask questions?"

Félix said, "No. We'll bring it into the secure area. It'll be in with so many other containers no one will ever even notice it."

Duarte thought about logistics and said, "If we look at it in the port, someone will see us. It may tip them off."

Félix said, "We'll check it on the boat. Once it's off-loaded, they won't know which container we checked." His cell phone rang. Félix spoke quietly for a few moments and then looked up at the others. "We can do it right now if you'd like. The ship just docked."

Flame of Panama itself was an older freighter that appeared to be painted brown until Duarte looked closely and realized it was rust, a deep, well-earned rust that seemed to change the ship's personality. If the upper deck were white and lower hull black, the entire look would lift the crew's spirits. The way it looked now, even sailors had to think they had drawn the short straw.

No one even challenged them as they followed a customs inspector up the gangplank. The round woman in a Department of Homeland Security uniform waddled up the plank and then pointed to a lower container. There were two containers stacked on it and several on each side.

A giant padlock with a tiny keyhole sealed the container.

"We can cut it," said the customs inspector.

Félix shook his head. "No, we don't want to draw attention."

They waited while the customs inspector retrieved a set of keys from the ship's first mate. The first mate stayed back out of the way and didn't seem to want to interact with the group by the container. Duarte saw that he was a young man with a thick, short beard. His bushy eyebrows and protruding teeth gave him a slightly Neanderthal look. The man's eyes met his for a moment. Then the first mate slipped off.

The doors opened out like the double doors to a ballroom. The overwhelming smell of damp marijuana hit Duarte like a linebacker. Félix and the customs inspector shined in large flashlights, and they all stepped into the dank freight container.

Duarte had never seen so much illegal substance in one place. It was one thing to hear someone say "twenty thousand pounds"; it was another to see bale after bale stacked on each side of the container. There was a passageway between each stack to the rear wall. Each bale weighed about four hundred pounds.

Something crawled across the top of the highest bale.

Duarte jumped to the other side.

Félix said, "Always get rats or big spiders in these loads."

That didn't make Duarte feel any better.

Félix turned to the customs inspector. "No one'll bother this?"

"Not over in the restricted area."

"And you won't let on what we're doing?"

"Not until I'm cleared to. You guys bring in loads all the time. Used to be, before 9/11, our customs agents arranged for loads, too. Now they got shifted to immigration and cargo crimes."

Félix turned to the whole group. "Let's let them get this thing unloaded and secured."

Duarte was the last to hop out onto the deck. For some reason, he felt like looking around for the first mate. There was something about the hairy young man that didn't seem right. He helped shove one of the heavy doors back into place, then watched as Félix set the big padlock again. The heavy frame hung down.

"Damn," said Félix.

"What's wrong?"

"I set the keyhole facing the door." He tried to lift the lock, but was unable to unlock it. "Screw it. It'll be easier in the daylight if we ever have to open the thing again." As he turned, he added, "If we ever see Gastlin again."

14

JOHN "JUAN" MORALES HAD ASKED THE DEA TO TRANSFER HIM to Panama for a couple of reasons. The extra pay was nice, just like the cheap cost of living, but the real reason was he got to pick his post of duty when he got back to the States. That was about the only way he thought he might get back to Jackson, Mississippi. He'd been assigned to St. Louis right out of the academy and tried to use his ability to speak Spanish, as weak as it was then, to get to New Orleans or Atlanta. He liked being close to his family and his father, a Cuban transplant who taught economics at Mississippi State. His mom, a former Miss Magnolia, didn't speak any Spanish and really had a poor grasp of English, too, but John had taken after his father and learned just enough Spanish to pass a fluency exam.

When he saw the posting for Panama, he put in for it, and to his surprise found himself living in the capital city a few months later.

So far he had found that most of his responsibilities were related to running errands for the guys in the States. They'd need some documentation about a resident or maybe a photograph of a boat docked at one of the marinas. It wasn't too hard, and he was just biding his time to go home anyway.

Right now, as the city slowed down and even the prostitutes started to come in off their perches on the street corners in lower-class neighborhoods, John was starting to get discouraged about finding the snitch that had given Félix Baez the slip. Morales had been in the DEA academy with Félix, two of only three Hispanics in the whole class at the Quantico, Virginia, facility. They had bonded, and Félix's easygoing manner and positive attitude had gotten John through some long weeks. His experience as a Mississippi state trooper had not prepared him for the challenges of tough academics, long hours and rigorous physical training.

John Morales had already checked his sources at the airport; no taxi driver had seen the portly American. His stuff was still in the cheap hotel room the DEA had supplied him. He had not been admitted to any hospital. John was starting to think he was holed up with a prostitute somewhere in the southwestern section of the city. That was why he was prowling those streets now.

He felt his cell phone vibrate and saw it was a local cop who was a friend of his.

"Diego, what'd you got?" he said in his heavily accented Spanish.

"Juan, my friend, I think we found your American."

"Great, where?"

"The main dump on the north side."

"Oh shit. How long has he been dead?"

"Hard to say."

"You sure it's him? You saw his photo."

"Still hard to say."

"Why? If you found him."

"We found most of him."

John froze in his tracks. "Most of him?"

"No head, his left hand is missing and three of his fingers on his right hand." There was a pause and the police investigator said, "Never mind, I think one of my guys just found one of his fingers. No luck on the hand or head."

"Jesus, Diego, what happened to him?"

"My guess is he crossed the wrong man."

"Where you gonna take him?"

"The main morgue."

"Will you let me know the autopsy results?"

There was a silence. Then Diego said, "Unless we have a suspect and motive and some cops who are interested, I doubt there'll be an autopsy. This isn't *CSI Miami*."

John didn't want to insult him, so he said nothing. He knew things were different here in Central America. "Keep me posted. I'll check with you tomorrow."

John Morales started home, but realized his stomach was a little upset. He wondered if he went to Staub and the national police, if they would be any help. He checked his watch and realized he better wait until tomorrow to call Félix. There was nothing he could do now anyway.

Cal Linley had worked for the Port of New Orleans for sixteen years. In that time, he had seen everyone with a skin color darker than his move up the ladder. Here he was, still a miserable off-loader. Sure, the pay was okay, but he had to work shifts and rarely had a weekend off. That worked to his benefit now. He stood in front of the container from *Flame of Panama* with a key for the padlock direct from the president, Mr. Jessup, who would be very happy with his efforts. He didn't know what they wanted out of the container, but he had detailed instructions on how to retrieve it and whom to give it to. The big shits at the National Army of White Americans didn't think he was fit to know exactly what he was retrieving from the container. He didn't care. He'd been told it was a step in the start of a revolution. He liked that idea. Set the country going in the right direction for a change. Not listening to them Commies at CNN or *60 Minutes* who always made it sound like regular people were stupid and the United States of America caused all the grief in the world.

Now he paused in the so-called restricted area. He wasn't worried.

The lone security guard was also a member of the faithful, a cop who'd lost his job because he'd used some instant justice on some punk who was stealing stereos out of cars. When he'd appeared in front of the all-colored review board, he'd just resigned on the spot. Been here at the port ever since.

Cal found the container, a twenty-footer set in the corner of the restricted area. He fumbled for the key and, with the flashlight tucked under his right arm, had to lift the lock because some moron had put the keyhole facing in. He flipped the lock upside down, then shoved in the small key. With a little twisting, he shook the lock free of the doors. He had to turn his wide frame sideways to make it down the aisle between the nasty bales stacked on each side. He realized they were bales of pot, but that was none of his business, nor was he interested in why pot was in with this cargo.

He squeezed through to the rear wall and tapped it with the long screwdriver he had brought with him. The hollow twang echoed in the container. He looked around, surprised at the volume of the tap.

He stooped low and unscrewed the thick, heavy screw holding the two halves of the wall together. He reached for the upper screw, but was short by a foot. He tugged one bale of pot over and stood on it, easily reaching the upper screw. The sides of the wall then slipped out and revealed another two feet of the container.

Tucked to one side was the package he had been told to retrieve. It was completely covered in a wooden crate. He nudged it and nodded. They had told him a little more than six hundred pounds.

He shoved back the bale of pot and then walked out to his pickup truck parked at the entrance to the restricted area. He pulled the old open-bed Ford next to the container and then lowered the tailgate. He had an appliance handcart and slipped it out. He had to do some fancy negotiating to slip the cart between the bales of pot, but found that with the crate on it to steady the cart, it was easy to pull out. He left the crate strapped to the cart and was able to tip it into the bed of his truck. The crate was about four feet long and two feet wide. He had no clue what could be in there that might start a revolution, but he was going to get it to the kid from Omaha and get it to him now.

He went back to the container and tried to reset the false wall, but found that he had popped the bracket holding one side out of the container wall. He just lugged out the two pieces of sheet metal and stuck them in the truck as well.

He looked inside again. He saw a clipboard with some documentation hanging inside the container. It wasn't in English, so he just left it on the wall.

As he left, he reset the lock and didn't even think about leaving the keyhole facing out like every shipper knew to do. He just did it out of habit.

ALEX DUARTE WATCHED FÉLIX BAEZ MAKE SOME NOTES BUT
knew it was bad news. Félix said into the phone, "Yeah, John, I'll hold."
He looked at Duarte, his pockmarked face dark. "They found Gastlin's
body. He'd been cut up pretty bad."

Duarte considered this. He knew it was wrong, but he was trained to
look at situations first. This meant their case was over. Now they had to
find out who had killed him and why. Was it related to the case? Was it
Ortíz?

Duarte said, "Have they done an autopsy yet?"

Félix shook his head. "No, and they might not. They're not even certain it's him. They have his torso and a finger. He's missing his head and
left hand."

Duarte held his breath. He hadn't heard of anything like that since
Bosnia.

Félix looked away from the phone like he was on hold and caught
Duarte up on the conversation. "The finger is whole, but they're not
going to check DNA."

Duarte knew they needed to know if it was Gastlin as quickly as possible.

Félix listened on his phone some more. When he looked up, he said, "I don't know, Rocket. This doesn't sound like they can even confirm it's him. Got any ideas?"

Duarte thought about the problem and the red tape that would be involved in getting the body to the U.S. for examination. The Panamanians could say they didn't even know if the victim was American. He didn't know how they operated down there. He just pictured Byron Gastlin in pieces in a drawer in a foreign morgue. He shuddered. No one deserved that. Then he thought about who would miss him if something like that happened. Gastlin had to have family that would care. Duarte had not talked about the drug dealer's personal life with him at all. He hadn't cared at the time.

Who would miss Duarte? His folks, of course. Alice. He froze. Alice could help.

He tapped Félix on the arm as the DEA agent listened to the other agent in Panama.

Félix looked up. "You got an idea?"

"I do."

"I'm all ears, man."

"We want this off the record and fast, right?"

"Yeah, the faster we find out the better."

"If someone prints the loose finger and faxes it, there might be enough of the print to identify or maybe not. If not, we're screwed."

"So?"

"If they mail the loose finger, we could have someone print it quietly, without any attention to it, and do it fast."

"I'm not following you, Rocket."

"Can your man get one of the severed fingers?"

"What? You loco, amigo?"

"I can get it identified without too much administration if they can get it to the U.S."

"You mean the FBI? I don't know."

"No, Félix. Alice could print him. He was booked into the Palm Beach County jail. It'd be quick."

"Snap, Rocket. That's a balls-up idea. Would she do it?"

"I don't know. See if you can get a finger first."

Félix spoke into the phone for a few more seconds. He looked back at Duarte. "He's with a cop at the morgue now. He's gonna check. Man, that's one stone-cold cool squeeze you got."

Duarte nodded.

"Why don't you publicize her more?"

He thought about it and almost shrugged, then said, "Because I'm an idiot."

Félix held up his hand as he focused back on the person on the phone.

Duarte heard him say, "No, really. Your pocket. Man, you are dope." He looked at Duarte. "All we need is a mailing address."

Cal Linley pulled to the side of the road about a mile from the little hotel in Metairie where he had been told to hand over the crate to the guy from Omaha, Ike. He wanted to go straight there, but his curiosity had gotten the best of him, and he couldn't resist. He had to see what was in the box. It was heavy, and it was important. They had had help in Panama and here, or else all that pot never would've made it through security.

He parked his old Ford F-250 in the parking lot of a closed grocery store. There was plenty of light from the streetlamps, and he lowered the rusty tailgate and hopped into the back. He rapped the crate with his knuckles and then tried the end by tugging on it. It didn't budge.

He went back to the truck's cab, dug into the rear-seat compartment and pulled out the extra tire iron he carried, as much for protection as for use in helping other people with flats. The narrow edge of the iron fit into the gap between the boards of the crate, and he peeled off the end.

He peered inside, but couldn't see anything. There was a soft metal foil, like lead wrapped around some kind of machine. He used his flashlight to look deeper. All he saw were wires and a shiny cylinder and some electronics.

He had finished the ninth grade at Pancetta High before being expelled for hitting a smart-ass Mexican kid in the head with a two-by-four. He was never charged, but he never went back to school either. His experience with electronics was limited. Mostly he used a lift to unload ships for minimum union wage and that was it.

He knew he wasn't prepared to make a rocket or even a firecracker, but he thought he had figured out what was in the box. Based on what he had just seen and what he had been told by President Jessup, he figured he was carrying some kind of equipment that concerned the oil business. He knew President Jessup used to be a big shot in the oil business in Houston. This thing he was carrying had something to do with funding a revolution to make America safe again. The machine he was looking at right now had to do with oil wells, maybe a new drill head or something that stopped oil flow. It was all making sense now.

He looked at the machine again and thought, Or maybe it's some kind of stolen technology that the National Army of White Americans will use to make a fortune and fund their political party better.

Either way he was happy to be a part of it.

He closed the box, hammering the nails back as best he could with the edge of his tire iron.

Five minutes later, he was knocking on the door to room nine at the Starlight Motel. The big U-Haul truck was parked in the slot right in front of the room.

It was now almost four o'clock in the morning. He saw a light flick on behind the cheap curtains. A younger man with short hair peeked out and nodded. A few seconds later, the door opened.

The man said, "You Cal?"

"I am." He eyed the muscular young man.

"You got the package?"

"In the truck."

"You know what it is?"

"No idea."

The young man smiled. "Good."

16

ALEX DUARTE LISTENED TO THE PHONE RING AND CHECKED HIS G-Shock wristwatch again. It was an hour later in West Palm Beach, so he was catching Alice at home before seven. He didn't like calling so early, but this was important, and he didn't want to make this call on an official sheriff's office phone line.

On the third ring, he heard her bright voice say, "Hello."

"Alice, it's Alex."

"I knew it was you. No one but my family would call this early, and none of them are up at this hour. How're you?" Before he could answer, she added, "Miss me? You must, to call this early. What time is it there? Five to six?"

"Still dark." Now he felt bad that the main reason he was calling was for a favor from her lab. He thought and said, "Getting ready for work?"

"Yeah, gonna hit the gym after work today. When will you be home?"

"Hard to say."

"Everything okay? You sound like there's a problem."

"We had a setback."

"No one is hurt, are they?"

"Sort of." He paused. She'd raised the question. He charged ahead. "Our informant went missing in Panama, and we think he's dead, but they can't identify the corpse."

"Was he disfigured? What happened?"

"He was murdered, that's clear."

He heard her take a breath. "Is Félix okay?"

"Yeah, he's here in New Orleans with me."

"Why don't they print the body?"

"That's what I asked, but I had another idea."

"What's that?"

"What if they sent his finger to a local police agency in the U.S. who already had his prints on file?"

"Why would they cut off one of his fingers?"

"They're already off."

"Oh, I see." She sounded ill. Then she caught on to the nature of the call. "So you didn't call because you missed me, you called to ask me to print an unattached finger."

"Both."

"Alex Duarte, you're a lousy liar. That's one of the things I like about you. Don't try it now."

He smiled and said, "Could you print the finger and match it to this guy Gastlin who was booked in the Palm Beach County jail?"

"It feels like I do a lot of forensic work for you off the books."

"And I appreciate it."

"How much?"

"A lot."

"How will you show it?"

"Dinner?"

"At least." She added, "How on earth will you get a human finger into the country?"

"Customs worked it out. A DEA guy will deliver it to you sometime tomorrow."

"You were pretty sure I'd do it."

"You're a very helpful person. I didn't see you saying no. We need to know what happened to Gastlin. The next step will be looking for the killer. It won't be easy."

"At least I'm easy."

Duarte didn't know how to respond to that, but he was good at just keeping his mouth shut.

William "Ike" Floyd watched the U-Haul truck from the big bay window of the diner while he ate a stack of pancakes with Cal Lindsey. They had loaded the crate with little problem, and Ike knew he couldn't stay at the rundown hotel. He went ahead and packed up his few clothes and decided he wouldn't turn down the older port worker's offer of breakfast.

Cal asked, "So where's the thing go now?"

Ike looked at him, remembering the words of one of the leaders of another group he used to belong to who said, "Never trust anyone who asks too many questions." The FBI always had people trying to get into the groups. The old leader of the American Nazi Party claimed the federal government hated white people, that's why they'd left the black groups alone. He looked at Cal's simple, long face and didn't think he could be a snitch for the FBI. He had a little experience in the matter and knew you couldn't tell by looking at someone, but it didn't matter right now. He just told the truth.

"Don't know exactly. I'll check for messages later." Ike figured if this guy was a snitch he'd ask about the messages and where he checked.

Instead, Cal said, "President Jessup says you were into some serious shit for us a while back."

Ike had to smile. "Can't talk about it."

"You think this is as big a deal as that shit?"

Ike considered it and said, "Yeah, if it works, it'll be bigger. There's a long way to go and a lot to do until we know for sure."

Cal finished the last bit of his scrambled eggs and wiped his mouth.

"I need to check in at the port. The beauty of a union job is someone will always cover for you. I'm off-duty at seven so I can go home and get some rest." He pulled out a pen and wrote a phone number and his name on a napkin. "This is my home number. Call me if you need more help."

"You're a good man, Cal."

"Anything for my country."

Félix Baez sat at the end of the long conference table in the administrative office of the Port of New Orleans with his arms folded and his mouth shut. He didn't care for the way Lina Cirillo had acted toward Lázaro Staub. Sure, the colonel was tall and handsome. Félix realized he had a certain charisma and obviously wielded some power back in Panama. But Félix didn't think that was any reason for Lina to hang on his every word and offer to show him around the city.

He thought he had staked his claim on the FBI agent. They had gone out twice for dinner and drinks back in Florida. He had paid both times. Now her full attention seemed to be focused on Staub. Shit.

Even as he thought about Lina, he knew his real source of unease was the fate of Bryon Gastlin. If the body they had found really was Gastlin. He held out hope that some other tubby white man in boat shoes and shorts had been killed and Gastlin was hiding out in Costa Rica. Unlike in the movies, the loss of an informant in real life could be very traumatic. Gastlin was Félix's responsibility. He'd possibly been killed because of something the DEA had had him do. Félix had promised him he'd be safe. Of course the possibility existed that he'd simply been robbed and murdered, or killed as a result of some other crime unrelated to Ortíz. But in all likelihood Félix would never know. The Panamanian cops were overwhelmed with street violence. Gastlin was just another statistic. And he was heavy on Félix's mind.

Lina said to the group, "Well, what now?"

Duarte looked at Félix since it was his agency's pot. Félix said, "Who the hell knows? I guess we pack it up and write off the case."

Staub spoke up, using his broken English for Lina and Duarte's benefit. "I contacted the investigators of the homicides, and they will do all they can to solve Mr. Gastlin's murder."

Félix spit out, "That mean anything?" He didn't want to hear from the Panamanian.

Staub looked at the DEA man with his dark eyes. "It means they will do all they can."

Duarte cut in before anyone was offended and said, "The gun case is closed, that much is for sure, but I can help you clear things up here."

Félix sighed. "We might as well get the pot into evidence. Customs has a facility here." He was glad Duarte was here to keep him from fixating on how he had let down Byron Gastlin.

An hour later, Félix and Duarte were at the container with a couple of customs agents and a step van.

Félix said, "Shit, this don't seem like fun anymore. Ortíz is off the hook, and Gastlin is dead."

Duarte nodded and patted his friend on the shoulder. He had seen plenty of grief in Bosnia from the locals involved in the war and from the military guys caught between the Serbs and Croats. That didn't mean he knew how to comfort anyone, but he was there for his friend if he needed anything. Duarte just had a hard time figuring out what people needed.

Félix stepped up to the container and dug out the keys from the front pocket in his pants.

Duarte said, "Wait a minute."

"What's up?"

"You notice anything odd about the lock?"

Félix looked at the shiny metal padlock. "No."

"The keyhole is facing out."

"So?"

"When you locked it, you had the keyhole in, remember? We didn't worry about it then."

Félix slowly nodded. "Yeah, I guess. What's it mean?"

"I don't know, but let's handle the lock carefully and see if anything is missing before the customs guys walk over."

Félix held the lock with two fingers as he worked the small key. It popped, and he fed it through the door latch.

Duarte picked up a crumpled paper bag from the littered ground and put the lock into the bag. Quickly they stepped inside, the smell of the pot soaking into their clothes and nasal passages. Duarte's eyes watered a little.

The load looked intact. They walked through to the rear of the container.

Félix said, "Looks like it's all here."

Duarte looked at the walls closely and the load of pot. "I think there was a wall here. See, the last two feet of the container has a clean floor and the walls aren't as dingy."

Félix looked closely at the indents in the sides of the container and the floor. "Snap, man, you may be right."

"Someone took out the wall last night."

"But why? How much more scrutiny do you get than bringing in a load of dope? Especially a load that the cops know about. It'd be crazy to hide anything in it."

Duarte shook his head, considering the possibilities. He heard the customs guys walking from their van. "Let's keep this quiet for now."

"Why?"

"Do you know who came in here?"

Félix thought about it, looked quickly at the approaching customs agents and shook his head.

"We got the lock." He stepped to the front of the load and pulled a few old sheets of the manifest off the hanging clipboard. He crumpled them and put them into the bag with the lock to keep it from moving around. "I bet Alice can tell us whose prints are on this thing."

"Damn, that girl is going to expect a lot from you now."

"She deserves a lot."

They stepped out of the way as the customs agents started to unload the marijuana bales.

William "Ike" Floyd sat in a Starbucks, chatting with a woman about his age, maybe a little older. He had a coffee or whatever the fucking place called a regular coffee, and the woman, whose name was Faith, had one of the fancier kinds with whipped cream that was the size of a 7-Eleven Big Gulp.

"You from New Orleans originally?" He smiled and looked right at her. He thought that most men probably found her attractive with her blond hair and pretty smile, but she didn't do anything for him. His main interest was in her computer.

Faith said, "I'm from Houma, but I'm here today because of a job interview. That's how come I got my computer with me. I'm checking my e-mail to see if anyone tries to contact me about other job interviews while I'm in New Orleans."

He smiled and took a sip of his coffee. "What do you do?"

"Mostly secretary work, but I can work computers good, too. The jobs haven't come back so much since Katrina."

Ike nodded, knowing that women liked to talk about themselves.

"Where are you from?" asked Faith.

"Omaha. I'm just here on business."

"What business you in?"

He hesitated. "I'm in shipping. We got a load that came through the port." He ran a hand across the computer. "In fact, is there any way I could check my e-mail really quick on your laptop?"

She paused, her green eyes running over his face and chest. "Yeah, I guess. This wireless Internet is a little slow."

"It's just a Yahoo account."

She nodded and slid the small Sony Viao across the little round table to him. In his button-down shirt and casual jeans, he knew he looked respectable, but add in the story about a decent job and he felt that this woman really might be attracted to him. He could understand for a moment what men saw in women. Not just the emasculating, nagging, overbearing women like his mom, who'd virtually left him parentless at sixteen when she ran off with a nigger musician from Chicago. He felt his blood pressure rise.

"You okay?" asked Faith, placing a hand on his arm.

Ike looked at her. "Yeah, why?"

"You just blushed really red in the face."

He looked down, embarrassed she'd seen what the memory of his mom could do to him.

"It's all right. In fact, it's kinda cute. I don't see men blush much anymore."

He liked this woman's voice. Then he remembered the computer and what he needed to do. He started navigating to his Yahoo account and, just like before, brought up saved drafts. He saw a new one among them and opened it.

It was short and direct. "Meet me at five today at the far end of Alamonaster Boulevard Bridge next to I-10. I have made arrangements for someone to accept the package in Houston. It will be a couple of days. O."

He closed the e-mail as Faith said, "When are you going to Houston?"

He snapped his face to hers. "Why'd you read that over my shoulder? You think I can't handle my own e-mail?"

"No, that's not it. I didn't mean to pry. I was just making conversation."

"Dammit. I just used your computer. Didn't give you permission to pry." He stood up.

"Wait. Why are you so angry? I didn't mean nothin' by it."

He decided this was as good a time as any to head out the door. He'd been lucky and had crammed the big U-Haul truck into two empty slots in the rear of the trendy coffeehouse. He'd have to make sure he knew how to find the Alamonaster Bridge and figure out where to meet Ortíz. He was glad he'd finally see this guy face-to-face. His size and conditioning would impress the Panamanian. And he needed some more cash. This beaner sure sounded like he had plenty of cash.

He was out the door and turning the corner when he heard Faith call out to him.

"Wait, don't be mad."

He turned and she surprised him by running straight to him and placing her small hands on his arms. She leaned in close, brushing her breasts against him.

He softened a little. "Don't sweat it. I'm just not used to worrying about other people." She followed him as he turned and slowly walked toward the truck in the empty rear lot.

"What're you hauling? Is that your truck?" She pointed at the U-Haul.

Suddenly he realized she knew too much about him. What if she figured out who he was and what he was doing after she watched the news in a few days? He might have to be on the run, but there was a chance he could pull this off without being identified. The obvious problem was that she'd be a loose end.

He looked at her delicate face as she turned her haunting green eyes up to him.

DUARTE WAS ON HIS CELL PHONE, SMILING AT THE SOUND OF Alice's voice again.

He said, "Hey, it's me."

"Wow, two calls in one day. You might really miss me. I think that's probably a first for Alex Duarte."

"Could be." He was surprised she knew him so well after only a few months of sporadic dating.

Then she really amazed him. "Unless you're calling for another favor?"

He didn't speak.

She raised her voice slightly. "Oh my God, that's it. You need another favor. What is it this time? Carbon-date a rock? Get a DNA sample from a cigarette butt?"

"You can do that?"

"What?"

"Get DNA from a cigarette?"

"Yeah, sure." There was silence on the line, then Alice said, "I'm waiting. What's the favor?"

"Lift some prints from a padlock."

"When will I get it?"

"Tomorrow. I just sent it overnight express."

"You were pretty sure of yourself."

He kept an easy tone. "Alice, this could be serious. I just want to keep it simple for now."

"How'd you pack it? Will it be stable and not disturb any potential prints?"

"I packed in a small box with some paper wadded up and holding it in place."

"That sounds pretty good."

"Will doing these things get you in any trouble?"

"Less trouble than dating you."

"Alice, you're the best."

"You better show it when you get back."

"Thanks." He waited to hear her, but there was silence. Almost like she expected him to say something else. Then he did. "I gotta go. I'll talk to you soon."

She didn't even say goodbye, so he hung up.

Ike looked at Faith and knew with certainty that he couldn't just let her walk away. The problem was he didn't know what to do with her. He didn't know who would miss the young lady. He didn't know how hard it might be to silence her or if she'd fight and escape. That would bring way too much heat on him.

He felt in his pocket for his buck knife. The only thing he had ever used it for was opening boxes and once for cutting chicken at a new place off Florence Avenue in Omaha. He looked into her eyes, and even with his limited experience, realized she wanted him to kiss her.

Slipping the knife out of his pocket, he said, "You wanna see what I'm haulin'?"

"Sure." She took a small step back then fell in step with him to the truck. He used the only extra key he had to the sturdy Master Lock. The door slid up easily as he kept track of where she was standing.

He stepped up into the truck. "C'mon." He motioned her up with his empty left hand, the knife still folded in his right.

Once she was inside, he opened the knife in front of her and acted like he was prying off one of the boards to the crate.

"What is it?" she asked, inching closer to him.

He gripped the knife, saying, "It's unusual. I was tapped special just to transport it because of my record for this kind of stuff." He flexed his arm, knowing she had no clue what he was poised to do. He had never killed anyone up close before.

Faith ran her small hand over the wooden crate and stared at it like it was a magic lamp.

The fact that his first up-close victim was a woman didn't make it harder; it didn't surprise him either. He had spent so little time with women other than his mom, that he didn't really understand the differences between them and men.

Ike looked at her, with the knife still ready. He knew he had to keep her quiet but couldn't seem to force his arm forward. No matter how important this was to him and the country, he could not seem to will his hand to plunge the knife into her exposed stomach.

As her shirt inched up her midriff, she leaned closer to him, looking for something other than a kiss.

"Shit," he shouted.

Faith cowered slightly. "What? What is it now?"

"Look, you'll thank me for this later, but for now, I'm gonna have to close you in here."

"What?"

"And if you make any noise, like scream or pound on the door, I'm gonna have to kill you." He held up the buck knife. "You understand?"

She stared at the knife with a new expression.

He raised his voice. "You understand, Faith?"

She shook herself out of her daze and stared at him for a moment. "Why? I'll keep quiet." A sob crept into her voice.

He slid the door down and slapped the lock back on it as he muttered, "I know."

18

ALEX DUARTE SAT WITH THE OTHER INVESTIGATORS AROUND A
conference table at the Port of New Orleans and said, "I don't know
what else we can do. The pot is in evidence. Gastlin is dead. I'd say the
case is closed."

Félix, who continued to glare at Lina every time she touched Staub's
arm or spoke to him, said, "We got the pot, that's something. But we
can't forget Gastlin."

Lina nodded. "I'm gonna stay in New Orleans a day or two longer.
Lázaro knows the city a little, and we're going to look around."

Duarte remained silent, but he wanted to see if Alice could lift any
prints off the container's padlock before he left. He and Félix felt like
they owed that much to Byron Gastlin. If the person who'd gotten into
the container knew anything about Gastlin in Panama, Duarte intended
to find out, and he didn't care what it took to get the information.

Lina said, "Let's all go out tonight."

Félix looked at Duarte, who shrugged.

Staub said, "A wonderful idea."

"How about we meet at five?"

Staub said, "I'm sorry, I have the errands to run. What about seven?"

Lina smiled. "Sure."

Duarte and Félix just nodded. Duarte was distracted by how much he had relied on Alice for forensic work. The ATF had a good lab, but if he went through channels, it would take weeks to get anything back. He didn't think Lina would even believe his theory that someone entered the container. Besides, she had a different agenda, and Gastlin's death wasn't part of it. She was focused on Ortíz's contacts here in the U.S. He also doubted she would approve of what he was willing to do to find out if the two incidents were related.

Félix mumbled to him. "Let's get out of here."

The two men stood, and Lina said, "We'll meet you in the hotel lobby at seven."

Duarte said, "Can't wait." And realized that he might have been sarcastic for the first time in his life.

Lázaro Staub rented a Chevrolet Impala from the Hertz office in the lobby of the hotel. He didn't want the others to see he had a car. He left early, around three o'clock, so he could see a little of New Orleans before his appointment. The colonel drove down Robert E. Lee Boulevard and looked out over Lake Pontchartrain. The white mansions on the other side of the street looked like they had survived the last two centuries without seeing any turmoil. That was not the truth. He was an amateur historian, and several trips to New Orleans over the years had taught him the hard lessons of the region. He knew that the American Civil War had reached this far, as had the War of 1812.

He knew the story of how Andrew Jackson, one of the country's most aggressive and bloodthirsty presidents, had fought the British near here in the swampy bayous surrounding the city before ascending to the nation's highest office. The arrogant Old Hickory didn't even realize the War of 1812 had been over for almost two weeks when he drove back the British.

He looked at the mansions and wondered how they would've fared against Stealth bombers.

Staub had also read about the floods after hurricane Katrina and laughed at the government response. When it was time to invade a small country like Panama, they could muster overwhelming strength, but when their own citizens were in need, the country moved like a snail.

He drove slowly through some of the streets near the French Quarter and past Tulane University. Finally he crossed the I-10 bridge and could see a U-Haul truck already parked near the base of the bridge. They were both an hour early. He was glad that this man took the matter so seriously.

Because of his status in the country as a visiting Panamanian official, he was not supposed to possess weapons. One of his assistants had circumvented this prohibition by bringing in a Beretta for him on the ship. Now he hid the automatic pistol under his loose shirt.

As he pulled the small white Chevy next to the truck, he was surprised at how large William "Ike" Floyd was. His broad shoulders and short legs made him look more simian than most, but at five-nine he was still impressive. Staub would hate to find himself engaged in an unarmed fight with him.

He stood from the car to his full six-feet-one and nodded as Floyd approached him.

"Mr. Ortíz?" said the man.

"Yes, William, I am Mr. Ortíz. It is an honor to finally meet you."

Pelly scowled at the small cook who had lingered at his private cabin after delivering a sandwich. The man scurried away like one of the many rats on the ship. He knew his appearance, when he didn't shave enough, terrified the superstitious sailors. That was *their* problem. He was no happier that Colonel Staub had sent him with this load than the sailors were that he was aboard.

He ate and then cleaned up in his small cabin. After shaving and changing into a clean white button-down shirt, he decided he'd see a little of New Orleans. He didn't need anyone's permission to leave.

Using a fake identification card in the name of Juan Rodríguez, with an immigration visa that listed him as a "deck worker," he walked right through security at the port and into the streets of New Orleans.

He took a cab to Jackson Square and wandered around the famous plaza. He smiled at the silly street performers, like the man who juggled bowling balls or the woman who swallowed swords, but kept his money to himself. He resisted the subtle nods of women he knew were there for business and not for meeting the man of their dreams.

He looked around at the nonstop festival that seemed to go on in New Orleans and had to admit he didn't mind this part of his boss's crazy plan.

As he reached a corner of the square with the Jax Brewery to one side, Pelly slowed and noticed a man leaning against the fence that separated the cement from the grassy inner square. The man stared straight ahead with hazy blue eyes. He wore several different shirts over one another and filthy cutoff blue jeans. But it was his face that Pelly stopped to study. While everyone else passed by without a glance or at least without trying to stare at the destitute man, Pelly saw the root of what might have caused this man's problems: He had an uncorrected cleft palette like none Pelly had ever seen. It virtually separated his face. He had a normal lower lip, but his upper disappeared up his face, causing his nose to be disfigured as well.

Pelly silently reached in his pocket, pulled out his wad of cash and, without counting it, dropped the entire bundle into the man's pouch around his neck.

The man's eyes flickered at Pelly's face and seemed to recognize someone who knew what physical appearance could mean.

Pelly patted the man on the shoulder and continued his walk through the square. He saved his energy because he knew that now that he had given away his money, it was a long walk back to the port.

C all me Ike; everyone does."
   "Fine, Ike. You have our package inside?"
"I do."

"Excellent. You will have to take it to Houston from here. I'll contact someone I know there who will get it ready for you."

"Great." His eyes darted back and forth over the deserted rest area parking lot.

"Is something wrong, Ike?"

"Well, there is one small complication."

"What's that?"

"I have to silence a witness."

"Here, in New Orleans?"

"Well, actually here, in this parking lot."

"I don't understand."

"There is a girl who saw me on the e-mail, and I'm afraid she knows too much. I got her locked in with the package."

"You mean she's still alive?"

Ike nodded as he looked down at the ground.

Staub didn't like the sound of this. Not only was it messy, but he was concerned Ike hadn't had the guts to kill her wherever they'd been before this.

"Let's talk to her, then. I need to see the package anyway."

Ike slowly slipped the key in the lock and then slid the door in one motion straight up. Before the door was all the way up, a young, well-built blond woman sprang from the truck, almost landing in Staub's arms. He didn't hesitate to wrap one arm around her chin and one around the back of her neck and twist with all his strength. It was a technique he had learned in the defense force, but he had practiced it on several prostitutes and informants.

The woman's head snapped to one side, and she went limp in his hands. Her legs and arms hung loose, and her eyes remained open and staring at Ike.

"Damn" was all Ike said.

"Any other problems I should know about now?"

19

AFTER LEAVING A CREOLE RESTAURANT THAT IMPRESSED STAUB but seemed expensive to Duarte, the four investigators without a case wandered down to a small bar and took a seat on the balcony because it was quieter than inside.

Félix had ordered too many beers for his thin frame and was starting to show the effects. He leaned into the balcony railing and yelled down to people passing by on Bourbon Street. Occasionally someone looked up.

Duarte tried to scoot his seat farther away, so they would think he was sitting at the next table.

Lina said, "Félix, cool it."

"Why? Does it embarrass you?"

"No, it's embarrassing you."

"I'll be heading back to the hotel. I'm tired of the company."

Duarte started to stand to help his friend, but Félix held up a hand and said, "Nope, I'm going alone." He careened through the small patio and disappeared down the stairs.

Duarte cleared his throat and said, "He's actually upset about Gastlin. He didn't mean any disrespect."

Staub nodded. "I understand it is hard to be responsible for someone else's death."

Duarte said, "I don't know how responsible he is, but he feels responsible."

"And I am afraid, with as many murders in my country, chances of solving the crime are not promising."

"We have a few ideas. We haven't given up yet."

Staub leaned forward. "What ideas?" He fidgeted with a cigarette, then realized he couldn't smoke inside.

Lina joined in. "With what jurisdiction?"

"With proper interest in finding out what happened to one of our sources. I admit it has a personal element, but who would be upset if we were able to find out if his death was tied to the load of pot?"

Staub said, "You are correct, Alex. No one can argue that."

Duarte noticed the colonel's English and accent had improved dramatically. It almost seemed familiar to him somehow. He watched as Staub's dark eyes shifted from him to the stairs, where Félix had left.

Pelly sat on a deck chair and watched the line of workers enter one of the big buildings that prepared containers for shipping. He had been down to the French Quarter twice, but Colonel Staub had told him to stay put tonight. He didn't want to risk the FBI, DEA or ATF agents seeing him. It didn't matter to Pelly; those tall, red drinks gave him a horrible hangover.

At least he didn't worry about how he looked tonight.

It was eleven o'clock when his cell phone rang. Colonel Staub said in Spanish, "I'm just outside the port. I don't want a record that I came in. Meet me at the coffee shop just down the street." The phone line went dead.

Pelly nodded to the ship's captain, not that the captain was his boss. That notion was put to rest the day some of Staub's associates took the man's ten-year-old son and cut off his left ear. Once he explained what could happen to one of the captain's three daughters, the man had been cooperative. For five years they had utilized the ship, which had a different name every year. The captain was paid and the ship made more money than most freighters, but it was prudent to keep it looking like a rundown garbage scow.

Whenever the ship was loaded in Colón, Colonel Staub had men supervise it, and there was no problem. So far, the old ship had chugged into the U.S. eleven times. Three times right here in New Orleans, and they had never had a hitch. The loads had been discovered three times, once in the Port of Palm Beach, once in Miami and once in Galveston, but each time the person listed as the shipper had been blamed, and the rusty old tub had sailed on without trouble, changing its name once more.

Pelly nodded to several of the crewmen, too. They didn't know exactly who he was, but they knew he was no sailor.

Pelly used his fast stride to make it to the coffee shop in a matter of minutes. He paused once to look into the window of a jewelry store. There was an emerald necklace that he thought his mother might like. He briefly caught his reflection in the window and, seeing the light reflect his hairy face, turned quickly and moved on. He had been used to the taunts as a child. Monkey Boy was the one that had stuck. Even after all these years, he didn't like to see his face in a mirror.

He walked directly to the small table outside the coffee shop where Colonel Staub sat by himself.

Staub said, "Any problems on the ship?"

"No sir. They plan to leave early tomorrow morning."

"You might have to stay."

Pelly hesitated. He didn't like being away from home and particularly didn't like this big, dirty city. "They haven't discovered that you are also Ortíz, have they?"

"No, but I have a job for you."

"Whatever is needed, boss."

"The ATF agent. You haven't met him."

"The well-built guy with dark, short hair?"

"Yeah, that's him, Duarte."

"I saw him on the ship. What about him?"

"He may be too smart for his own good."

"I could handle him tonight and still make the ship before it leaves."

"No, we have to make it look like an accident."

"Or maybe a botched robbery."

"Perhaps." Staub considered the idea and then said, "That's very good, Pelly. But we have to act fast. He is looking into Gastlin's death."

"No problem, boss. Just give me the details of where he's staying. I can get someone to help here. We have several contacts."

If his boss had decided that this guy Duarte needed to go, then he needed to go.

A lice Brainard arrived at the office an hour early and took care of all of her assigned duties. She wanted to have enough time to see about Alex's padlock and arrange to fingerprint the severed finger the DEA was going to deliver. The idea of handling a severed finger didn't faze her personally. She had fingerprinted dead bodies a number of times; this wasn't much different. But though the lock was no big deal, the finger was way outside the lines. Technically, it should be done over at the medical examiner's office, because it was part of a corpse. It made sense, though, that with only one available digit, she should print it instead of some DEA agent who could screw it up. It was also more secure than faxing a print up for identification. It was gross, but smart. She could be fired for doing it in the lab, but she knew her way around and wasn't worried what might happen.

As she considered what she was risking for a guy who hadn't even introduced her to his parents, her intercom buzzed.

A male voice said, "Alice, there's a FedEx guy with a package."

Five minutes later, alone at her station, she carefully opened the package from New Orleans. She pulled out the two crumpled sheets of paper from the box, then carefully removed the lock with a pair of long-nose pliers. She picked up the box and looked for a note or card. Anything. She unfolded the sheets of paper. They were in Spanish and appeared to be some kind of shipping invoice. But no note from her supposed boyfriend.

She sighed. That was just so Alex Duarte.

Dusting the lock was no problem. She immediately had three decent thumbprints. There was a mark or two from the handling of the lock and the shipping, but they were identifiable. Probably AFIS quality. She was hoping the giant database of automated prints might yield a hit.

Before she could even clean up, she had another call. The DEA agent with her special "package" was here. Alice had him escorted back to the lab.

She was surprised how young he looked.

"I'm Carl Spirazza with the DEA. A mutual friend asked me to deliver this to you."

Alice looked him in the eyes. "You know what's in here?"

"I was told."

"And you guys can mail stuff like this?"

"Nope, but I was told you were cool and it was a favor. We all owe Félix for one favor or another." He paused and said, "Besides, Alex Duarte is a hard-ass. If he can find out who did this, he'll do something about it."

"You know Alex?"

"The Rocket? You bet."

She smiled at how her quiet, unassuming boyfriend was known by every cop in the county. She left on her latex gloves and used a razor to slit the corner of the small box. She tipped it up and a small plastic bag, half the size of a sandwich baggie, dropped onto the table with a meaty, sickening sound.

She used thick tweezers to open the baggie and extracted the slightly shriveled finger. There was not much blood in the bag. She held it up and examined it closely. Then she saw something that made her hesitate. She better call Alex.

In the little hotel café, Colonel Staub sipped some coffee at a tiny table with Félix Baez and Lina Cirillo. They had said little since all sitting down at about the same time.

The colonel was lost in his own little world. After snapping the girl's neck in the U-Haul the night before, he had felt almost drunk with excitement. His erection had been so intense that he had found two different prostitutes. Neither had satisfied him, and he resisted the urge to kill them. He was not in Panama and couldn't cover his tracks as well here in New Orleans.

He looked up and smiled at Lina, knowing that the FBI agent had no idea about him. They were much too focused on Mr. Ortíz.

Staub believed he could get this idiot American, Ike, to complete the mission, and then he would go back to his life in Panama while the U.S. government spent the next fifty years looking for "Mr. Ortíz."

He smiled because life was good.

Alex Duarte stepped out of the hotel lobby to use the curb to stretch his Achilles tendon and calves. It was cooler than Florida, and even though he preferred not to run in traffic, he decided it was early enough that he could make do on the sidewalks of New Orleans. He wasn't ready to leave the city yet. Something about this whole case didn't sit right with him. There was still work to do. Perhaps, with some evidence, they could charge Ortíz with the killing under the relatively new federal kingpin statute. He knew he now had a clear objective. Any army officer with a clear objective had a much better chance of completing his assignment, and Duarte's was to identify Ortíz and have him extradited to the U.S.

He stepped off the curb and used one hand to balance himself against a sign. He let his heels dip and felt his leg muscles stretch and tingle. He intended to run an hour today. It had been a stressful week.

As he stretched, his cell phone, tucked in his shorts pocket, rang. He flipped it open. "Duarte."

In a mock deep voice, he heard Alice say, "Brainard."

He smiled.

She said, "You always sound so serious when you answer. What is that?"

"Four years in the army."

"I guess so. That stuff never leaves you."

"I hope not."

"Well, I was calling to say I got your note tucked in with the padlock."

Duarte thought about it, but couldn't remember sending any kind of note. He remained silent.

"It was a lovely note."

"In with the lock?"

"Yeah, you remember how you said, 'This is so great of you to do that I'm including this thoughtful note of thanks'?"

He had to smile at that. She had him. "I'm sorry. It's just been so busy."

"I'll pretend the shipping invoices were notes in Spanish to me. Oh, wait. Neither you nor I even speak Spanish. The better to keep up the illusion."

She let him hang for a second before she added, "Are you getting a chance to slow down at all?"

"Yeah, a little. I'm gonna run in a few minutes."

"Wow, running in New Orleans, tough job."

"Wish you were with me."

He felt the pause, but knew that for a change he had said the right thing.

Alice said, "That's sweet and, coming from you, almost incredible."

He smiled as he stepped up from the curb, listening to Alice's laugh.

Then she shifted gears. "There's something I need to talk to you about before we have the young DEA man dispose of the finger. And I should at least say he is going to dispose of it illegally because no one can know it was mailed here and was examined outside the M.E.'s office."

"What do we need to discuss? Was it Gastlin?"

"Yes, it matched his prints here."

"Something else?"

"There's blood under the nail of the finger."

"So?"

"So it's probably not his. He scratched his killer, so skin and other evidence is under it."

"Usable evidence?"

"Does the term 'DNA' mean anything to you?"

"Really? You can get DNA from the sample?"

"No guarantees, but probably. The issue is whether it could be used in Panama. They don't have a DNA database. And if they have no clear suspect, it won't matter. We can't enter the sample in our database because of how it was obtained."

Duarte looked up and down the street as he thought about what to do. At the corner, across the street in front of a doughnut shop, he noticed a dark, shaggy young man. He looked directly at Duarte, then seemed to melt behind a wall. Something was familiar about him.

Alice said, "You want me to take the sample?"

"Do you mind? I mean, is it a big deal?"

"Depends on what I get if it is a big deal."

He kept looking at the doughnut shop for the man he had just seen.

Alice said, "I guess I get something really great if it's a big deal."

"Huh?"

Alice said, "What's wrong that you can't talk to me for more than a few minutes without losing interest?"

"I'm sorry, I just saw someone who looked familiar. If you could take the sample, we'll see if we can use it."

"I also have at least one name for you from a print off the padlock."

"Really? Who?"

"He's a longshoreman who lives in Gretna, Louisiana. He has four arrests. Two for theft and two for battery. One of those was on a cop."

"Nice."

"He left his thumbprint on the lock. I don't know when, but he did." She read off his home address.

Duarte ran it through his head and knew he had it stored forever.

They talked a minute more, and Alice said, "Miss me?"

"Yes. Yes, I do."

"When are you coming home?"

"Soon."

They exchanged goodbyes and Duarte flipped the phone closed. He looked back up at the doughnut shop and suddenly realized who the man he had seen looked like: the first mate of the *Flame of Panama*.

IKE HAD NOT DRIVEN FAR FROM NEW ORLEANS YET. HE HAD
stayed the night in a Motel 8 right off I-10, near Gonzales, Louisiana.
He had spent several hours looking for the right place to dump Faith's
body. He was still a little freaked out by how quickly and casually Mr.
Ortíz had twisted her neck and killed her. There might not have been
blood, but he wouldn't have called it clean and neat. Her bowels had let
go and she started to stink almost immediately. He left her curled up in
the rear of the truck Then, a few miles east of Lutcher, he pulled behind
a Wal-Mart and tossed her over the side of a giant Dumpster. Her body
made a thud on the other side that could only have been made by something dead.

Despite all he had been involved in years earlier, he had never seen a
dead person up close. He knew from the news and what people had told
him that there were corpses because of what he had done, or at least
what he knew was going to be done, but it never occurred to him just
how unnerving a dead person looked. When Faith's eyes stared at him
with no thought behind them and her body flopped around like a bean-
bag doll, he got a glimpse of death. He thought it might be worse

because he had been talking to her and had the feeling she was a nice person. He remembered her smile and the smell of her fancy coffee drink when she leaned in close to him and spoke.

He saw the sign for Lafayette and knew that even though it wasn't even lunchtime yet, he needed a beer. Maybe several. He whipped off the next exit faster than the big rental truck was built to do. He felt it slide a little to one side, then settle as he took it down the ramp to the light. About five blocks off the interstate, he saw a bar and grill sign that said simply BEER AND GOOD FOOD. That was the ticket as far as he was concerned. He pulled the big yellow truck to the side of the building and parked in the far end of the lot. There was a Camaro and two pickup trucks in the lot up next to the white building. He locked up the rental truck and then quick-stepped past the big bay window and through the glass front door. He noticed his hand shake as he shoved open the door.

The five customers, two waitresses and bartender all looked up at him as he headed straight to the bar.

The fat, biker-looking bartender said, "The lunch rush is early today. What'll ya have?"

"What's on draft?"

"Icehouse and Lite."

Ike said, "Two Icehouses and a hamburger."

"You sound like a man with a plan." The bartender drew the beers and then stepped into the kitchen.

Ike sucked down the first beer in two gulps. He grabbed the second one when the young man a few seats down at the bar said, "Rough day already?"

Ike paused and looked over at the man, about twenty-one with light hair and dazzling, green eyes. "Rough night. Today is just recovery."

"Know the feeling."

"I doubt it." Ike noticed the man's eyes still on him. He held off on gulping the next beer and said, "My name is William, but my friends call me Ike."

"I'm Craig, but my friends call me Craig."

Ike smiled at his humor, especially because his eyes shined as he spoke. His clear skin had a rich, moist look to it. He slid over to the stool next to Ike.

"You staying here or just passing though?"

Ike turned on the stool to face the young man. A little older than Ike liked them, but still plenty young enough. "I could be convinced to stay a little while." He was sure he hadn't misinterpreted the man's message, even if he was in western Louisiana.

"That might be arranged," said Craig, as he reached for his own beer and Ike joined him.

A lex Duarte had stuck the phone back in his pocket and finished his prerun stretch. He searched for the man he had just seen with the amazing resemblance to the first mate of the *Flame of Panama*. He had been unnerved by the man's sudden appearance. Had he imagined it?

He shifted his thoughts to Alice and what she was risking to help him on what was probably a futile effort. As he jogged down the street, he pictured her pretty face and infectious smile. He started to trot, allowing his body to warm up slowly. That man . . .

He made it to the end of the street, where a canal forced him to swing onto the next street and reverse directions. He could see the upper floors of his hotel, so he didn't think he could get lost as he picked up his pace.

When he was just about even with his hotel, a small man stepped out from a parked car so quickly that Duarte bumped into him on the sidewalk.

Duarte slowed to a stop, spun on his right foot, and in three steps was at the man's side, helping him up.

"I'm sorry. I didn't see you."

"Chíngala," He looked at Duarte. *"Pendejo."*

Duarte used his limited Spanish. *"Lo siento."*

Then he caught another figure out of the corner of his eye. He turned and saw another Latin man with an automatic pistol pointed at Duarte. Then a third man stepped from the same doorway. That man had a knife. The older, short man he had bumped looked up and smiled at him. *"Chulo pendejo."*

The man with the gun said something in Spanish.

Duarte shrugged. "You're making a mistake."

"What, you don't speak Spanish?"

"No, I don't like robbers." He had the man closest to him by the arm before the others could react. He heard the gunshot before he saw the flash. At least that's how it seemed.

DUARTE DIDN'T PANIC AT THE SOUND OF THE GUNSHOT. HE HAD heard them before, up close and from long range. The problem was that he had seen the muzzle flash and was temporarily blinded. He kept his grip on the man he had grabbed by the arm and then, since he couldn't see, decided it would be best to put him out of action. He twisted the arm until it was elbow up, then Duarte dropped his right forearm across it. He felt the joint crackle and shatter as the man dropped to the ground.

The ATF agent had to move to avoid being shot and fell behind the car at the curb. He heard another shot and felt a sting on his arm. Looking down, through his clearing vision, he saw a little blood but not a serious wound. The next shot showed him why. The gunman had shot the windows out of the Nissan that Duarte had hidden behind, and the glass from the first window had cut his arm. He knew there were still two men on the other side of the car.

He peeked under the vehicle and saw a set of feet in work boots coming to the rear of the Nissan. Duarte waited to time his spring. He crouched, and a second before the man came around the trunk of the small car, Duarte was in the air. He struck the man like a Miami Dol-phins linebacker and leaned his head down so he would catch the man on the chin.

The man never had a chance to aim the pistol, and the force of the blow knocked him hard against the next car. He was unconscious before his body stopped toppling onto the ground. Duarte looked for the hand-gun, then stole a peek under the car to see where the third man was standing.

The gun was too far under the next parked car to reach without exposing himself. He popped up and saw a younger man with a semiau-tomatic pistol. His hand shook as he scanned over toward the car con-cealing the ATF agent.

Duarte darted low behind the car to a better position and hoped to grab the fallen handgun when he heard a vehicle rumbling down the street. The old pickup truck swerved in close to him, making him roll to the curb. The man with the broken elbow flopped into the bed. The man with the gun scooped up his unconscious friend and struggled to pile him into the bed of the truck, too.

He thought about trying to reach the pistol under the car when he realized one of the men from the truck was now under the car and had a hand on the gun.

Duarte sprang up as the man fired from under the car. The sound was deafening. The round hit the curb, spraying concrete under the car. Then the man jumped up and returned to the passenger compartment of the big Dodge pickup truck.

The driver gunned the engine and then took the corner fast enough to send the men in the back into the side of the bed.

Duarte scanned the street quickly for more threats and to make sure no one was hurt. No one else was on the street. Not even in any of the old shops. He looked at the cut on his arm and again realized it was minor.

He took a few deep breaths, shrugged, and started to jog back to the hotel.

Alice Brainard had her sample properly stored in a 1.5-milliliter plastic tube, but she was not a DNA scientist. She worked with them and liked them but didn't feel competent enough to develop the STR, or Short Tandem Report, sample and make a determination for identification. She knew whom to ask and how to ask him, and she felt a little guilty for doing it. She even felt guilty for knowing how to do it, but it could help Alex, and she knew he didn't blow things out of proportion.

It was just before lunch, and she planned to work out instead of eat, which was common. What was different was that she changed up in the lab instead of the gym. She also wore shorter pants and a leotard top instead of a T-shirt. She looked like one of the women at the commercial gyms she often made fun of, the ones who put on makeup to work out, the ones who wanted to be seen more than they wanted to be fit.

Then she waited until Scott Mahovich was in the lab alone. She liked the DNA scientist as a person, as a quiet, geeky kind of guy. She knew he stole glances at her when she was at her station. She knew he kept track of whether she was dating. She was always pleasant to him, but didn't want to lead him on. Until now.

"Hey, Scott," she said, making sure he got a good look at her.

The DNA scientist remained silent for a moment as he ran his hand over his near–crew cut. "Hi, Alice." He fumbled for something to say. "Goin' to work out?"

"You should be a detective." She smiled and placed her hand on his arm. She noticed the blush in his face.

"I need to start back at the gym." He flexed his thin white arms, then looked at her. "I'm mainly an aerobics guy."

"I like to mix it up. Today is back and aerobics." She turned to show off her back and butt. How slutty am I? she thought.

When she turned back to him, he was just staring.

She decided to make her move. "Scott, you think if I had a lab task that wasn't, strictly speaking, on an official case, I could talk to you about it?"

"Yeah, sure. How is it not an official case?"

"It's real preliminary, and the submitting agency wants to keep it quiet."

"What is it?"

"DNA."

"From what?"

"Blood under a fingernail."

"That's easy."

"Would you help me? I'd love to learn more about the process." She leaned in close to the man, who was now shaking slightly.

"Sure. I'll help."

"But you can't tell anyone."

He smiled as she looked up in his eyes. He gulped and said, "I promise."

She gave him one more smile to seal the deal and then stood up on her tiptoes and kissed him on the cheek. "You're a champ."

As she walked away, she felt lower than she ever had since trying out for the cheerleading team in high school. She was pretty sure Alex Duarte was worth it.

Duarte came to a stop in front of the Marriott and saw Lina Cirillo on her cell phone in the lobby. As soon as she saw him, she flipped the phone closed and turned to him.

"What happened to your arm?"

"You wouldn't believe me if I told you."

"Try me."

"Someone tried to rob me, and this is from a shattered window."

"Just now?"

"Five minutes ago."

"What shattered the glass?"

"A bullet."

Now she raised her voice. "The robber shot at you?"

"Sounds unbelievable, doesn't it?"

"How can you stay so calm?"

"What should I do? It's over."

"I don't know, but if someone shot at me, I'd be upset."

"I *did* cut my run short. What else should I do?"

"Call the police?"

"Won't help. The guys are gone. I messed up one's arm."

"Maybe they can find him at a hospital."

Duarte thought about it and shook his head. "No. It'll just be a distraction. We have enough to worry about."

"So that's it?"

"I didn't say that. I'm wondering how random a target I was."

"Why?"

"Who robs joggers?"

William "Ike" Floyd could not believe how lucky he was. He had Craig in the cab of the rental truck talking about what they liked to do and feeling the interest the young man had in him. Now Ike wished he had shaved this morning before he left the Motel 8. He and Craig had shared lunch and a few beers, and Ike didn't give a damn about his schedule right now.

Craig brushed back his neat light brown hair. "So you're on your way to Houston."

"Yeah."

"When you supposed to be there?"

"I'm the boss. I decide. Why, you got something in mind?" He smiled and edged closer on the big bench seat.

Craig smiled, too. "Don't know, but I don't meet a lot of guys like you in Lafayette."

"What kind of guy am I?"

"Funny, good-looking."

Ike's heart rate started to rise. He felt some sweat on his forehead. "You have someplace we can go?"

"What about the back of the truck?"

"This truck?"

"Sure. What are you carrying?"

Ike wanted to tell him. He wanted to impress the young man and share his glory. He thought about the consequences of telling him the truth or just saying it was a crate. He looked into the young man's eyes. "Can you keep a secret?"

"For you, I know I could."

"C'mon." Ike slid back past the steering wheel and fished his keys out of his pocket. He walked to the rear of the truck, arriving at the tailgate at the same time as Craig.

He paused at the locked truck door. "Now, this is big. Big enough that it'll make you look at things different."

"Does it fill the whole truck? We still will have room for us, right?"

Ike was disappointed in the boy's attitude and at the same time happy he was so eager.

"There's room. I was just trying to show you I'm not a regular truck driver. I'm a visionary."

"What's that?"

"A person who can see the future."

"No shit. Like, can you tell me the Lotto numbers?"

"No, not that kind of seeing the future." Ike paused to gather his thoughts. "Like seeing how each of us can affect the future. I want to save the country."

"From what?"

"From what it's becoming."

Craig seemed satisfied with that. He also seemed eager to get in the truck with Ike.

Ike unlocked the door and then turned to the young man. "You have to give me your word of honor not to tell anyone about what you see."

Craig solemnly said, "I give you my word." Then he gave Ike a sly smile.

Ike threw the door so it slid into the slot in the roof of the truck. His heart felt like it was going to shoot out of his chest.

ALEX DUARTE COULD HAVE EASILY IDENTIFIED HIMSELF AND entered the port through the main gate. He still had an ID tag from the day before, but he didn't want any official record of his entry into the Port of New Orleans. He found a low section of chain-link fence, quickly scampered up the outside and dropped to the ground on the inside. He left the day-old badge on his collar. His plan was to stay away from everyone's attention, leave minimal evidence of reconnaissance. The fewer people who knew you were around the better. This was based on one of the many lessons he had learned in Bosnia, both in limited combat and from backing up the navy SEALs who had come into the country to capture war criminals. They had conducted several successful operations and used Duarte for a few minor booby traps and demolition jobs because of his duties with the combat engineers. It was these same SEALs who had shown Duarte the power of an "aggressive interrogation." It was a simple concept Duarte tried not to abuse. In the right circumstances, with proper justification and an individual who deserved it, fear and pain were excellent motivators. Duarte had been very careful in his use of the concept. It certainly was not approved of by the Department of Justice.

Duarte had used it only in vital and dangerous situations, but he considered almost being killed by robbers vital and serious. He didn't believe that seeing the first officer of the *Flame of Panama* before being accosted was a coincidence. He had some questions to ask, and if the man was not open to the interview, he might end up with another scar on the other side of his hairy face.

Duarte navigated the big port. He had thought about finding this Cal Linley while he was here but decided the man's house would be more appropriate and less public.

He finally found the dock where the *Flame of Panama* had been moored.

There was a large open space on the dock where the ship had been.

Duarte nodded to a man in a small, three-wheeled security cart. The patch on the man's dark polyester shirt read "W Security."

The older black man's eyes went immediately to the identification badge on Duarte's shirt, then he smiled and said, "How can I help you?"

"I was wondering if you knew when the *Flame of Panama* pulled out?"

"Sure, I had just come on duty. It left at six this morning."

"With everyone on board?"

"I assume so. They didn't make any fuss like they do when someone isn't back from leave. They had the pilot guide them out, and were out of sight before the sun was all the way up."

"Thanks," mumbled Duarte, wondering how he had seen the first mate at nine o'clock if the ship had left at six. He was certain he had seen him.

The old security guard said, "Have a good day, son."

Duarte looked up and nodded absently.

This might be a long day.

Lázaro Staub stood in front of the seated Pelly, looking down at him like he might strike the young man. The twenty-nine-year-old from the town of Yavisa, near the Darien Gap, had felt the heat before.

As a child he had seen Colombian drug runners take over his grand-father's small farm and treat the old man like a slave. When he was fifteen, Pelly had killed two of the drug runners with a hatchet. He had managed to keep his identity secret for two weeks as the drug runners tried to find out who had butchered their men. If it were not for a newly appointed narcotics officer named Staub who had led a raid into the town, Pelly would have been found out. Staub had stood up to the Colombians and given Pelly someone to admire. Four years later, Staub helped Pelly get on with the national police.

It was only after a few years of working with the colonel that Pelly realized his righteous outrage wasn't about drugs, but about foreigners coming into Panama. Staub was crazy about others making trouble in his country. If he hadn't been seduced by money, Staub may have really helped the country. At least Pelly used to think he had a chance.

Now, in the café, Staub had allowed his voice to raise because he didn't believe, even if any of the people in the kitchen spoke Spanish, they would have any idea what he was talking about.

Staub stopped and faced Pelly. "I told you this son of a bitch, Duarte, was sharp, didn't I?"

Pelly nodded, trying to look bored.

"I also told you to hire good men. You knew someone here in New Orleans."

"I do."

"Those idiots? They couldn't handle a child. Duarte escaped like it was a classroom exercise."

"You're right, boss. He was tough. The boys said he was fast, too. They said he knew karate and surprised them."

"That's what we pay men like that for—surprises."

"I know, boss."

"You know, you know . . . You don't know anything." Saliva started to spray as he got angrier and angrier.

Although he wanted to smile at his boss's unraveling, Pelly remained still and silent. He occasionally saw the colonel get mad like this. Usually someone died when he got this crazy. Pelly knew he wouldn't do anything to him, but he also knew this guy Duarte wouldn't last until the weekend.

Staub said, "Now you have to make it look like an accident. After a robbery attempt, a second violent crime will arouse too much suspicion."

"How do I arrange it?"

"I'll call you when we're going out. Use a stolen car. Make certain you hit him dead on. I don't care if you have to back over him to be sure."

Pelly nodded, then said, "And how do I get back to Panama after I'm through?"

"What do you mean?"

"The *Flame of Panama* left this morning. I have no papers with me."

"We'll work it out when it's time. I may need you on the main job, too. This man William Floyd has not impressed me."

"I thought you needed an American to complete the assignment."

"I need an American to take the *blame*. Anyone can complete the mission."

Pelly realized he'd be in the U.S. for a while. He'd try and improve his English during the visit. He finally said, "I'll take care of Duarte if you need me to, but I'm not sure what he could do to hurt us."

"That's why you're not in charge. He is determined and smart, and that worries me when we have such big plans. You need to ask fewer questions and take more action."

Pelly glared at his boss. He had no idea what kind of action he might take if he got the chance. This whole mission was crazy and, more important, didn't earn them any money. He did not share his boss's sense of vengeance. He did, however, share his view of how helpful the right killing could be.

Ike looked over his shoulder into the noonday sun and saw how the light hit Craig's brown hair. Ike knew he should keep his mouth and the truck shut, but he had been bursting to tell someone what he was up to and what he had been entrusted to transport.

As the door slid up, Craig said, "You got this whole truck for that one crate?"

"I wasn't sure how big it was gonna be. It had to be covered, too. It might not have fit in a pickup with a cover."

Craig hopped up into the truck.

Ike took a second to look at the muscular young man's backside as he made the jump, then followed him inside. There were six pine two-by-four pieces of lumber he had thrown in the truck in case he needed them to stabilize the crate. He hadn't known it would be so heavy, and once they had it on the truck's wooden floor the crate had bit in and he could tell it wasn't going to budge. The lumber, all between four and six feet, lay in a small stack next to the wall of the truck bed.

Ike watched as Craig kneeled next to the crate and poked a finger between the boards. He was pleased to see the interest in the young man. Maybe he'd even have a companion for the trip to Houston.

Craig turned and said, "Okay, I give up. What is it?"

Ike smiled. "You sure you want to know? Once you hear it, you won't be able to forget it." He smiled, still sucking in the little gut he had developed just after turning thirty.

"I wouldn't have come in here if I wasn't ready for a surprise. Maybe if I hear a surprise, I'll give one, too." His smile and green eyes made Ike's knees go weak.

Ike squatted next to him and pulled on the one board that was loose. He figured he'd tease him a little more by showing him the metal casing and some of the wires he'd be able to see through the crate. "See if this gives you any idea." He worked on the board as Craig scooted to the side to give Ike room to work.

Ike pulled the board loose easily, his heart pounding and sending blood through his ears like a bass drum. Once he was done, he said, "Lookie here. What'd ya think?"

As Ike turned to see Craig's reaction, he felt a stinging pain in his shoulder and heard a loud slapping sound. He reached up and grabbed at his left shoulder and turned to see what had happened. He froze, seeing

Craig with one of the shorter two-by-fours in his hands, his arms cocked like Barry Bonds at the plate.

All Ike got out was "Wait . . ." when he saw the pine board rush toward his face and Craig's young, muscular body twist on his swing.

His vision went blurry, then dark. He felt like he was in an empty, dark hallway.

23

ALEX DUARTE DROVE PAST THE HOUSE IN A WORKING-CLASS neighborhood of Gretna, just outside New Orleans. The rental Nissan didn't look like a cop's or anyone else's who shouldn't be in the area. The sun had just disappeared behind a tall oak tree, and the light was fading fast.

He checked the piece of paper with the information Alice had found for him on Cal Linley. The longshoreman had lived at this address for eleven years and drove a Ford F-250 pickup truck registered to him and Ella Linley, whom Duarte assumed was his wife.

Duarte scanned the house and yard to see if there was anything that might cause him trouble. He knew to do a recon first. He had learned that lesson in Bosnia, where everyone had a gun—maybe not as many guns as Louisiana, but close. There was a chain-link fence and a gate for the backyard, and that probably meant there was a dog back there.

The F-250 was in the attached carport. Duarte could just make out a bumper sticker that said WHITE PEOPLE ROCK! He smiled. This guy was a cop-beating, racist thief. Duarte wouldn't have a problem questioning him.

He parked the Nissan in front of a dark house five up from Linley's, and casually strolled down the sidewalk without seeing anyone or feeling like someone was looking out at him from a window. He had a good sense of when someone was watching him, but you never really knew until they took action.

He walked just past the house that interested him, noticing the lights in the side window, probably the kitchen and in the rear room. He thought he saw the gray-blue flicker of a TV set as well. He turned on the property line and quick-stepped to the corner of the fence, then crouched.

Now he could clearly see the backyard, the side and rear of the house.

He stayed low and still for three full minutes, letting his eyes adjust to the growing darkness and ensuring no dog was going to bound out of the shadows at him. He'd still approach the guy like a cop, ID out and professionally, but he wanted to know all he could before he asked the first question. He crept toward the carport. As he passed the big Ford truck, he felt the hood. The slight heat meant the man had been driving in the past hour or so.

As he stood looking at the door that probably went to the kitchen, he saw the knob turn and a shadow behind the glass jalousies.

Duarte purposely stepped out into the light and reached for his wallet.

The door opened and a large man with a rough face and thinning hair stepped awkwardly down the two steps with a plastic bag of garbage in his hands. He never even noticed Duarte.

Duarte said, "Mr. Linley."

That made the man's head snap.

"What the hell? Who're you?"

Duarte held up his identification. "Alex Duarte, ATF."

"ATF. I don't talk to no damn ATF assholes. Besides, I ain't done nothin' with guns."

"I just had a few questions about a container at the port."

"Then go talk to the damn port director, sport. I got nothin' to say to you."

"Sir, can we step inside and speak?"

"No. I done told you to fuck off. What're you? Some kinda of Mexican that don't understand English?"

Duarte fought to hide his smile. This redneck had no idea what was about to happen to him.

William Ike Floyd felt like he was swimming, then he heard some noise. He opened his eyes and thought he was looking up at the sun until he realized it was a streetlight. An old round glass one that was really low. He lay still and felt something bite into his back. He had no idea where he was or what had happened. He started to sit up, but the pain in his head forced him to lie back down. But that hurt, too. Tiny, sharp rocks dug into his bare skin.

He sat up quickly, letting the pain sweep through his body but feeling the need to clear his head. He looked at his lap and legs. He was naked. Naked and outside. But where?

He tried to stand, but lost his footing and tumbled back to the rough, dirty street. He looked up at the low streetlamps and narrow road, then realized he was in an alley. In the alley naked, sore and, most important, without the truck.

He finally got to his feet. He raised his hand to his head and felt the sticky blood along his hairline.

A gust of wind whipped down the deserted alley, and he shivered. He looked around for some discarded clothes or even some garbage to cover up, but saw nothing. For a nasty-ass alley, there was little usable trash.

He had no idea what time it was, what town he was in or even how seriously he was injured. All that paled next to the most important question that the beautiful and deceitful Craig left him with: Where was the truck and its cargo?

ALEX DUARTE STOOD IN THE SMALL LIVING ROOM OF CAL LIN-
ley's house. He wasn't sure if the big longshoreman realized yet that
this interview was likely to fall outside the Department of Justice guide-
lines.

Linley had a nervous timbre to his voice now. "Look, I told you I
didn't want to talk. I told you not to come inside. What the fuck is
going on?"

Duarte didn't speak. Instead he let his gaze drift to a wall with photos
and shelves filled with memorabilia. He purposely ignored Linley and
stepped to the shelves for a closer look.

He had his left hand lightly holding his right fist in case he had to snap
it out quickly, but he thought he had Linley right where he wanted
him—nervous and confused.

Then Duarte realized what all the memorabilia was. The photo of
Hitler in front of the Reichstag, a sketch of Nathan Bedford Forrest, the
founder of the Ku Klux Klan, a photo of a much younger Linley receiving some kind of certificate from a man in a uniform with a swastika on
the arm.

Duarte looked over at the smug, smiling moron.

Duarte said, "So this the kind of stuff you're into?"

"Ain't no law against it."

"I'm Hispanic."

"I'm sorry for you. But I ain't saying shit, and you can get your ass outta my house before you regret it."

Duarte smiled. Just enough to show Linley that he wasn't intimidated, but in reality he wanted the big man to give him a reason to break a few bones.

Linley backed away a step, the sixth sense of a street fighter kicking in. "What the hell does the ATF want with me anyway?"

"I told you. Information about a container out at the port."

"What container? The fucking port has thousands of them."

"You know which one. You opened it night before last." He leveled his eyes at the man.

Linley remained quiet and still.

Duarte turned to face him. "I have questions about that container and what was in it."

"I told you I ain't sayin' shit."

"We'll see."

"What's that mean?"

Duarte gave him a slight smile. "You'll see."

The music was a little loud to consider the sports bar "intimate," but it was cozier than Alice Brainard had intended. She thought that by telling Scott Mahovich that she'd have dinner with him and then suggesting McKenna's, he'd realize it was purely platonic. She knew that she was using the fact that he was attracted to her to get her own way and that it was wrong, but she had done it anyway. She knew Alex needed the information on the blood she'd scraped from the severed finger.

"This is nice," the DNA scientist said.

Alice smiled and nodded.

"We should do it more often."

She wanted to say that this was a one-time event, but she remained quiet.

"You like this place?"

"I come from time to time. Sometimes with my boyfriend." She hit the word "boyfriend" a little hard.

Mahovich looked stricken. "Yeah, he's an ATF agent, right?"

She nodded.

"That's who needed the analysis of the scrapings, isn't it?"

She hesitated and said, "Yes. Please don't say anything."

He didn't reply; he just seemed satisfied with himself.

She finished her grouper sandwich, enduring his stare and that stupid grin. He'd go on about how DNA science was going to be the next big frontier and that the sheriff's office wouldn't be able to pay trained personnel like him enough to stay.

Mahovich made a show out of pulling out a hundred-dollar bill to pay for dinner. "Does your ATF man take you out much?"

"Not too much."

"He doesn't know how to treat a lady."

"No, not really, but he's learning." That was one of the first accurate statements she had made during the entire evening.

As they left and walked out to their cars, parked side by side, she slowly brought up the one topic she was interested in talking to this jerk about.

"So, Scott. How long before you have a profile from the sample I gave you?"

He gave her a serious look. "Ya know, Alice, you can't rush this kind of stuff. I can't ignore one of the real cases brought to us by sheriff's deputies just so some hotshot ATF man can play detective."

She held her thoughts. "It's not like that."

"There is a way we could move things along."

She looked up at him as she leaned against her Honda. "How?"

He placed a hand on her shoulder and leaned down and nibbled on her neck. Just a quick bite.

It shocked Alice, but not as much as what he was inferring would speed things up. Without thinking, she balled her fist and swung at his goofy face, and felt the satisfying snap of her knuckles striking him in the left eye. He lost his balance and bounced off his Buick on the way to the asphalt parking lot.

Alice looked down at him. "You know what will move the case along? You saving your energy for the office."

A lex Duarte tried to look at life from other people's perspectives. That was one of the reasons he'd got along in Bosnia. He could see how the Croats and the Serbs thought they each had the high moral ground in the conflict. He'd come to support the Croats based on his personal relationships as well as on some of the Serb activities, but he understood how each side clung to their ancient hatreds. Back home, he listened to political debates and felt he had some things in common with Democrats and some in common with Republicans. At any time, one side or the other could make a decent point. That was why he was an Independent.

Looking at Cal Linley and then at the Nazi memorabilia on the shelves, he had a difficult time seeing his point of view.

"You a member of a racist group, too?"

The big man looked surprised by the question. "Why should I answer? So you can open a file on me?"

"Look, Mr. Linley, I swear to God there will be no record of my visit."

Again Linley was taken aback. Duarte didn't think he was smart enough to catch the subtle threat in the comment.

The longshoreman took a small step back. "What do you want, ATF man?"

"Answers. That's it. You tell me and I'll leave."

"What if I threw you out instead?"

Duarte didn't respond. He rarely did to threats. Instead he picked up a tiny statue of a woman holding a banner with a swastika. "This valuable?"

"More'n you could afford."

Duarte heaved it against the front wall, the small figurine shattering almost into dust."

"You crazy? What kind of federal agent are you?"

"One that needs answers." He leaned toward the shelves and then flicked a ceramic Black Sambo playing a banjo off the shelf and watched it break into a dozen pieces on the hardwood floor.

"That's Americana. It's art. I spent my whole life collecting it."

Duarte looked at the shaken man and said, "The *Mona Lisa* is art. That thing was insulting. Especially how *you* look at it." He bumped the shelf, and two candlestick holders with German writing on them clinked together then fell over.

Linley shrieked, "Dammit! Cut that out."

Duarte didn't acknowledge him. Instead he reached over and picked up a beer stein with a glass bottom.

"No, not that. It's engraved to me personally."

"From who?"

Linley hesitated, then said, "The commander of the Aryan Army."

Duarte shook his head. "What was in the crate?"

"I told you, I don't know."

Duarte dropped the stein straight to the ground. He heard the man say "Okay," and in a lightning-quick flick of his hand and bend of the knees, he caught the mug an inch off the ground.

Duarte said, "I'm listening."

"I did take something from the container, but I swear I don't know what it was exactly."

"What do you think it was?"

The big man scratched his chin as he formulated an answer. "I just saw the metal and some wires, but I was thinking it might be some kind of machine."

"To do what?"

He hesitated and finally said, "I think it has something to do with oil wells."

"Like how?"

The tall man shook his head. "I ain't sure, but I think it might be a drill head or maybe even something to fuck up the oil flow."

"How'd you figure that out?"

"I ain't stupid. I know the folks bringing it into the U.S."

Duarte had a lot of questions, but decided to go with "Where'd you take it?"

"A motel over in Metairie."

"Who'd you give it to?"

Linley paused, appraising the ATF agent again. Duarte lifted his hand with the engraved stein.

"Okay, okay. I gave it to a young fella from Omaha."

"Look, you're dragging your feet. Just tell me the whole story, and I'll be out of here. Keep stalling, and I might have another accident." To emphasize his comment, he lowered the stein, but flicked a cast-iron tank a little bigger than his hand off the shelf, then while it was still in the air he kicked it hard. It flew in a straight line directly through a windowpane on the side of the house. He hadn't meant to aim for the window, but he wouldn't admit it to this moron.

Linley yelled, "Would you cut that out? I'll tell you." He took a breath and said, "His name was 'Ike' and I called him on a pay phone in Omaha. The president of the National Army of White Americans, Mr. Jessup, hooked us up. All I did was deliver the crate to him. Mr. Jessup spent his whole life in the oil business."

"The NAWA? You're kidding me, right?"

"Nope. We're allowed representation."

Duarte sighed, then said, "How much they pay you?"

"Nothin'."

"Then why'd you do it?"

"To help my country. They is gonna use whatever it is to help build a stronger country."

Duarte eyed the man. "A stronger country for whom?"

"Americans, you dumb-ass. You seen what's going on in this country? We need to do something, and I done my part. I ain't ashamed of it either. Figured the association has some way to set things straight."

"Like what?"

The big man's eyes shifted, then he said, "Maybe taking control of oil production. Hell, I don't know." Sticking to his same story.

Duarte questioned him some more about "Ike" and the motel. At least he had a lead.

When he had all the information he could use, Duarte said, "Look, Mr. Linley. Give me the phone number to this Ike and whatever else you know, and you can forget I was ever here."

"But I'll know by my smashed stuff."

Duarte looked at the remains of the few items he'd broken and at the hole in the window. Then he looked up at Linley. "Believe me, you got off easy."

IN THE LOBBY OF THEIR HOTEL, ALEX DUARTE SHOOK HIS HEAD. He had just recounted all that Cal Linley had told him the night before.

Lina looked at Félix, then back to the ATF agent and said, "Oil doesn't fit in with our sources here in the U.S. I don't see it as a possibility."

He looked over at Félix. The DEA man had seemed more and more disturbed by the death of his informant, Gastlin. Often cops took the full brunt of responsibility for the deaths of people who worked for them. Duarte had seen the subtle signs that Félix was being eaten alive by this. Félix had made a note of Cal Linley's name on a small pad.

Félix finally said, "He does sound a little crazy, bro. Why would he do shit like that for no money? And what would 'help the country' in a crate that fit in the back of a truck? Could oil equipment be more valuable than pot?"

Lina sounded interested now. "What would be more valuable than the pot?"

"Coke or maybe even heroin. That would bring in a hell of a lot more cash than pot."

Duarte sighed. "There's something wrong here. It may have to do with our load, and it maybe points to Ortíz."

Lina said, "Or it might distract us from working on the case. It could work both ways."

Duarte nodded and said, "Regardless, I'm staying a few more days until I'm satisfied."

Félix said, "I'm with you then, bro. Maybe I can help." He paused and then said, "You really think this guy Linley might know something about Gastlin?"

"He might know someone who does. It's a long shot, but I feel like I have to follow up on it."

Lina became more agitated and said, "You're both foolish. It was a load of pot, and you feel guilty your snitch got killed. That's it."

Duarte kept his dark eyes on the FBI agent. "Lina, it's not like I'm asking you to jump in on this. I just have a few leads to run down. Maybe it is nothing."

"You have a report on your interview?"

"No report on that interview."

She shook her head like a frustrated teacher.

Duarte let her calm down a little and said, "Have you seen the colonel? I've got a few questions for him."

Lina shook her head. "No, he's been gone since early this morning."

Félix shot a look at her. "Keeping pretty close watch over him, aren't you?"

"That depends, Félix."

"On what?"

"On whether it's any of your fucking business." She turned and stalked off toward the elevators, leaving Duarte and Félix in the little sitting area of the hotel lobby.

Lázaro Staub let his eyes burn at the terrified man from Omaha who was sitting on the trunk of the rented Impala. Pelly leaned against the car's driver-side door with that perpetual smirk under his five o'clock shadow even though it wasn't yet nine in the morning. And he was in a town named Lafayette, about three hours from New Orleans.

Staub shook his head and glanced at Pelly. "I'm surrounded by idiots. First you and your hired asses, then this moron manages to lose our package altogether."

Ike said, "There were just too many of them. I'm sorry, Mr. Ortíz, but they surprised me."

"I'm afraid you'll be in for a horrible surprise if we don't have the truck with my package back in our possession in the next few hours." He looked up at the clear sky and the expanse to the north. "How big is this town?"

"What, Lafayette? I dunno, hundred thousand maybe."

"Where would one take a rental truck?"

Ike shrugged and shook his head.

Pelly cleared his throat.

Staub looked at him, "What? What is it, Pelly?"

He started in Spanish.

Staub said, "Speak English, so we don't have to translate for this idiot."

"If you look at it like a business, who would want the truck?"

Staub thought about it until he heard Ike say, "The rental company?"

Pelly nodded. "For parts, if the truck is not working. Perhaps the reward, no?"

Staub's narrow eyes darted from side to side. "You may be right, Pelly." He looked at his assistant. "Get on it." He glared at Ike, wondering the exact cost if he were to eliminate this problem right now.

Duarte showed his ID to get into the New Orleans office of the ATF. The office had moved since Katrina and seemed a little cramped in the temporary building on the outskirts of New Orleans.

He needed some analytical help and knew the best person for that would be one of the office's intelligence analysts. After a few greetings and small talk, he caught up to a young agent named Hugh O'Conner who had been through the academy with him.

The New Orleans agent slapped Duarte on the back. "Heard you were out here on a case, but I thought it was at the port."

"It was. I'm just doing some follow-up."

"How's South Florida?"

"Good."

"Miss the army at all?"

"Nope."

O'Conner smiled. "Still the talkative one, huh, Alex?"

Duarte just smiled and said, "You guys have a 'go-to' analyst?"

"Yeah, doesn't everyone?" He looked down the hall to a tall, pretty woman with red hair. "Jan Stern is the best. She's got the lowdown on every database you can think of."

"Will she give me a few minutes?"

"Jan? Sure. Loves Latins. Lived in Spain for a while. She'll do anything you ask."

"Thanks."

"Still all business."

Duarte shrugged as he started toward the analyst. He eased up to her cubicle and smiled. "Jan, hello. I'm Alex Duarte from the West Palm Beach office."

She looked up from her report, then smiled herself. "What can I do for you, Agent Duarte?"

"I need to identify someone, and all I have is a description and nickname." He pulled out the registration sheet from the motel in Metairie where Linley had said he delivered the crate. It had taken a while to find the exact motel, but the owner was cooperative if it meant getting rid of a federal agent. "His registration at a motel just says 'Ike Floyd, Neb.'"

"No problem." She scooted out a second chair and slid it next to her. "Have a seat, and we'll see what we can find."

After a half hour of more conversation than he wanted but some dynamite computer work, she had narrowed it down to five possibilities for "Ike" Floyd in the Omaha area.

As he prepared to leave, she said, "How long you out here for?"

"Few more days, at least."

"Are you free for dinner?" She had a bright, flawless smile.

He smiled and knew his answer immediately. "I'd like that, but I have a girlfriend." He'd finally taken the plunge.

William "Ike" Floyd had tried to strike up a conversation with the man named Pelly, but so far he hadn't had much luck. He wasn't unfriendly or nasty, just focused on finding the truck. He spoke English. He had an accent, but he knew what words to string together and how to put in a little inflection. In most sentences. But he didn't have much to say.

They pulled up to the fourth place that rented U-Hauls. This was a grimy, former gas station that wasn't one of the nice, roomy corporate sites.

Pelly nodded. "This kind of place might buy stolen parts."

Ike looked over at the man whose face seemed to grow darker with hair by the minute and said, "You think we got a chance? What if he doesn't want to say anything?"

"If he knows something, he'll talk."

Just the way the trim, furry man said it made Ike believe it. Ike pulled the rented Impala into the lot next to the old station, and they walked through the empty office and into the covered work bay. Inside, a sloppy, fat man in a T-shirt too small for his girth unscrewed the grill to a step van.

Ike said in a low voice, "I think that's my truck."

Pelly stepped into the bay and said, "Excuse me, sir."

The fat man jumped at his voice and turned to face his visitors. He stood to his full six-three and tried to pull down the greasy white T-shirt. "What can I do for you boys?"

Pelly smiled and eased closer. Ike noticed him reach under the back of his shirt for his automatic pistol. He had seen how quick Ortíz was to kill. The image of Faith's open, staring, dead eyes was still burned into his head. He was about to see another version of the brutal way these guys did business.

WILLIAM "IKE" FLOYD DIDN'T KID HIMSELF. HE KNEW HE WAS involved in something that would have the cops all over him if they pulled it off. Of course, he had thought that once before and still never had had to answer for his role in that incident. He had to admit he wasn't comfortable with seeing people killed right in front of him. Even though Pelly had moved his Beretta .380 from the rear of his pants to the front, Ike didn't give the fat mechanic much of a chance for surviving this encounter.

As the big man waddled slowly closer to them, he passed a greasy hand through his wavy blond hair. There was an oily fingerprint on his nose.

"Hey," he hesitated, his eyes fixed on Pelly's gun. "What can I do for you?"

Pelly nodded at Ike. "Make sure is right truck," he said, his accent bleeding through.

Ike quick-stepped past the mechanic and over to the U-Haul step van and peeked into the cab. His Doolittle Industries ball cap was on the dash, and he recognized the small tear in the truck's bench seat. He looked back at Pelly and nodded. He elected to stay next to the truck.

The nervous mechanic turned so he could see both Ike and Pelly.

Ike knew Ortíz was ruthless. He had seen it firsthand. Pelly didn't have the sophisticated manners of Ortíz, but with that thick stubble and muscular arms, Ike knew the younger man was no pussy. He seemed more approachable than Ortíz, even eating a Big Mac with Ike at lunchtime while Ortíz made calls from a diner. Ike figured the boss didn't want to be involved in the grunt work like this.

Yeah, Pelly seemed okay, but that didn't mean he wouldn't think twice about shooting the behemoth in the head if he had to.

Then Pelly started to speak in that slow English he had. He looked at Ike but spoke for the mechanic to hear. "I know this gentleman is a businessman. He deals with stolen trucks. That's for profit, no?" He looked at the mechanic. The man was shaking hard enough for Ike to see the fat strips on his back jiggle.

Pelly continued. "I am also a businessman, so I can see what he wants. He would prefer I pay him five hundred American dollars to find out where our crate is and who took it. He knows that involving the local police in a murder investigation doesn't help me or him." He looked at the mechanic. *"¿És verdad?"* Then he translated, "Correct, no?"

The mechanic stole a glance at Ike, then stared back at Pelly. "That's right, that's right."

He was panting like a dog on a hot day.

Pelly leveled his gaze at the man. "So who took it?" He rested his hand on the pistol grip.

The mechanic didn't risk being slow with the answer. "Craig Gaines and some of his buddies took the truck. I just paid them fifteen large for it. There weren't no crate or nothing in it when they delivered it."

"And where is Craig Gaines?" Pelly let his hand drop off the gun.

"About four or five blocks over near the railroad tracks." He wiped his sweaty forehead, leaving a smear of black grease. "Fourth house in from the main road. Has a green Camaro out front."

Pelly nodded and smiled. "We will make this deal, my friend."

The man's legs were shaking now.

Pelly kept his placid face. "If we go to Craig Gaines's house and you have warned them, or they are not there, or we do not recover our property, I will make sure you do not see the sunset." Pelly kept his hairy face pleasant. "If we get the crate, we will not say we saw this truck here and you will never see us again. Is this not fair?"

The mechanic nodded furiously.

"Now, do you have any guns here?"

"Why?"

"Because if you do not answer me, I will shoot you."

"In the office. Cabinet behind the desk. Right at eye level."

Pelly looked over at Ike, who scampered past them again and into the office. In the cluttered room, he squeezed past a stack of boxes to get behind the desk and in front of the metal, nicked–up cabinet. He had to jiggle the handle to force open the door. He found a small SIG-Sauer auto pistol in a nylon holster on the shelf, just about his eye level. He grabbed the pistol, then paused. On the same shelf, over to the side, was a wooden crate without a top. Set inside like eggs in a carton were six old–style grenades like the ones in an old John Wayne war movie. He slid out the small crate and tucked it under one arm, then hurried out to Pelly.

"I found something extra."

"What?"

"Look." He held up the crate of grenades.

Pelly smiled. "Put 'em in the car."

"What about the gun?"

Pelly looked at him. "Keep it. You may need it." He looked at the mechanic. "No calls or travel for the next two hours. Understand?"

"I do, I do, sir, and thank you."

Pelly turned, and Ike fell into step with him.

Pelly said, "You see, money can solve a lot of problems and save a lot of trouble."

Ike said, "But he knew you'd shoot him if you had to. Even I could tell that."

"He better hope we get the crate and the boss doesn't come talk to him. Then he'll wish he'd only be shot."

The pretty analyst, Jan Stern, had come up not only with five possibilities for "Ike" Floyd, but with their driver's license photos as well. Now Duarte was on his way back out to Gretna to have Cal Linley point out the man to whom he'd given the crate from the container.

Duarte had thought he could eliminate two men from the list. One was in his forties, older than Linley had described, and one had a funny eye placed way over on the right side of his head. Duarte thought Linley would have mentioned that if the man he had dealt with looked like that. But he had to be sure, so he turned his rented Taurus down Linley's street, then slowed.

There was a mass of emergency vehicles in front of the little house.

He parked and wandered to the edge of the crime-scene tape. He showed his ID to a uniformed officer standing next to the tape. "What's going on?"

The younger, thick-necked cop said, "Someone found a dead guy inside."

"Cal Linley?"

"Think so. You know him?"

"Sort of." Duarte knew he'd have to let the lead homicide detective know that he'd talked to him. He wondered what the chances were of this murder being unrelated to his case. Just about zero, he figured.

Right now all he had was one name in Omaha. He knew where he was headed.

PELLY PREFERRED HAVING THE DULLARD AMERICAN, IKE, IN THE
front seat with him as he drove around Layfaette. He was an idiot, but he
wasn't constantly putting on an act or ordering Pelly around. Now with
the boss in the car and Ike stuck in the backseat, Pelly once again had to
take directions to a house he had already been past. It was like having a
wife.

He took the Impala past the house slowly, noticing the activity. Obviously the mechanic had not made a call. One young man sat on the front
porch in a faded plastic chair, sipping a beer. Another man leaned into
the hood of a green car in the grass of the front yard. It looked like two
more people were inside.

"Good, Pelly, good," Staub said, like he was watching a porno movie.
"I'm impressed how you found them."

"They may not have the crate."

"But they'll tell us where it is."

"How can you be so sure?"

His employer just chuckled.

Pelly knew the boss was going to use his own means to question these men, whether they were efficient or not. He looked over his shoulder and saw the fear on Ike's face. For a tough-looking guy, he didn't seem to have much stomach for violence. He looked sick right now.

Pelly said to the passenger in the rear, "Ike, when we pull around and stop, you can watch the car."

The American spoke right up. "No, no. I'll go in. I want to make sure they tell you the truth." He added, "Can I bring a grenade?"

Pelly shook his head and pulled the car around and parked directly in front of the house, still attracting no attention. He had his Beretta in his waistband. He'd save the grenades for later.

The three men headed up the front walkway. Pelly was alert to an ambush, but so far the man at the car had not looked up and the man drinking a beer had only nodded to them. Pelly had been on many raids with the national police and had a good sense of when things were not as they appeared. These men were so complacent he thought it was a trap at first. Then he realized they were just Americans and so used to security that they took it for granted.

The man on the porch let the front legs of the chair he was leaning back in touch the ground. "You don't look like no cops."

Pelly would've gotten right to the point, but Staub said, "No, my friend. We are here to chat."

"Chat?"

"That's right, chat with you young men." He looked back at Ike, whose eyes were nervously darting from the porch to the windows. Staub said, "Do you recognize anyone?"

Ike shook his head, then said to the man, "Is Craig here?"

Pelly wondered: If Ike had been ambushed and had had to fight off several attackers, how had he gotten the man's name? Perhaps he'd gotten it from the mechanic, but now Pelly was curious.

The man on the porch just waved them inside. "Craig is in watching TV or something."

Pelly stepped through the open front door with Staub and Ike behind him.

In the main room a young man and teenaged girl sat on a wide, ratty couch, watching a TV set on top of a coffee table. They didn't even look up from the TV to their visitors. Pelly noticed that they were holding hands. The girl had long brown hair and acne on her cute face. He could relate to that, something that distracted people from how you really looked.

The young man glanced up and casually looked over at the intruders. Pelly noticed that when his eyes fell on Ike, he flinched and then sat up.

Staub smiled, realizing the man recognized Ike. He pulled the pistol Pelly had brought on the *Flame of Panama* for him. He let the man see the gun, then said, "I believe you have something that belongs to me."

Now the girl jumped at the sight of a man with a gun.

The man stood up and thrust out his hands. "Wait, don't do nothin' crazy."

Staub walked over to him and calmly placed the barrel on the head of the girl sitting next to him. "I assure you it won't be crazy."

The man's eyes darted over to Ike and said, "He tell you how I got the truck?" His voice cracked. Oddly, the girl just looked up at Staub with her big brown eyes, not acknowledging the danger she was in.

The man's voice picked up on the urgency of the situation. Pelly knew he had no idea that his girlfriend had little chance of surviving this.

The man said, "I'll tell you how I got it. I'll tell you everything." He stared at Ike. Pelly noticed his new comrade flushing red in his face. This might be interesting.

D uarte had found a flight from New Orleans first thing in the morning and was on the ground in Omaha, driving a rental car, by nine o'clock. He had not told Félix what was happening for several reasons. One was that the DEA man had become more and more agitated as the death of his informant had eaten at him. He could see it in Félix's manner and the gradual ebbing of his natural good humor. Duarte didn't want to raise false hope in his friend.

The other reason he had not included his friend on the trip was that he didn't want any witnesses. In case he had to resort to his way of questioning, he'd rather not put someone else on the spot. With the death of Linley, the case had taken an ominous turn. He still didn't know what was in the crate, but the possibilities scared him.

By ten, he had eliminated one suspect. Darrel Floyd was a computer programmer who worked from home. Even with his less-than-perfect interviewing skills, Duarte knew the anemic-looking, thirty-five-year-old who was busy playing War Craft on his PC was not involved in anything concerning illegal drugs and murder.

At the apartment of the second man on his list, Duarte got no answer to his knocks. He hated the idea of waiting until the evening, when most people were off work, to talk to the man, but as he left the building, he saw a hand-scrawled note on one door that said "Manager."

A rap on the door brought a short, round woman in her midsixties, wearing a brown muumuu and flip-flops.

She looked Duarte over and said, "We got no vacancies."

He said, "I was looking for one of your tenants."

"Who?"

"Mr. William Floyd."

"Ike? Why you want that moron?"

"I need to talk to him."

"You a cop?"

"Would that surprise you?" He didn't offer any identification.

"Not at all. That boy had a job, but them people he hangs out with, they is trouble."

"What people?"

"Them Nazi or Klan people. Whatever they is callin' themselves nowadays."

"You think he might be over there?"

The lady shrugged her shoulders, and Duarte thought he might know how everyone else felt now. He didn't own the patent on shrugs.

"You know where he works?"

"Nope. Like everyone else in this town, he's some kinda telephone solicitor." She paused, looking down the hall. "You trustworthy?"

"Yes, ma'am."

"I don't know if you're a cop or not, but for twenty bucks I'll let you in his apartment, as long as you don't take nothin'."

He had the twenty in her hand before she could change her mind. He followed her down the narrow hallway to William Floyd's apartment.

Inside the cramped one-bedroom apartment, Duarte checked a pad of paper on a small table with the telephone. The old landlady stayed by the door and watched to make sure he didn't steal anything. He searched a small, one-drawer desk and found a pocket-sized address book. He was about to take it, then remembered his pledge to the old landlady. He turned and held up the black book. "I'll throw in another five bucks if I can take this."

"Done."

He found a brochure for the Omaha chapter of the National Army of White Americans. He held it up and showed the landlady the address. "That around here?"

" 'Bout three miles off Forty-second. Maybe ten minutes away."

Duarte nodded and looked around some more. He found a single sheet of paper. Cal Linley's phone number was scrawled on it. There was no doubt now. This was "Ike." For his own good, he better have some answers for Duarte.

He thanked the landlady and got directions to the address on the brochure. Fifteen minutes and two wrong turns later, he was looking at a duplex. One side was quiet, but the other had loud George Thorogood guitar twanging out of the windows. A lanky young man with a shaved head stood by the front door. Duarte doubted he was a chemotherapy patient. One part of him almost hoped these idiots gave him a reason to question them harshly. Either way, he was about to get some answers.

28

WILLIAM "IKE" FLOYD WATCHED AS MR. ORTÍZ KEPT HIS GUN barrel on the girl's head. She had shown no interest in the gun since he had placed it there. She reminded Ike of a hound dog who didn't know what a gun could do.

Craig said, "You wanna know what happened?"

He looked from Ortíz to Pelly, not knowing who should hear the story.

Ike's heart started to beat harder, and his grip tightened on the pistol in his hand. He was about to get smacked in the face by the truth, and he had to do something quick. He couldn't let Craig tell them how he had tricked Ike.

Without thinking, he raised his pistol and said, "Where's the crate, Craig?"

When the young man hesitated, Ike started to jerk the trigger of the slim SIG-Sauer .380. Three of the first five rounds caught Craig square in the chest.

Ortíz instinctively stepped back, away from the gunfire.

Craig dropped onto the couch without another sound, snatching silently at his chest for a moment until he went still.

Once Ortíz had backed away, the girl stood up. The seventh shot from Ike's gun had caught her in the throat and she tumbled next to her boyfriend, her big eyes staring at Ike.

When the small pistol was empty and the slide locked back, he stepped up to the couch. He looked down at the lifeless Craig, satisfied he had gotten his revenge. The girl squirmed next to him on the couch, using her small hand to try to stop the blood pouring from the wound in her neck. A gurgling sound escaped from her that turned Ike's stomach. After a few seconds, she lay still, too.

Ike heard the door burst open and saw the man from the porch. Pelly raised his gun to the man's head and said, "Where's the crate from the truck?"

The man's eyes popped when they fell on the dead couple in the living room. He stammered, "The satellite?"

Pelly said, "What satellite?"

"The one in the crate."

Pelly looked over to Ortíz. Then back at the man. "Yes, the satellite."

"It's in the garage in the back."

Ortíz said, "I'll stay with our friend. You two check the garage."

Ike followed Pelly out the door and through the house. He still held the empty pistol. He couldn't believe he had just shot a man up close. He'd shot a girl, too, but that was an accident. He was becoming a killer.

They didn't encounter anyone else in the house as they searched for the back door to the one-car garage. Going in through the kitchen, they found the bomb in the middle of the clean garage with only the top of the crate torn off.

Pelly stood on his toes and looked out of one of the windows built into the wooden garage door. He turned back to Ike. "The man working on the car has headphones on. He's still there."

Ike, still shaky from the adventure, said, "How're we gonna move this thing?"

"We'll get another rental truck. The fat mechanic earned his stolen one."

Duarte casually walked up to the duplex and waited for the man standing by the front door to look up. There was no need to be rude. Yet.

The man's eyes came up to meet Duarte's. He said, "We're not buying."

"I'm not selling anything."

"Then get lost."

Duarte tried not to smile. "I'm looking for Ike Floyd."

"Who're you?" The man's angular face made him look angry even though he didn't sound like it.

"I'm the guy looking for Ike."

"Oh, a smart-ass. You look like you might be an Italian or Spanish smart-ass."

"I'm from Florida, and I need to talk to Ike. Where is he?"

"Look, Mr. Florida." Now he sounded pissed off. "I don't care who you are or what you are. This is a private club, and by lookin' at ya, I doubt you could join."

Duarte kept a calm expression. Something like this made him realize how little his heritage mattered to most people, but when he found an idiot like this, it was all he could do not to take his head off. Instead he simply started to step around the wiry man.

The man tried to grab Duarte's arm as he said, "Wait a minute. I said . . ."

That was all he got out once Duarte had bent the man's wrist in the most unnatural downward position.

In a quiet voice, he said, "No loud noises or you won't write any letters for more than a year. Understand?"

The man nodded furiously as he hunched his whole body, hoping for the slightest relief he could get.

Inside it looked like a comfortable museum, with couches along the walls and shelves of knickknacks. On the walls, vintage posters of the Ku Klux Klan and Nazis hung in an orderly fashion.

Duarte said, "You guys love your memorabilia, don't you?"

The man just said, "Let up, let up."

Duarte did slightly and said, "Where're your buddies? I need to talk to someone about Ike."

The man nodded forward, and Duarte could see two men inside a small room off the hallway. He thrust the man with the sore wrist inside the room, then stood in the doorway until they were done bouncing off one another.

A wide man, who resembled a pro lineman, stood up from a chair that looked like a kid's prop next to him. "Who in the hell are you?"

Duarte kept it short. "Look, guys, I just need to talk to Ike Floyd. You know where he is?"

The man Duarte had seen at the door massaged his wrist and said, "I think he broke my fucking arm."

The lineman and the third man, a real young guy about Duarte's size, stepped toward him.

It was on.

29

WILLIAM "IKE" FLOYD NODDED TO MR. ORTÍZ AND PELLY. SITTING in the new Ryder rental truck that Mr. Ortíz had secured, he was anxious to get on his way and put some distance between him and these two. The men from the house had fled, and Ortíz didn't seem to care.

Mr. Ortíz looked at Ike and said, "Take no more chances. Contact me in three days. Pelly and I must handle some problems and then we will meet you in Houston. Is this clear?"

"Yes, sir."

"You surprised me back there. You were decisive."

Ike didn't tell why he was so decisive. He couldn't let them find out how he was tricked. Craig got what he deserved. He tried not to think about the girl bleeding out from her neck wound.

Mr. Ortíz said, "I do not believe the men who fled will go to the police. That was a criminal enterprise. They will run."

Ike nodded. He hoped this crazy Panamanian was right. Then he said, "What about the mechanic? He saw Pelly and me. He could link us to the killing."

"Pelly and I will decide if we need to talk to this man." He patted the step van's hood. "Now you must go."

Ike nodded to Pelly, who looked like he had grown his winter coat in the course of the day. Then he pulled the van out onto the street. He was headed to Houston, but first he needed to sleep. Maybe for a long time. It wouldn't take long to get to the Texas city, and he knew he couldn't call for a few days. He was going to sleep; the only question was where. As his eyes blurred from the wave of exhaustion and relief that swept over him, Ike realized he was going to have to find a place here in Lafayette if he wanted to stay on the right side of the highway and not run the van into an embankment.

He saw a little motel with a yellow sign that said THE CAJUN INN. He slowed the big step van to swing into the parking lot of the motel.

Duarte had yet to punch one of the three men who continued lunging at him inside the headquarters of the National Army of White Americans. He simply kept dodging and feinting and watching the men miss him and often stumble onto the hard, wooden floor.

The big lineman couldn't maneuver well enough past the shelves of statues and memorabilia. He knocked off several pieces, then froze, cursing his size.

For fun, Duarte turned and kicked over a shelf, sending little ceramic figures flying.

"Stop," yelped the big man, then he crouched for another shot at Duarte.

Duarte took the lunging man's arm and redirected him into the nearest wall, literally knocking out the drywall with the man's head. The big man stumbled, then collapsed on the floor.

The thin man with the sore wrist now had a metal shelving support he swung like a sword. He whipped it past Duarte's right ear, then stepped up to deliver a blow to the top of Duarte's head. The ATF man stepped to one side and watched the heavy metal support slip past him and end up breaking the big man's arm as it came to rest on the floor. The man still made no sound.

The third man stood motionless as the one with the sore wrist yelled. "C'mon, Sean, kill this motherfucker."

Duarte had had enough of this skinhead and swung his right foot into the man's jaw, sending him to the floor near the heap of his giant friend.

Now Sean realized this wasn't going his way. He turned and started to run away from Duarte down a hallway. In three quick steps, Duarte was close enough to shove the man and send him flying to the floor.

Duarte ducked his head down the other hallway to ensure that no one else was in the building, then went right to the man named Sean. He was the only conscious one, and due to his youth he might be more inclined to talk, and talk fast.

Duarte stood over him. "Sean, I'm in a hurry. You can tell me where Ike is or I can *make* you tell me." Duarte cracked his knuckles. "Which is it gonna be?"

The young man held up his hands. "Last I saw him was Kansas City."

"What was he doing there?"

"He rented a U-Haul there. About five days ago."

"Why?"

"It had something to do with a crane." The man's voice had a noticeable quiver.

"A crane?"

"Yeah. He asked me if I knew anything about these U-cranes. Maybe they're rentals like the vans."

Duarte talked to the young man and got a clear idea of where he needed to go next.

The drive to Kansas City was three hours, and in the little rented Cobalt it felt like five. The manager was immediately helpful as soon as he saw Duarte's ATF identification.

The older man brushed back his longish gray hair with one hand.

"Since the bombing, we don't take no chances in this part of the country. I worked in Oklahoma City. I don't care if it's Ryder, Budget or us, anyone in the Midwest will help you. We don't need subpoenas or nothin'."

Duarte nodded. "Thanks. I just want to know if a guy named William Floyd has rented a truck and maybe if he gave you an idea where he was going."

The manager punched up a computer on his desk and said, "Yep, has a step van for ten days."

"Say where he was going?"

The man smiled. "Doesn't need to."

"Why's that?"

"Because we have a GPS in that truck."

"You have GPS service in your vehicles?"

"Not all of them. Just a few of the vans. They been disappearing down in Louisiana and we wanted to see if a GPS or LoJack would solve the problem. It's not public knowledge or nothing. Just the big, corporate stores use them. We stuck a unit on that truck because it was new and like the others that have gone missing."

"Where on the van is it?"

"We seal them in the front bumper with the unit wired to the battery for power. No one would even notice it unless they were looking."

"Does that mean you can tell me where the truck is right now?" Duarte was amazed at the breaks you could catch if you just did a little follow-up.

The man called up a new screen on the computer. "It's just like putting a Nextel phone with GPS on the bumper. Here, look." He slid to the side so Duarte could look at the screen. "See, it interfaces with a mapping program, and it sends a signal once an hour." He looked at the data. "This van has been in Lafayette, Louisiana, for two days now. Right on this street." He pointed to a map on the screen.

Five minutes later, Duarte had a hard copy of the map and was figuring the fastest way to Lafayette after a few hours' rest.

A lice Brainard was just cleaning up everything at her workstation when Scott Mahovich came to her door.

"Is it safe for me to come in?" His black eye had turned a pus-yellow color.

"Are you going to do anything stupid?"

"I don't plan to."

"Then you may enter." She was only half playing. She didn't like men who took women for granted and especially those who took liberties. It wouldn't have been so bad except that she hadn't thought Scott was like that. He had always been so quiet and shy. She wondered if Alex would be upset if he heard. He'd probably think it was funny.

The DNA scientist said, "I'll have a profile from the blood tomorrow. Do we have a suspect yet?"

"Not that I know of."

"Is the ATF going to reimburse the county for the work I did?"

"Are you going to be able to handle a sexual harassment suit or another smack in the face?"

"Point taken."

She smiled, knowing she owned this guy now.

IN HIS KANSAS CITY HOTEL ROOM, DUARTE ROLLED OVER AND answered his cell phone on the second ring. He had slipped back into a pattern of insomnia which had plagued him for years after his service in Bosnia. Now, as he felt more and more like he had missed something obvious about the killings, he was awake, lying in bed, when the phone rang.

"Hello," he said, before even checking the clock.

"I knew you'd be awake."

He smiled at the sound of Alice Brainard's voice.

She continued. "I bet you already worked out, too."

"Nope, I technically haven't been to sleep yet."

"Out partying with Félix?"

"Not exactly."

"Then what happened?"

"I'm not sure. I'm caught up in the follow-up to our case, and it's taking more time than I thought." He didn't intend to worry her with the details of more bodies.

"At least I can tell you we have a profile from the blood under your informant's fingernail. All you need is a suspect."

Duarte thought of the *Flame of Panama*'s first mate. "I may have one."

"Can you get a comparison sample from him?"

"By what I suspect right now, if I can draw blood on this guy we should have plenty."

"That sounds like a good, determined ATF agent." There was a pause. "How're things in New Orleans?"

"Good, I guess, but I'm in Kansas."

"Why Kansas?"

"Long story."

Alice said, "When are you coming back?"

"Soon as I can. We have a few loose ends to clear up."

"We'll have a great homecoming date when you do."

"Can't wait."

They exchanged goodbyes and he looked up at the clock. It was 5:55.

Thanks to Alice, Alex Duarte had already eaten breakfast and traveled all the way from Kansas City to Lafayette by eight in the morning. It had been pure luck to meet a pilot with the Department of Homeland Security, a former customs agent who was flying down to Houston the next day. Duarte had spoken to the uniformed man in the lobby of the hotel, and the good old boy from Dallas had remembered when, before 9/11, both customs and the ATF had been under the Treasury Department and sometimes worked closely together. He knew some of Duarte's friends from the ATF office in Miami and gladly let Duarte take one of the empty seats in the sleek Gulfstream jet. The pilot made a quick stop in Lafayette and was on his way again.

Now, in another damn rented Chevrolet Cobalt, he slowly cruised down Talbot Street, looking for an obvious place where the rented U-Haul van might be stashed. He had checked with the Kansas City U-Haul manager, who'd said the van was still in the same spot.

As he drove, Duarte realized the GPS unit might just be in a trash can. But he had to try. He had to admit to himself that he had no idea where this was going. He didn't know what had been taken from the cargo container; he didn't know why Byron Gastlin had been killed; he didn't know who'd killed Cal Linley. All he knew was he had a lead, and he was going to follow it.

Duarte almost stopped the little Cobalt in traffic when he looked up and saw the U-Haul sign on the dingy little building that looked like a former gas station. The van had to be there. He wondered if it had been turned in as he pulled the Cobalt into the tiny lot.

Inside, the business presented no more of a professional look. Ancient posters of 1970s vintage cars pulling U-Haul trailers were stuck on the walls without pattern, a small office with a desk piled high in paperwork was empty.

Duarte peeked through an open door into the two-bay garage. It was hot, but the bay doors were closed and a large man with blond hair leaned under the hood of a van. Stepping inside, he said, "Excuse me," in a loud voice.

The giant man in a filthy, white T-shirt that had to have been dirty when he put it on this morning, straightened up and looked toward Duarte.

"Help you?"

"Maybe. I'm interested in a van."

"I only got trailers left. Three of 'em out in the back. Should get a van back tonight."

Duarte got a sense this guy was nervous. "What about the one in the bay?"

The fat mechanic waddled a little closer, blocking Duarte's view of the van. "This here one is down for a while."

Duarte stepped into the bay.

The mechanic said, "Sorry, bud, but you can't come out here. Insurance reasons."

Ignoring the mechanic, he started to pass the giant man.

The mechanic reached out to grab Duarte's arm until the ATF man said, "Don't try it unless you want to work a ratchet with your left hand."

The man knew threats when he heard them and quickly withdrew the hand.

Duarte looked in the cab of the van, then in the glove compartment. He found the paperwork signed by William Floyd. He turned to the mechanic. "This is the van I'm looking for." He knew not to mention the GPS. This guy may have rented U-Hauls, but he was not part of their corporate structure.

Duarte said, "Where's the man who was driving this?"

The fat man shrugged. That was annoying.

Duarte took a quick step closer to him.

The mechanic said, "Look, I don't want no trouble."

"Then you better answer some questions."

"What was in that truck that made you Spanish people so interested?"

"Someone else was by here?"

"Yep, and he paid me five hundred bucks for information. What are you good for?"

"I won't break your arm for having a stolen van."

"How you know it's stolen?"

"Because the company doesn't have it as returned, you're stripping it, and you got the bay doors closed when it's a hundred degrees in here. Now you gonna give me some answers or am I going to take your right arm in my grip?"

The fat man played with his blond curly hair for a minute and said, "I like your threats better than the monkey-looking guy's. I think he would've kilt me if I didn't talk."

Duarte knew exactly whom he meant: the first mate from the *Flame of Panama*. "Talk to me, and you won't see me again."

"That's what Monkey Boy said."

Duarte was ready to get some answers.

Twenty minutes later Duarte drove past the house where the fat mechanic had told him he had sent the other man who "looked like a monkey." Duarte knew the description and that the man was likely the first mate of the *Flame of Panama*. He had Félix Baez going through the DEA in Panama right now to find out his name. Whoever he was, he was smart enough to get ahead of Duarte and had at least some cash. The mechanic admitted to having been paid five hundred bucks to tell the man where the van had come from.

The men who had questioned the mechanic, and by the description of the second man, Duarte thought it might be his William "Ike" Floyd, had asked for another van to replace the partially disassembled one the mechanic had hidden in his shop. That meant they would've arranged for transportation from this area, because the fat guy had no more step vans.

The man didn't look too happy when Duarte made him call the manager in Kansas City and say he had the van. He gave the fat mechanic a hard stare until he admitted that he had bought the van knowing it was stolen. The U-Haul manager from Kansas City was shouting over the phone. Duarte figured there would be a U-Haul franchise open in Lafayette in the next few days.

The house he had driven past was quiet. There was no Camaro in the front yard as the mechanic had said, but there was a work stool and a few rags where it looked like someone had been repairing a car.

Duarte finally parked the rented Cobalt two houses away and walked down the deserted sidewalk and straight up the path to the front door. He knocked hard and stepped to the side. He heard something inside the house like a radio or TV. There didn't seem to be an air conditioner running, and all the windows were closed.

He tried the handle. Open. He pushed the door as he called out, "Hello."

Immediately he sensed something wasn't right. He stepped inside and drew his Glock before his brain registered exactly what was wrong. He looked down the messy hallway, with magazines piled on the side and several empty bottles. The familiar odor was what had put him on edge. He had gotten used to it as a young man in the army. American soldiers might not have seen widespread combat in Bosnia, but the atrocities by both sides made up for the lack of U.S. participation. Duarte had been with units that uncovered mass graves or found slaughtered families on a number of occasions. His specialty with explosives as a combat engineer had given him the chance to work with a number of different units.

Now he smelled death and knew exactly what it meant. There was a body in this house.

He eased down the hallway, not positive he was alone in the old wooden structure. His SIG-Sauer was in his extended right hand and pointing anywhere he looked. He came to the living room and saw the two bodies on the couch. He noted quickly that they were a man and woman but went right past them to clear the rest of the house.

Two minutes later, he was back in the living room, holstering his pistol. He was careful not to disturb the crime scene. The man was about twenty-three, with light brown hair. He had been hit in the upper chest four times. He lay at a slight angle. The woman, who was really more of a girl, about eighteen, lay at the opposite angle with her head touching the man's head. She had been hit in the neck. The blood from all the wounds had turned much of the old white sofa dark brown.

With the TV screen in front of the couch, the bodies looked like a young couple on a date watching TV.

Duarte looked for the phone to make sure the 911 call went to the right police agency. This case was turning bloody, and Duarte was no closer to the answers that he needed.

31

PELLY WASN'T HAPPY WHEN HIS BOSS CALLED HIM AT DAWN. HE had heard somehow that the ATF agent was on his way to Lafayette, and he wanted the fat mechanic silenced. He also wanted Pelly to stop Duarte if he could find him.

With no traffic, Pelly had made the drive from New Orleans in under two and a half hours. But he was still annoyed.

Pelly waited until a middle-aged man with a young boy had hooked up a rental trailer to his pickup truck and left the old U-Haul building where the heavy mechanic worked. Now there shouldn't be anyone else inside the office. He didn't like the idea of going back on a business arrangement, but Staub had insisted, and he had a point. There was no guarantee the mechanic would remain silent for long.

He waited in the small parking lot for several more minutes, then walked quickly to the front door and ducked inside.

The office was empty again, so he pulled his small Beretta from his waist and turned toward the garage bay. Stepping inside, he didn't see the mechanic, so he leaned down and spotted the man's legs on the far side of the same van that had been stolen. The fat man still didn't notice him.

Pelly stepped farther into the big bay, the pistol dangling at his side.

As he was about to call out, he heard a deafening blast, and the window of the van next to him shattered. Instinctively, he fell to the hard floor of the garage and searched for the source of the shot. A second booming blast blew holes in the side of the van just above his head. It was a shotgun. He barely heard the racking of the slide over the ringing in his ears. He scurried to the rear of the van and stole a peek to the back of the bay. Somehow the mechanic had surprised him.

Wedged in between two shelves of parts, the fat mechanic had a pump shotgun up and scanning the bay. Pelly picked up an old air filter and tossed it to the front of the van on the side away from the mechanic. The man turned toward the noise and fired again, racked the slide of the weapon, and fired blindly again.

Pelly saw him fumble in his front pocket for another round and knew the shotgun was empty. He took the moment to rush the man. He had his pistol up, but didn't fire. Instead he wanted to make sure the shotgun was out of his hands while it was empty and the man didn't expect an assault.

Pelly threw himself into the giant man as the mechanic's girth seemed to swallow him up. Pelly wondered if the man had any bones in his huge body as he was enveloped by fat. The shotgun clattered onto the floor and the mechanic bounced off the wall, then stumbled away from the gun. Pelly was lucky the giant didn't fall on top of him. He would've had a hard time wiggling out of that situation.

Now Pelly stood over the fallen behemoth with his gun out, but not pointing at the man.

The mechanic, panting, flat on his back, held his hands in front of him. "I'm sorry. I had to tell him."

"Tell who?"

"The other guy. He didn't offer me any cash, but I could tell he'd hurt me if I didn't tell him who took the truck."

Pelly realized he was too late and would have to explain things to the boss. He didn't speak, just pointed the Beretta at the man's blond head and squeezed the trigger three times. It was nothing personal. Just business.

After telling the local cops all he knew about the house, Alex Duarte had found out that his source of information, the fat mechanic, had been found shot to death in his rental shop. Duarte had already told them about Cal Linley, so now it looked like the Louisiana cops had four bodies that were tied together. That was a big deal.

To Duarte the real worry was whatever was in the crate that was worth killing four people over. The more he thought about it, the more concerned he became.

He had called Lina as he left Kansas to tell her he was on his way to Lafayette but gave no details. He didn't like sharing information with someone who didn't return the favor.

He didn't intend to stop until he had answers to his questions.

He knew this case had some deeper meaning.

ALEX DUARTE WAS HAPPY TO TURN IN THE LITTLE COBALT NOW
that Félix Baez had driven a DEA Bronco from New Orleans to meet
him at the crime scene. He had briefed the DEA man on what he knew
and endured his countless questions about why he had not been included
from the start.

He had listened to Félix's theories of how Lina was in New Orleans
with Colonel Staub for all kinds of lewd reasons and finally said,
"Maybe she's working another angle of the case."

"No, bro, she's giving him that pussy."

"I don't know, Félix. She seems to be pretty interested in her job. She
knows something she's not telling us."

"She's an FBI agent; that's what they do." He scowled out the window
as they looked for the third rental place on their list. "Just something
about that babe. She's got a butter face, but, snap, her body is tight."

Duarte looked over at his friend. "Butter face?"

"Yeah, you know, man, everything she's got looks good but her face."

"I don't think that's too fair."

"It's not fair she's fucking the colonel either."

Duarte shut up, knowing he wasn't making the situation better. On Moss Street he noticed a Ryder truck backed in the front of a motel called the Cajun Inn. The yellow truck was smaller than the U-Haul he had seen earlier in the day. He slowed the little Cobalt as the hotel came up on his right.

Félix said, "What 'cha doin', bro?"

"Just noticed that rental truck. The way it's wedged in the front like that."

"C'mon, I'm already trusting you enough to go to the rental places with you. Let's not waste time on wild-duck chases."

"Goose chases."

"I was raised in Miami. I couldn't tell the difference between a duck and a goose. I don't wanna chase either. I wouldn't mind getting back to New Orleans and keepin' Lina from makin' a mistake."

Duarte gave in and sped up instead of turning into the motel.

Duarte looked over at the truck as they passed. He had a feeling he was making a mistake, but Félix had a point. They could always come back.

Pelly drove his own rental car far behind the older Ford Bronco that the ATF agent, Duarte, and his partner, Baez, rode in. He had followed Duarte from the house where they had recovered the crate. Pelly was patient. He'd know when he had a chance to act. It had taken Pelly a good thirty minutes to figure out what the two men were doing. Then he realized they were looking at truck rental places. This was one smart cop. He knew, probably because of the dead mechanic, that they had lost their van. This guy thought ahead.

Pelly smiled, enjoying the challenge of a man who knew his business and how to handle things. He had heard from the men he hired that the ATF agent had moved like a cat when the fake robbery went down in New Orleans. Now the man had their scent.

Pelly had called Staub but could tell his boss was involved in something else. His guess was that the colonel had a scent of his own. He had not personally seen the FBI woman. In a way, it was a relief to see Staub interested in a woman under normal circumstances where he didn't have to whip her or cut something off to be satisfied. In another way, Pelly was not happy that the man was distracted from business again.

Colonel Staub had hardly listened when Pelly told him that Duarte was looking at rental companies. Staub was convinced they were quiet enough to hide their activities and that the extra cash they had given the manger of the Ryder rental store would keep his mouth shut. He told Pelly to use his judgment and hung up. What the hell did that mean? It meant that whatever he did, Staub would have a reason to blame him if something went wrong.

Pelly saw the old Bronco slow near a hotel a few blocks ahead. The sign out front read THE CAJUN INN and had to slow himself so he wouldn't creep up on the federal agents. Then the Bronco took off again.

As Pelly got closer, he saw what had caught their attention. A Ryder step van, just like the one they had rented for Ike to take the device to Houston, was parked in the small hotel's lot.

Pelly slowed his rental car. It couldn't be. No one would be that stupid. He touched the automatic pistol in his waistband and pulled into the lot. He wouldn't call Staub on this just yet.

He'd just use his judgment.

Colonel Lázaro Staub stood on the tiny balcony of Lina Cirillo's hotel room at the Marriott in New Orleans, smoking his last Camel. Lina seemed somewhat fanatical about her dislike for cigarettes, so he hadn't pushed it and stepped outside while the FBI agent freshened up.

Staub had not been blind to the signals the FBI agent had been throwing his way since he had arrived in New Orleans. He also realized that Félix Baez had been interested in the odd-looking FBI agent, too. It was obvious that any attention she showed him bothered the DEA man tremendously.

While Staub had no real sexual interest in the woman, he did see the value in playing along. She might know something he was not aware of. He had heard the phrase "Pale Girl" used in a conversation and felt it would be beneficial to learn the meaning of this code name.

Physically, Lina was too skinny and fit to interest him. She didn't have nearly the right girth in her breasts, and her face lined up like a kid's drawing. Besides, he didn't think she would respond to the type of domination he would be interested in showing her.

After a few minutes in the bathroom, Lina stepped out onto the balcony and looked out over the city.

"Looks like Katrina didn't hurt the Quarter too much."

Staub nodded, dropping his cigarette and snubbing it out on the concrete floor. Stepping closer to her, he said, "This is where the white tourists come. Of course the government protected it." He placed a hand on her back and started to rub.

She looked up into his eyes and smiled.

He felt nothing from it.

Lina said, "You think there was anything in that container besides pot?"

He shook his head, "Not unless it was something more valuable, and that is doubtful. What do you think, my dear?" He moved his hand to her shoulder and slid in closer to her.

"I have no idea. Duarte seems convinced."

"I think this case is over except for the singing of the fat lady. Soon I will return to Panama and you to your job in Washington." He looked into her eyes now and said, "Perhaps we should make use of our time wisely, no?"

She didn't move, but didn't answer either.

He decided to keep asking questions. "Why are you here from Washington anyway?"

"Just helping."

"But why not a local agent?" He went to kiss her, and she stepped back, holding up her hand.

"Because I know when to say no."

The clean, professional atmosphere of the Ryder truck rental center was in sharp contrast to the dark and dingy U-Haul franchise where the fat mechanic had told Duarte about his scam and was later found dead. After trying to reason with the clean-cut manager here, Duarte secretly hoped the same fate might await him. It wasn't like the sandy-haired man of thirty-five was part of the case or vital to any testimony or had even done anything wrong, so Duarte certainly wouldn't use any of his special techniques on him, but the man still had an annoying tone.

"I understand you need information," said the man, "but I will not divulge anything to you unless you have a warrant."

Duarte kept his cool in the rear office where he and Félix were crammed together behind a spotless desk with a nineteen-inch computer screen. Duarte responded, "We don't need a warrant, only a subpoena. And we won't need that if you could just tell us if you rented a step van in the last twenty-four hours."

The manager shook his head. "Nope, not a word until I see proper authorization."

Duarte said, "Sir, this could be important. If you've rented a truck, then we'll get you a subpoena. Can you tell us that much?"

"No. This is not Nazi Germany, my friend. I will not divulge private information."

"I don't need private information yet. Just info on if you rented a truck."

"No dice, and I don't have time to continue to argue the point with you gentlemen. Now, unless you have a warrant, I will say good luck and goodbye. Unless you are not really law enforcement personnel, you'll heed my wishes." He stood up behind the desk.

Félix, who had not said a word, stood up and stepped around Duarte to the side of the desk, blocking the man's exit. "You're right, mother-fucker."

Duarte noticed he put on a thick Cuban accent, but it got the man's attention.

Félix continued. "We're not cops; that's why we don't got a warrant."

The manager swallowed hard and plopped back into his cushioned chair.

"You see we ain't cops, and this ain't no fucking social visit. The men who rented this truck owe us money, and we need to collect. So here's the scoop. Answer the question or your typing skills will go to shit with six broken fingers. But it won't matter anyway, because you won't be in the office with a full body cast on. Do you got it now, man?" His voice had risen through the whole tirade.

The manager looked hypnotized, then nodded as a bead of sweat ran down his high forehead. "I understand what's going on now. I apologize." He said in a remarkably calm voice. He swallowed hard, still looking up at Félix.

"Did someone rent a truck in the last day?" Félix leaned in close to the man.

"Yes. Yes, sir."

"Who?"

The man fumbled with the computer. "He listed his name as Robert Merrick."

Duarte perked up at the familiarity of the name until he realized what it was: the Elephant Man. Hadn't Michael Jackson tried to buy his bones, or something?

Duarte said, "What'd he look like?"

The nervous manger looked between the two men several times and then said, "A little like a caveman."

Duarte knew they were on the right track.

33

WILLIAM "IKE" FLOYD ROLLED OFF THE CLEAN, WARM BED AND
stood inside his small room at the Cajun Inn just off Moss Street. He had
slept more than eleven hours and he felt like a new man, even though his
face still hurt from where Craig had smacked him with the board. Then
he thought about Craig's fate and his girlfriend's, too. Ike realized he had
actually killed someone. Shot them at close range. He was a killer. He felt
more confident, like maybe he belonged with the men with whom he
was now involved.

He had matured in the past two days. He was no longer interested in
cheap sex with unknown men. He had a purpose, an important role to play.
He was going to deliver the package to Houston and then see if it worked.

He pulled on a pair of jeans, realizing he was sore in other places
besides his head.

He peeked out the curtain to check the truck, parked right outside.
He leaned in close and looked as far down the hallway as possible and
saw an older maid talking to someone. He could just see the man's head
as it bobbed slightly as he spoke to the woman.

Then he felt a chill as he realized it was Pelly.

Back in the old Bronco, Duarte kept his voice flat. "Anything you want to talk about, Félix?"

"No. Why, bro?"

"You were a little rough on the manager in there."

"That douche bag? He deserved it. Talkin' to us like a couple of wetbacks working in his garage. Besides, aren't you the one who thinks this truck is a lead in Gastlin's murder?"

"Maybe or maybe more."

"Besides we scared that asshole so much, thinking we were dopers, he'll never mention our visit to no one."

"Wish he woulda told us more."

"Hey, a hairy caveman rented the truck without ID for an extra five hundred bucks. That sounds like our man."

Duarte said, "We'll see if we can put it out for all cops to look for."

"For what reason? We need a little more info."

Duarte considered this and realized he couldn't answer why he was looking for the Ryder van other than he had a feeling. He looked at Félix and said, "We may have another lead."

"Where's that?"

"The head of this National Army of White Americans."

Félix looked at him. "The NAWA?"

"I know it sounds stupid."

"How do you know the leader?"

He held up the address book he had taken from William Floyd's apartment. "Floyd has his name and address in here. We can verify it with one of the analysts."

"What's this redneck's name and where does he live?"

"His name is Forrest Jessup, and he lives in Biloxi. That's less than an hour from New Orleans. What if we pay him a visit?"

"Sounds good, bro."

Duarte said, "But first let's just check that van at the Cajun Inn to be on the safe side."

P elly checked the outside of the parked rental truck, then stepped up onto the truck's running board and peeked into the cab. There was nothing that identified it as the one they had rented for Ike, but it sure looked like the same one and was only two miles from where they had rented the step van. He hoped Ike had more sense than to stay in Lafayette, but he wouldn't be surprised if the moron had just driven here and stayed.

He looked down the row of doors facing the highway. The parking lot was empty except for the truck and two rented Dodges parked next to each other in front of rooms five and six. An elderly black woman pushed a cart in front of room four and stopped, then used a passkey to go inside, wedging the door open.

Pelly touched the Beretta tucked into his belt under his loose shirt and started to the open room. As he got there, the maid stepped out into the breezeway.

She gave a visible jump when she saw him. He didn't know if it was just his quiet approach that startled her or his appearance.

"Excuse me, I'm looking for a friend."

The woman eyed him carefully.

He held out a twenty-dollar bill.

She snatched it and said, "Who dat?"

"Excuse?"

"Who you lookin' for?" She kept her eyes on his face like he fascinated her.

"He drive the van?" Pelly pointed.

"Room one. Big white man."

Pelly smiled and nodded.

Then she surprised him by slowly raising her hand and touching the hair on the side of his face. He had not shaved since the night before, and it was grown in almost to his eyeballs.

The maid smiled and slipped back into the room, this time closing the door because she apparently had been through this drill before.

Pelly started down the breezeway to the room.

William "Ike" Floyd had no idea what to do or what Pelly would do when he found him. He had seven rounds of the light .380 ammo in the single clip he had reloaded after he had killed Craig and the girl. He didn't think he'd stand a chance against Pelly.

On the other hand, he had seen the furry assistant to Mr. Ortíz be very reasonable on some issues.

He quickly gathered his few belongings and pulled on his T-shirt. He decided to tell the truth and see what happened.

He pulled open the door like he didn't know Pelly was even in the area.

Before he could step out the door, the scary-looking young man was in front of him.

Ike kept cool. "Hey, Pelly, what are you doing here?"

"I could ask you that, too."

"Too tired to drive. I was just leaving right now."

Pelly looked over Ike's wide shoulder into the room, then back at his face. He seemed to be weighing his options, his hand resting at his belt buckle. Ike knew why.

Finally, Pelly said, "You know the boss would kill you if he found you still here."

"Why? I got three days till they need me in Houston."

Pelly nodded. "I know, I know." He seemed to relax. "You must leave *ahora*. Uh, now. The boss won't find out."

Ike let out the breath he didn't realize he had been holding. "Thanks, man. I owe you one."

He hurried up into the cab and let Pelly help direct him from the tight spot. He intended to get right on the road and be in Houston in a few hours. Then he'd worry about food and anything else he needed.

Pelly saw the big Ryder step van drive away and start in the wrong direction until Ike had to pull a U-turn and head up toward I-10. Pelly wasn't sure he'd used the best judgment as far as Colonel Staub's plans went, but he had made a good business decision. There were already too many bodies in this little town, and they had not even delivered the package yet.

His concern now was that the ATF man would return. He knew from the guy's past behavior that he would be back to check the van and probably the registration to the room. Pelly considered his options.

He could wait and shoot it out with him. He had seen Duarte in action and didn't necessarily want to risk that confrontation. He could forget it and head back to New Orleans, but that just put one problem off until later. Then he remembered the old army surplus grenades they had taken from the fat mechanic. He knew he'd find a purpose for the old ordnance. But this would have to work out perfectly.

The door to Ike's room was still open. He looked into the small room with its messy bed and noticed a back door. He walked through and saw that the old, creaky door opened onto a dilapidated tiny patio with thousands of cigarette butts in the grass surrounding the concrete. Pelly looked down the wall and saw that each patio was in the same shape. This was how they considered the room "nonsmoking."

He hustled back to his car and popped the trunk, grabbing two of the old grenades. Inside the apartment, he shut the front door and cut the strings to the curtains. He took another look outside and saw a communal gas grill in the rear of the middle room. He checked the area and then walked quickly to the grill. The tank felt like it was about half full. With a little effort, he had the tank loose and was back in the room. He set the tank a few feet behind the door and tied the grenades to the leg of the bed right behind the tank. He straightened the pins so they would slip out easily and then tied his last length of curtain cord through the grenade rings and to the door handle. When someone opened the door, there would be one hell of a blast.

He knew he couldn't just leave with this trap set. He left through the back door and visited his friend the maid again.

She didn't look surprised when he entered the room she was cleaning.

"What 'chu want now?" asked the old black woman.

"My friend, he left. But I have another hundred dollars for you."

"What I got a do?" She kept her clouded eyes on his face.

"Do not clean room one until I check back with you. Do not go in there."

"Uh-huh. And what else?"

"If anyone asks about the truck, give them a key to room one."

"For how long I gotta wait. They expect me to do the cleaning."

"I will return, if no one shows up in one hour." He handed her the five twenties. "Not bad for an hour of work."

She snatched the money like he might change his mind.

As he backed out of the room, he said, "Remember. No one goes into room one except if they ask who was in there."

"I ain't stupid. I heard you."

He smiled, feeling the hair bunch around his eyes. He slipped back to his car and pulled across the street into a mini-mart lot. Before he had stopped the car, he noticed the old Bronco rumble into the Cajun Inn.

He smiled at his timing.

ALICE BRAINARD HAD DONE ENOUGH WORK FOR THREE FORENSIC scientists since she'd arrived early at 6:55. By that time she had already worked out and had breakfast, or at least a protein shake. She was hustling because she didn't want to feel like her work for Alex Duarte had cost the county anything, especially after Scott Mahovich's remark about billing the ATF for his DNA work. What a dick.

As she concentrated on one more form, she heard a deep male voice at her office doorway.

"You look busy this morning."

She looked up and smiled at the tall, blond man in the Palm Beach County firefighter's uniform. "Hey, Jeff, what're you doing down here?"

The man, who had been the January photo for the firefighter's calendar the past three years, gave her one of his copyrighted smiles that melted most women and had a definite effect on Alice. "Doing a demo on unusual instruments we use, and had to pick up some things from the lab."

"What's that one?" She pointed at the small box with what looked like a microphone in his hand.

"An old-style Geiger counter."

"We had radioactive stuff?"

He switched on the instrument. "Here, I'll . . ." Before he could finish his sentence, the machine started to make a whooping alarmlike sound.

"Damn," he called out over the sound. "Usually the fire alarms have radioactive material, but it's weak. Never had 'em set this off so quick." He looked up and stepped away from her office to the alarm on the ceiling in the other room. As he did, the sound faded, then stopped.

He called into her. "Wasn't the fire alarm."

Alice heard the whopping again, then saw the object of several of her fantasies, Jeff Jacobus, step back into her office door.

"Alice, what've you got in here?"

She raised her own voice. "I have no idea."

As he stepped closer, the whooping raised in pitch. Next to her desk, the noise was almost shrill. He swept her desk and stopped near an empty bottle of Gatorade.

"I drank a radioactive Gatorade?"

He lifted the bottle with his free hand and swept the area again. "Nope. It's these pink papers."

She looked at the shipping invoices that Alex Duarte had used to secure the lock for fingerprints.

He looked at her, all traces of his charming smile gone. "Alice, where'd you get those papers?"

Duarte pulled into one of the many open slots in front of the rooms of the Cajun Inn. The Ryder step van was gone.

Félix said, "He couldn't have gotten too far. Let's look for him."

Duarte shook his head. "He could go in any direction. Let's see if it was really Floyd staying here."

They slipped out of the faded, old Bronco and turned toward the office. Duarte took a second to survey the area. He noticed one room door that was wedged open with a maid's cart.

"Hang on, Félix. Might be easier talking to the maid than the manager."

"Especially after the last prick manager we had to deal with."

Duarte motioned for Félix to stay there as he crossed the small lot to the open room. He called out as he approached the cart. "Hello."

After a few seconds, a short, elderly black woman popped her head out of the room.

"Office is up der." She pointed toward the front of the lot.

Duarte smiled. "I was wondering if I could ask you a question."

The woman perked up like she expected a question. She looked down the breezeway toward the first room.

"What 'chu wanna ask?"

"Do you know who drove the Ryder rental truck that was here?" He pointed to where he had seen the truck parked.

"I seen him. White man."

"Big fella from New Orleans?"

"I guess."

"Do you know what room he had?"

"Room one."

"Did he check out?"

"Yep."

Duarte hesitated. He could go to the office, but he would like to see if anything was left in the room.

As if reading his mind, the old woman said, "You wanna see the room?" She held up an old heavy metal key.

He took it and smiled. "I'll get it right back to you."

She nodded and turned back into the room.

Duarte waved his hand for Félix to wait as he checked the room. He could see in the open windows of each room as he walked down the breezeway. He stopped in front of room one and noticed the curtains were drawn and hanging a little funny.

The key slipped into the scarred door handle easily. He turned the handle, but paused. He had an odd sensation that everything wasn't as it should be. He shrugged off the feeling and slowly pushed open the door, aware of his SIG-Sauer P229 on his hip under the loose shirt.

L ázaro Staub sulked in his room, annoyed that Lina Cirillo was just a tease and not a woman who appreciated his position and power. He was not used to being rebuffed, especially by someone without the classic shape that he required from his women. She was built like an athletic man, not a full-breasted and luscious woman.

The more the colonel thought about how she had completely ignored his charisma, the more confused he had become. Did she not realize that he literally held life and death in his hands or at his command? No one ever refused him. Not in Panama and not here in the United States. She was only an FBI agent. He was the head of the national police narcotics unit and one of the richest men in all of South America.

He thought back to his betrayal by the first and only woman he ever thought he loved. The day he found that whore with his father, doing the same things she had done with him. This was close to that feeling. Not a rage, but more of a determination. An urge to dominate her and anyone like her. He could do things to her she couldn't imagine. But he could. A good beating with a leather strap or riding crop would go a long way to showing her what an error she had made by rebuffing him.

He stood up from the bed and realized he was sweating though his shirt and his face was drenched in salty moisture.

He stepped into the bathroom and wiped his face with the towel on the rack. Looking in the mirror, the first thing he noticed was that the twitch in his left eye was going off like a car's turn signal. What had this woman done to him?

He looked at his face and shoulders in the mirror, mystified that any woman would be able to resist him. Even if she didn't know about his wealth, he didn't see how she had backed away from his advances. He was so angry he had to spit into the sink.

She'd pay. The only question was, who would go first? The troublesome ATF agent or the silly female FBI agent?

Now he had a real reason to stay in the U.S. until his missions in life were complete.

Alice Brainard had puzzled about the fact that the shipping notices had given off such a strong signal to the fireman's Geiger counter and was now concerned enough to have moved them into the lab. Not that she thought she'd get sick from it, but why take chances? Working in a lab with chemicals and other things had taught her that being careful was a real plus.

She had looked on the Internet and spoken to one of the other forensic scientists about the possibility of something being contaminated by a cargo. No one seemed to know the answer.

She started checking and learned that U.S. Customs used small radioactive "pagers" that would set off an alarm if they came in contact with a ship that was carrying anything radioactive. She called over to the customs office in the Port of Palm Beach and couldn't get anyone but a machine on the phone.

Finally it started to bother her enough that she decided to take one of the shipping notices over there herself.

She had already slipped it into a plastic evidence bag and now into an old metal box that had been sitting unused for years in the crime scene room. She lugged the box to her Honda and decided today she would eat lunch in Riviera Beach, conveniently right next to the port. She had her sheriff's office ID and hoped she'd be more successful talking to someone in person.

35

ALEX DUARTE OPENED THE DOOR TO THE HOTEL ROOM A CRACK and tried to see inside. The bright sunlight made it difficult to see into the gloomy room. For a reason unknown to him, he slid his right hand to the butt of his pistol. He leaned into the door and opened it a little farther.

The room still remained too dark to see anything. He went ahead and pushed the door inward, feeling it catch slightly on something. For a moment, he thought he might be finding another dead body. That was starting to get old.

As the door opened all the way, with his hand still resting on the knob, he looked into the room and saw the white propane gas tank. Then he thought about the slight catch in the door and saw the loose curtain strings on the floor.

His mind just reacted and he pulled the door to him, hoping to contain the blast he knew would come.

He saw the flash in the crack of the door and heard the blast just as the door was about to close.

Orange flames peeked out all around the door, and the window next to him blew out.

At the same time, he felt the door fly loose from its hinges and lift horizontally off the ground, with him still holding on.

He flew across the breezeway and into the parking lot like he was riding a magic carpet instead of a propane gas–powered door.

He made no sound as the explosion filled his eyes and vision.

He caught a glimpse of Félix instinctively ducking as he passed by him on the floating door.

Pelly smiled when he saw the old lady give Duarte the key and then go back to minding her own business. He couldn't have planned it more precisely. It was almost like the ATF agent was following his script.

Then Pelly saw him hesitate at the door. He opened it a crack and paused. Had he detected the trap?

Pelly thought back over his actions and tried to see if he could determine what he might have done to give away his plan.

Then Duarte pushed the door open.

Pelly let out his breath, knowing the pins had just been pulled from the grenades, and when they detonated so would the propane. He involuntarily squinted his eyes.

Duarte jumped back outside, but it was too late. The flash of the explosion reached Pelly before the sound.

That was one less problem as far as Pelly was concerned. The ATF man wouldn't bother him or the colonel again.

36

ALEX DUARTE FLINCHED AS FÉLIX BAEZ TREATED A CUT ON HIS head with some peroxide they had bought on their way back to the hotel in New Orleans.

Considering the size of the blast and the damage to the hotel room, Duarte was still amazed he had gotten away with only a few cuts and some singed hair on the right side of his head.

Félix said, "You sure we shouldn't have stayed and talked to the responding cops?"

Duarte shook his head. "No one was hurt." He jumped when the peroxide and cotton struck an open wound. "Except me." He took another breath. "I don't want to give anyone a reason to take me off this case. Someone is going to a lot of trouble to keep us from finding out everything. That pisses me off."

Félix smiled. "I've never seen you pissed off." He paused. "Or happy or sad or tickled or annoyed."

"Yeah, I got it, I got it."

Félix chuckled. "I never seen a flying ATF man. You looked like

Aladdin floating across that lot." He laughed louder. "And the old cleaning woman. She looked like she seen a ghost."

Duarte slipped past Félix and stood, stretching out his back and arms. He wouldn't admit that anything was sore from the blast. But everything below his eyes did hurt.

"Okay, Félix. Tomorrow I'll find this Jessup character over in Biloxi."

"What time should I be ready?"

Duarte held up his hand. "Not on this. I can handle it. You need to stay on Lina and see what she knows. She's got the source, Pale Girl, and anything Staub learns. I don't think she's been sharing like she should."

Félix snorted. "That's not her, that's the damn FBI. Fucking Bunch of Idiots. They don't like to share nothin'."

Duarte nodded, feeling the exhaustion wash over him. He was glad Félix had agreed so easily to staying in New Orleans. Another reason Duarte hadn't wanted to take him was that Félix had been rough on the Ryder manager, and Duarte didn't want to risk what he'd do to the head of a racist organization, especially with what he felt about Gastlin's death.

Félix told him to relax and get to bed early, then the DEA man headed out to eat.

Duarte nodded and eased back on his bed, still in his clothes.

He heard the door close and started to slip into sleep immediately. Everything seemed to catch up to him at once. As he drifted off, he jerked awake thinking he had heard another blast. How many had he heard in his thirty years? More than most people heard in a lifetime. As he started to drift off again, he realized this might not be the deep restful sleep he had hoped it would be.

The young agent from ICE, which stood for Immigration and Customs Enforcement, appeared genuinely interested in answering any of Alice Brainard's questions. She didn't think her position at the sheriff's office had anything to do with his attitude either. She could tell it was more the position he had in mind for the two of them. He was young and buff—the customs guys always seemed to have time to work out—and had a cute face surrounded by lots of light brown hair like a surfer's.

He wore a dark blue uniform and took more than ten minutes to explain his complex and dangerous duties around the Port of Palm Beach.

She smiled and said, "I'm sure it's hell, but what do you do if there's something radioactive on one of the ships?"

"Run." He laughed at his sharp wit.

"I mean, how would you know?"

"Oh, we have these pagers that sound and take a sample of the emission."

"The pager ever go off?"

"Oh sure. Maybe three or four times a year."

"Is it scary?" She really wanted to know, as well as make sure the young Homeland Security ICE agent thought she cared so he would still help.

"No. The first couple of times we got excited, but now we know it's a false alarm. Big loads of timber or tile can set 'em off. Sometimes a larger instrument of some kind with a radioactive gauge on it."

"Why would tile set them off?"

"A lot of organic things have natural radioactivity. We send the readings from the pagers to the RAD team so they can analyze them. They usually get back to us within an hour or so."

"How do they know what it is?"

"They can tell by the alpha emissions if it is fissionable and from enriched uranium or plutonium. Something that can be made into a weapon."

She nodded, her scientific mind trying to understand the process as well as the reasons to do it. She could tell the guy was just reciting what he had learned in a class. He had no more idea about fission or the uses of enriched plutonium than a manatee, but he had been told to recite what he had learned. He did it well and looked good doing it.

Alice said, "Let me get something I found and see if your pager goes off and takes a sample of it."

"I gotta go get the pager."

"Where is it?"

"Locked in my desk."

"Does everyone do that?"

"No."

"Good," she sighed.

"Only the guys with the pagers. They're expensive, and we don't want to be held responsible for them."

"So it's possible that something could enter the U.S. undetected?"

"Yeah, if the pagers aren't out that day or if the container went directly to a special area and none of the customs inspectors went into the area. It could happen."

"Great." She turned to run out to her car as the ICE agent went to retrieve his pager. She'd find out what had contaminated these pages. Discovering things was her job. And her calling.

Alex Duarte tossed and turned for several hours. When his eyes opened, it was only three hours later, about ten-thirty in the evening. He had dreamed about Bosnia, as he usually did. But not about the Drina River and his dreadful mistake. During the Bosnian conflict, he had attempted to stop a Serbian tank by blowing a bridge it was crossing. Shrapnel from the explosion had accidentally killed a Croatian boy on the bank, down the river. Tonight he didn't dream about the agony he'd gone through after the incident.

He dreamt about small bombs in enclosed places. The SEALs blowing in a door in Sarajevo, his improvised device that had blown a Serb command post, the effects of a grenade on a British SAS barracks. He had seen them all up close and often relived the experiences when he slept. It had robbed him of a full night's sleep ever since he had returned from eastern Europe.

Now, with a few years' experience in not sleeping, he knew when his night was over. Instead of fighting it, he often used the time to work out, catch up on reports or read one.

Tonight he knew exactly what he could do.

He got up, already dressed, and washed his face, cringing slightly at the bruising around his right eye caused by his ride on the door.

He took his gun from the small safe in the closet and strapped the Glock on his right hip. Tonight it was slightly cooler, so he slid a light tan windbreaker over his shoulders to cover the gun.

Within a few minutes, he was on his way out to Biloxi, Mississippi, to the home of Forrest Jessup, president of the National Army of White Americans.

The trip east on I-10 was quick on a weeknight near eleven o'clock. It was dark, and he got little sense of the damage from hurricane Katrina on the trip east. He found his exit and then the three turns that took him to a nearly deserted street with two houses at the front of the block and Jessup's lone, clapboard house on a good rise at the end of the street. There were several cars parked along the dark street as Duarte eased the rented Ford toward the house.

He parked directly in front in a deep shadow. As soon as he stepped from the small car, it seemed to disappear. He hesitated. The late hour and the distinct possibility that Jessup had moved from the house because of Katrina made Duarte pause.

Then he noticed a single light coming from what he would guess was the kitchen off the long, twisting driveway to the street.

He felt for his pistol out of habit and started up the long driveway.

Pelly looked in the mirror of his room at the Napoleon Arms hotel in New Orleans. The older, family-run motel fit his needs perfectly. It wasn't fancy like the colonel's chain resort in the Quarter, but it was clean, he could park directly in front of his room and he knew all the escape routes. Just like he had been taught in the academy.

In the mirror, he saw his skin. He had shaved, then used the lady's hair removal system on his face like a doctor back home had shown him.

His skin was clear and normal for a change. He smiled as he ran his hand over it, and then his severely trimmed eyebrows. He looked completely human. His teeth were a little pronounced and ears too wide on his head, but that wasn't unusual. It was these features combined with his hair that made people scared and wary of the man who looked like the missing link. Or a gorilla.

He intended to go out on the town tonight. He had nothing to celebrate. He had seen his little grenade and propane bomb go off and the ATF man fly across the parking lot, only to get up, apparently unscathed and quick as ever. He had fled from his vantage point across the street and knew he'd have to deal with the ATF man again. But that was his job. He didn't let it bother him.

Right now all he cared about was his lack of facial hair. He had two hours until he looked like the Wolfman again. He lifted his shirt and saw the long tufts of hair from his chest. He'd worry about that if he got a girl back to his room. Right now he had a clean face, and he was going to use it.

ALEX DUARTE CREPT ALONG THE WALL OF THE DETACHED garage, keeping his eyes on the front door. He had noticed the great number of abandoned houses on the street and wondered if anyone would even hear him if he ran into problems. Or caused them.

He tried the knob of the front door. It was open. Now he had to make a choice. Knock as ATF agent Alex Duarte or just use terror tactics. As a federal employee, he could explain that he was investigating Gastlin's death and the activity around the container. Perhaps say that the dead Cal Linley had given him Jessup's name. Convince or trick the man into spilling what he knew. The other choice was to skip all pretense and slip into the house and just scare the man into talking.

Somehow, although the first choice was the proper one, Duarte knew how much easier and effective the second choice was. He hoped it wasn't because he knew that this man led a group of racists who thought that blacks and Hispanics were lower forms of life and that Jews were evil. He hoped he was willing to use his special methods because he had grown increasingly troubled by what was in that cargo container or what Gastlin knew that would lead to so many murders in the

United States. Either way President Jessup was in for a shock during this interview.

Duarte slipped into the small entryway and stood in the dark for a few seconds. He could see the light from the TV and a small lamp coming from the next room. In addition to the television, he heard voices. He took a few quiet steps down a short hallway. On the walls he noticed the same kind of photos he had seen in Linley's house and the clubhouse in Omaha: photos of men in white robes or Nazi uniforms, one photo showing a black man hanging from a tree with the year 1963 scrawled in faded ink in the corner.

Duarte shuddered. He had seen ethnic violence in Bosnia, but somehow the old history books didn't get across the horror or the violence here in the U.S. over racial issues. Now, in the house, with a man who might have participated in such acts, he understood that it wasn't limited to Serbs, Croats and Muslims.

He leaned into the TV room and blinked to make sure of what he was seeing.

An older man, whom he assumed was Jessup, was bound in a chair and another man stood over him with a pistol. The gunman stood back slightly, his face obstructed by shadow. He was lean, with dark hair. His movements from side to side showed his agitation.

Duarte couldn't hear what was being said, but knew he had his killer caught in the act. His heart raced at the thought of solving this case. His mind hummed with the questions he had for both these men.

As Duarte drew his Glock and eased into the room, the killer's head snapped up. The pistol he pointed at Jessup's head fired, blowing blood and brain matter toward Duarte. Without any hesitation, the killer raised the gun and fired two more shots in the ATF man's direction, forcing him to retreat into the next room.

Duarte controlled his breathing, then realized he had blood on his face. He touched it with his fingers. Had he been hit? He felt for a wound, then realized it was Jessup's blood. He heard the killer scramble through the next room. Duarte darted toward the front door and fired as the figure passed by the hallway. It was unaimed, but it looked like he might have struck the assailant.

Duarte raced to the door and then took a quick peek to make sure it was safe. When he was able to look out safely, he saw the figure running, apparently not wounded in the legs. The man almost ran into the rental car parked in the shadows. As he slowed, the killer casually aimed his pistol and blew out one of the car's tires, then fired twice toward the house, causing Duarte to instinctively duck back into the house.

Duarte felt something by the door and touched it with his left forefinger. Blood. He had hit the assailant. As he heard a car down the street race off, he knew he might have another lead. He walked back into the TV room just to make sure Jessup was dead. It was obvious the way the man's head lolled to one side, but if that wasn't enough, he had a gaping hole which had leaked out all possible brain and fluid into a sickening little pile on the floor.

Duarte moved on to the kitchen. He found a baggie and napkin in the kitchen. As he left the house undisturbed, the only thing he took was a sample of blood from the front door.

This was a scene he wouldn't tell the cops about. No one would believe him. Now he had to find out what was in that cargo container.

Pelly stopped at a bar very close to Colonel Staub's hotel—wouldn't it be a kick if his boss were in there and didn't recognize him? The big Marriott would have cast a shadow over the little club at the right time of the day. He nodded at the bouncer as he entered, detecting no scorn or jokes from the thick man. If he had to, Pelly knew he could make the power lifter regret he had such big, slow muscles, but he didn't have to. The large man didn't say anything but "ten-dollar cover."

He moved through the crowded dance floor and to the less-busy bar. He rubbed his face out of habit and felt some slight bristles but no real hair yet. It had been thirty-five minutes since he shaved. He thought he had at least another hour and a half before things got out of control and he started getting looks again. He had a razor in his pocket for a touch-up if needed.

He looked around, and at the end of the bar he saw a single woman with an empty bar stool next to her. Conveniently, it was the only empty one at the bar. He approached it casually and said in his best English, "Is this stool available?"

The woman looked up from her drink and nodded her head.

Pelly smiled, trying to figure out if the woman was attractive. She had dark, seductive eyes and a sharp jawline, but there was something asymmetrical about her face that seemed odd. Pelly knew the feeling and thought fate might have put him next to this woman.

He leaned into her, catching a whiff of the straight bourbon in her glass. "Are you visiting New Orleans?" He spoke just loud enough to be heard over the sound system that was playing some dance mix he had not heard before.

The woman looked up. "I don't live here. No." She gave him a crooked smile. "What about you?"

"I am from," he paused because he didn't want to give too much information, but he didn't want to be a peasant from Panama to this American bourbon-drinking woman. "Spain. I am from Spain in Europe." He smiled as he unconsciously rubbed his face with his right hand.

"Where in Spain?" She turned to face him as he had hoped.

"Madrid."

"Oh, Madrid is beautiful."

"Yes, yes, it is. And that is where I was born. Madrid."

She smiled and held out her hand. "Hi."

Pelly took her somewhat large hand and said, "My name is Arturo Pelligrino, but my friends call me Pelly."

"Hello, Pelly. I'm Lina."

WILLIAM "IKE" FLOYD PULLED THE RYDER VAN INTO THE PARK-
ing lot of a diner on the outskirts of Houston. It wasn't dark yet, but he
was a little tired. His run-in with Pelly as he was about to leave Lafayette
had spooked him, but the hairy Panamanian had not seemed to care too
much where Ike had slept. What did it matter, really? He had to wait
until Mr. Ortíz contacted the person here in Houston who knew what
to do with the damn thing in the van. He had told Ike it would be a few
days. He obviously didn't expect Ike to go without sleep and food for a
few days, so what did it matter if he was in Louisiana or Texas? The
locals all acted the same down in this end of the country. The accents
were hard to tell apart, and it seemed like everyone wanted to pick a
fight or steal your stuff. Ike didn't think he'd miss Omaha and its steady,
comfortable life, but after the beating Craig had given him and then the
comments Mr. Ortíz had made, Ike wondered if he wouldn't have been
better off staying at home and just trying to expand his chapter of the
National Army of White Americans. Or maybe just getting a promotion
to major.

Ike did wonder what would happen to him if he was caught on this mission. This time he hadn't already fucked up and been forced to do what he had done. This time there were no excuses. He would carry this out, and things would change. Things would change, and he'd be famous.

He just didn't see how he would be able to enjoy it at all.

I nside the diner, he picked at a cheeseburger and thick, undercooked French fries. He still had to find a computer to check the e-mail account, get a hotel room that would be secure for the van, too, and then worry about Mr. Ortíz contacting the guy who knew what to do with his cargo.

As Ike ate, three men came in the front door. Two were older than Ike, in their late thirties. The third was a decade younger and seemed to have a little more interest in fitness. The trio were all in dirty jeans and filthy T-shirts. Each had a small backpack. The younger one wore a T-shirt with no sleeves, and his large upper arm bore an intricate tattoo with a swastika in the center.

They started to sit at the counter, but the man behind it held his nose and sent them to the booth next to Ike's, as far from the counter as they could go. All three shambled along, as one patron or waitress after another gave them dirty looks. Ike knew the looks well. They were not being shunned because they were dirty or possibly homeless. It was the tattoo and the fact that the oldest of the three had a German cross around his neck on a leather string. These men were being discriminated against for pride in their race.

As they came closer, Ike looked them in the eye and smiled. The oldest one, with a shabby mustache, saw the gesture and returned it, nudging his friends so they would also see the friendly face.

They stopped in front of Ike. "Hey, brother," said the older, scruffy one, "you recognize the symbols of race and power?"

It was the slogan of the White Aryan Men of America, an organization that tried to unify all the splintered white-power groups.

He answered with the second part of the slogan. "And I adhere to the laws of God's selection." It was the first time something like that had ever happened to him. He felt like beaming. Like he had stumbled on allies in the midst of a war.

The man asked, "Can we join you?"

Ike held out a welcoming hand.

"I'm Charlie. This here is Chuck and Charles."

"You're kidding, right?"

"Nope. Just chance that we all met up at a rally in Little Rock a month or so back. We all used 'Charlie,' but thought it'd get confusing if we called each other Charlie all the time. We rolled dice to see who got what handle." He smiled, showing missing teeth all across his upper plate.

The younger man eyed Ike's food like a wolf on a farm. The waitress didn't seem interested in visiting the table again.

Ike slid the plate to the center of the table. "You guys want some?"

All three men reached at the same time. After a minute of concentrated munching, Charlie looked at Ike. "Thanks, brother. We're mighty hungry. Not many people stop for three grown men hitchhiking. Best we get is the back of a produce truck once in a while."

"Where are you heading?"

"West, maybe California. We been stuck here in Houston, working as day laborers for the past week." He looked around like someone might wait on them. "What about you? Live here or visiting?"

"Just got into Houston now."

All three men eyed him. Charlie said, "This ain't no place for a white man, brother. We been ousted from a shelter, robbed twice and generally treated like turds. This here place is full of them Katrina refugees, and let me tell ya, they are a rough bunch. New Orleans must be paradise with all their hoodlums over here."

Ike shook his head. "I can tell you from recent experience that New Orleans is no paradise."

"What are you doin' here?"

"Working for the Cause."

Charlie smiled again. "No shit? Need any help? We're outta work. You know how people discriminate against us."

Ike thought about his run-in with Craig and those disastrous results.

Then he thought about keeping an eye on the truck. These tired, hungry men weren't predators. They were members of the same kind of outfit as Ike.

"What if I told you I'd pay you in a couple of days for helping me? Would you be interested?"

"We gotta work with niggers?"

"Nope."

"We gotta get up early?"

"Maybe one of you at a time."

"We gotta lift anything heavy?"

"Nope."

"Then we're your men."

Ike realized that the early schedule and hard labor were what really bothered these men, but it didn't matter. He just needed someone to tell him if the rental van was being bothered. He nodded approval at his new friends.

Staub may not have been in this bar, but Pelly certainly didn't consider it time wasted. He couldn't believe this attractive girl with the broken nose named Lina had sat at the end of the bar, leaned in close to him and talked over the music for almost an hour now. She was fascinating in that she loved to do all sorts of sports and didn't seem to notice his condition in the least. Of course, he had already shaved twice in the past hour. Every time he went to the bathroom, he ran his razor over his stubble.

Lina had seemed very open to him except for what she did for a living. He didn't believe she was a female kickboxing champion, but he didn't want to risk calling her a liar. Not when she was being so friendly.

A song that Pelly did not recognize blared over the speakers, and Lina stood with a bright smile across her crooked mouth. "This is my favorite song."

Pelly said, "I am not familiar with it."

"You will be," said Lina as she took his hand and jerked him onto his feet. "We're dancing." It was a direct order, and she tugged him along behind her like a mother would a child.

He had not danced since one had been arranged for his grade school with the girls from a small school run by nuns. He remembered he liked the smell on one small girl with long, rich hair. Other than that, his experience with dancing was what he caught on MTV when he was somewhere with a satellite.

Lina held his hand as she started to bounce to the rhythm of the music. He felt the bass and instinctively knew to bob to the beat. Shuffling his feet slightly, he felt like no one could identify him as a hairy policeman/killer from Panama. Although he doubted that Lina had completely bought his story of being an art historian from Madrid.

They danced through the song, and then another, older-sounding song called "Shout" came on and everyone seemed to know how to dance to it. He just followed Lina's example.

A drunken woman with outrageously large, fake breasts, kept bumping into Lina and him during the song as her tall boyfriend attempted to spin her every so often. Pelly didn't mind it. In fact, he was enjoying his first night out on the town in the United States. Maybe this wasn't such a bad assignment after all.

Pelly found the rhythm to the song and enjoyed seeing Lina's form move to the beat. He felt his hair below his face mat with sweat, but knew it was unnoticeable under his long-sleeved shirt. He had shaved a small circle near his throat so he could leave his shirt opened one button.

Then the drunken, top-heavy woman seemed to turn an ankle and started to go down hard. Pelly twisted to catch her at an awkward angle, but it was too late. With her long nails she groped out, looking for a way to keep from falling on the dance floor.

She found his collar and grabbed on instinctively.

He felt his shirt start to tear and buttons start to pop even as he tried to catch the woman.

As she landed and rolled slightly, he felt the front of his shirt fall open before he could stop it. Even in the low light of the dance floor, he knew everyone could see him. He felt his thick chest hair untangle and fall out of the tear in his shirt. He touched his chest and realized the shirt was open almost to his stomach. Out of the corner of his eye, he saw the hair near his shoulder start to pop straight up now that it was free. Dark, tall, proud strands of hair he battled with daily. Now, when he needed to win the battle most, the hair had defeated him and escaped.

Then he heard someone with a thick New Orleans accent say, "Jesus, would ya look at that boy. He must be part monkey."

Pelly's fist was in the man's mouth before he could follow up the comment. Someone stepped up to grab Pelly, then fell to one side. Pelly turned and saw Lina, the girl he had just met, standing over him, her foot coming back to the ground after kicking the man who tried to accost him from behind.

Maybe she really was a kickboxing champ.

BACK IN HIS HOTEL ROOM IN NEW ORLEANS, ALEX DUARTE HAD tossed and turned for the few hours he laid in bed. He got up before dawn and turned on the TV, wondering if there would be any stories about the killing of Forrest Jessup just outside Biloxi, Mississippi. Now he saw some good reasons to have called the cops and explain what he had seen, but it was too late. He'd be tied up for days in the investigation. He wanted to find William Floyd and that truck and its cargo, then get Floyd to explain this whole plan and why so many people had died for it. Duarte had a hard time conceiving of people killing over a load of pot. He knew it had to be more. Cal Linley's idea that it would start a revolution was as cryptic as the kid in Omaha saying it had to do with cranes.

He kept in his mind the connection to oil and the Houston address of Forrest Jessup that the ATF analyst had found. The old man had been in the oil business as a "wildcat" or independent operator. It didn't look like the racist leader had ever made a lot of money in the business. Maybe the item Cal Linley had unloaded at the port had been for the oil business. He had to keep an open mind.

He stretched as he watched CNN until the earliest local news popped on. Shortly after seven, while he was up in the army resting position of a push-up, his three hundredth, his cell phone rang.

He popped up off the floor and found the Nextel with his ID and gun on the small desk in the room.

"Duarte."

"Even at seven in the morning, you answer like that?"

He smiled at Alice's voice.

"Even at midnight. Just habit."

"You doing okay?"

He thought about his night and then said, "Yeah, nothing new, really." His eyes moved over to the baggie with a blood sample in it. Was this the right time?

"Well, I have a couple of reasons to call other than just missing you and wanting to hear your voice."

He smiled. "It's nice to hear your voice, too."

"That's sweet." There was a pause until she realized he wasn't going to speak again. "I have two things to tell you. First, the DNA sample was not in the Florida Department of Law Enforcement database."

"Does that mean if I have a comparison sample I could send it to you?"

"If you had a sample, yes."

"I'll get it out this morning."

"How'd you get a sample so fast?"

"Don't ask."

She paused and then said, "I also found out that the shipping notices you packed the lock in are radioactive."

Duarte paused and considered this. "What form of radioactivity?"

"You know about all that stuff? I'm impressed."

"Did you get a particle spectrum?"

"Not yet. I wanted to ask you. First, a Geiger counter noticed them, then I took them to U.S. Customs to get a confirmation from one of their pagers."

"That's smart, Alice. Now *I'm* impressed. Did the customs guy give you a particle spectrum?"

"No, he just said they were probably around tile or something and, I quote, 'not to worry my pretty little head about it.'"

"Is he still alive?"

"He was too cute to punch. But it still scared me about the reading. You want me to insist he get a particle spectrum?"

"No, not yet. That calls in a whole bunch of other agencies. I want to find a reason that might get them moving from here and leave you out of the mix."

"Now tell me something besides work."

"Like what?"

"I'm your girlfriend, Alex. I don't care."

And to his surprise he did talk to her about things unrelated to the Department of Justice.

Alex Duarte sat at a booth in the outrageously overpriced restaurant inside the Marriott. It was nearly ten in the morning, and he was still waiting for Félix Baez to meet him. As he sat alone, he sketched out a little diagram with some of the major players in the case to see if he noticed any links he had missed before. He wrote in "B.G." for poor, dead Byron Gastlin and "W.F." for William Floyd. He just wrote a big "O" at the top. He felt certain the shadowy Mr. Ortíz had something to do with the overall scheme.

His concern came when he wrote "L.C." for Lina Cirillo at the bottom of the page. She knew more than she claimed. He also wrote "L.S." next to Lina's initials. Colonel Lázaro Staub appeared legit, but his trip to New Orleans and lingering presence had set off an alarm inside Duarte's head. Not a serious one yet, but the colonel might also be better informed than he claimed. His English had improved drastically in his short visit to New Orleans, and every day he seemed to disappear with someone for a while. Duarte decided he didn't want to take his eye off the colonel.

He looked up from his diagram and saw Félix crossing the restaurant. Duarte saw the look on his face and said, "What's wrong?"

"I got more bad news from Panama."

"What's that?"

"First I spoke to Staub, then I asked my buddy with the DEA down there, John Morales, to find out about the first mate of the *Flame of Panama*."

"Yeah."

"The captain was found dead on the ship. Two bullets in his face. No one knew anything about the crew. No records, no payroll, nothing. They already renamed the ship, and it's hauling something else."

"Dammit." He looked up at his friend. "Félix, does it seem like everyone involved in this case dies violently?"

Félix seemed to flinch as he slid into the booth. "As long as it's not you or me."

Duarte looked at the DEA man. "You okay? You hurt yourself?"

"Just banged up my arm a little. Out late on Bourbon Street."

"That why you look like you haven't slept?"

"I haven't."

"You look rough."

"C'mon, bro, we almost got blown up yesterday. I mean you flew across the parking lot on a door. Neither of us should look good."

Duarte nodded. He wanted to tell him about his visit to Jessup's house in Biloxi, but he didn't want to put Félix in the position of hearing about a crime and not being free to tell anyone. Duarte knew he had gone off the books on this case, and if he was going to get in trouble he didn't want to hurt his friend, too.

Félix didn't seem to care if they pursued any leads today. Instead he looked down at the sheet of paper on the table. "What's that you're working on?"

"Just a flowchart on the case."

" 'B.G.' is for Gastlin?"

"Yeah."

Félix smiled. "The two in the corner are for Lina and the colonel?"

Duarte nodded. "You're not the only one who thinks there's something fishy with them."

"What's the 'W.F.' for? White female?" Félix smiled.

Duarte hadn't noticed that the common police designation for a white female was the same as William Floyd's initials. Somehow it made a click in his head, but he couldn't put it together just yet.

Pelly waited just down the street from Colonel Staub's hotel for his boss. He worked his hand, opening and closing his fist. It was a little sore from his fight the night before. He had hit at least three grown men in the mouth. That always led to a sore hand. He could see the entrance to the little bar he had been in the night before.

He was sorry he hadn't been able to get to know the lovely Lina. She had backed him up in the ensuing melee and didn't seem upset by the hair that bulged out of his torn shirt. But he couldn't look at her dark eyes after the incident. He had simply fled, sure he had blown a chance to talk with the interesting self-proclaimed kickboxing champ.

Pelly liked to stay busy and concentrate on work, because when he didn't he realized he was lonely. He had been on few dates where he hadn't paid the girl at the end of the night. The more he thought about the events of the night before, the angrier he got. He wished he could see Lina again. He'd shave down his whole body. Maybe even get a wax if it would help.

From the front window of the diner, he saw his employer walking on the opposite side of the street like he was the king of New Orleans. In Panama, Staub was the undisputed boss, but Pelly doubted the Americans cared much about Panama. And he knew that was what motivated his boss. His idea of revenge made some perverse sense if anyone cared that Panama had been humiliated by the U.S. But now, years after the invasion, the people of Panama relied on the U.S. as much as they ever had. They needed protection and tourism as well as aid in the form of engineers and professionals for all kinds of projects.

Pelly knew it would be difficult to keep the U.S. from figuring out who was involved in an attack like this. Pelly knew it could hurt the country not to mention their own business, but his boss seemed hell-bent on carrying out his plans.

He stood as Staub entered the diner, then stepped over to the table.

Staub said, "Pelly, we should not meet so close to my hotel. I would not want Duarte to see you."

"I thought I'd make the meeting convenient for you."

"While I appreciate your concern, I think we should not come close to the Marriott again. Understand?"

Pelly just nodded.

Staub continued. "Now we have another issue and an opportunity."

Pelly just kept looking at his employer.

Staub continued. "In addition to Duarte, the ATF agent, we should probably take care of the FBI agent on the case."

"Won't that raise questions?"

Staub smiled. "We'll be gone in a day or two. We'll drive to Houston then fly home. We must set it up in such a way that there are no witnesses or that I can give misleading answers."

"What's the FBI agent look like?"

"It's a woman. Haven't you seen her?"

"Only from a great distance. I know Duarte and the DEA man."

"She has dark hair and an athletic build. If I had more time, I'd have some fun with her. She would not do well under the whip. On the other hand, she's not built for it either. Not enough meat."

Pelly felt disappointment that he had grown used to his boss's odd quirks. He had grown callous to many things in the years he had worked for Staub. He asked his boss, "How should I do it?"

Staub gave an evil grin and said, "I may have a simple, fast way to wrap up these two problems."

Pelly nodded. Unhappy, but willing to complete another task that didn't help their business in any way.

ALEX DUARTE HAD STARTED THE DAY ON A LIE BY EXPLAINING
to Lina Cirillo that his bruised face was the result of running into a door.
Félix knew it was from the Cajun Inn explosion and smiled smugly.

Lina just said, "Yeah, sure." Duarte was still trying to figure out which
piece of the puzzle she knew.

Félix Baez was still in his own little world, focusing on who had killed
his informant in Panama. Colonel Lázaro Staub seemed to have a voice
Duarte had heard somewhere, and his English was much better. He
wondered what the Panamanian cop knew about Ortíz and if he had
chosen to keep quiet.

Lina touched Duarte's arm and said, "We should shut things down on
this case. It's not going anywhere."

"No, Lina, you're incorrect. It's going somewhere. I just don't know
where it's going."

"You're chasing ghosts. Give it up or . . ."

"Or what?"

"The bureau might make you give up."

"Why? What the hell does the FBI care about a little dope deal or a dead informant?"

"It's the people associated with the deal who could hurt you."

"Now you have to tell me what's going on."

"Truthfully, I don't know. But the FBI can handle it without the assistance of the Rocket."

She used his nickname like an insult. He fought hard not to mention the radioactive reading from the packing slip. Sure, there were a hundred reasons for it. A previous load of timber or tile in the container or even the pot itself might have some natural radioactivity. But he didn't want to give up his single chip yet.

Colonel Staub wandered over from the elevators and greeted the three U.S. agents. He sat in his usual, stiff upright way and said, "I have several matters to discuss. It would be my pleasure to buy you breakfast at a little café I found several blocks from here. It is truly remarkable." He kept his dark eyes on Lina, with an occasional glance toward Duarte. Then he turned to Félix and said, "You may come, too."

Félix stood up, his long-sleeved shirt tight around his chest. "No, thanks. I gotta make some calls." He turned toward the elevator.

Duarte was going to decline, too, but he knew he'd never have his questions answered by avoiding the solutions. He needed to know what both the colonel and Lina knew. He had to put it all together.

He stood with the colonel and noticed Lina's less-than-thrilled attitude to a free meal and a chance to get some answers from the Panamanian cop.

Duarte hesitated at the front door, noticing the light drizzle for the first time. The weather summed up how he felt right now.

William Ike Floyd woke up and instantly regretted inviting the three men to help him watch the truck. All three were asleep on the floor or couch of the hotel room on the outskirts of Houston, their alternating snores sounding like a manufacturing plant.

The scruffiest of them, Charlie, was supposed to watch the truck until ten in the morning. He had clearly given up, and it wasn't even eight-thirty yet.

Ike knew there was a risk to having these guys here, but he'd made it clear that his cargo had no value and that they'd get paid when they were done with the mission. He didn't go into details on anything other than that they were to stand guard and that if he met with a Panamanian they were to act tough in case he needed them to. Right now he was more afraid of Mr. Ortíz than he was of three beaten-down white supremacists who had never been accepted into any of the white-power organizations—not even the Klan, and they accepted anybody, as long as you were white. The oldest Charlie claimed he had been a member of the Klan in Daytona but judged by his description it was not any Klavern officially recognized by the national Klan organizations.

He looked over the sprawled bodies, all shirtless and one only in his underwear, and thought, This is the most unattractive group I've ever seen. None of the men were what someone would call in shape. Charles, the youngest, had big arms, but his stomach had no definition. All were pretty hairy, not like Pelly but still with more than he liked. And most important, all of them were over sixteen. A definite turnoff. He could make exceptions, but it had a lot to do with how old someone looked.

He sat up in bed, then stood and shouted, "Hey, guys."

They all stirred, but no one jumped.

"Hey, get up."

Charlie, the oldest of the three, wiped his eyes and said, "Yo, dude, what's the problem?"

"The problem is that I let you guys stay here to help me keep track of the truck."

One of the others peeked out the window. "What's the problem? It's still there."

Ike looked over the group and realized he may have created another problem. He hoped he could handle this one by himself.

Pelly answered his phone on the first ring. He had noticed the light rain start to pick up, but it had not impeded his view of the alley where Colonel Staub was supposed to lead the FBI agent and Duarte. Pelly had his pistol and knew they'd be boxed in the narrow roadway with high walls on each side.

"Yes?" he answered the small cell phone.

"We'll be walking your way in a minute."

"Got it." He slapped the phone shut. Right now the alley was vacant. He could even try running them down with the car. That would make the colonel's explanation to the police more plausible.

On the street behind him, he had noticed a group of six small children and two women. He dismissed it as a preschool class. They were looking in the wide window of an antique-doll shop he had spotted when he'd pulled in the edge of the alley.

A large black man in a blue jumpsuit stepped out of a door in the alley and tossed a bag into a Dumpster recessed next to the wall. He left the door open as he disappeared back inside.

Pelly saw a pedestrian at the far end of the alley and realized it was the colonel with the two targets just behind him. He could tell one of them was a woman with dark hair. It was Duarte he had to watch out for.

Alice Brainard had been in front of her computer all morning. She loved doing research on things she knew very little about. It was a form of discovery, and she liked to discover stuff. If this had been the 1500s and she were a man, she would have been on one of Columbus's ships, or maybe one of the Spanish conquistadors'. She didn't agree with how they had treated the native people of Florida, but she liked their adventurous spirit.

She had been on her Dell looking into the role of the Department of Energy and their Radiological Assistance Program. She realized that Jeff

Jacobus, the best-looking firefighter she knew, had said that a lot of things gave off radiation, but she had no idea how many things were considered radioactive. Maybe she was jumping at nothing. Alex didn't want to raise a fuss about it just yet. He'd said it would get too many people involved in something that probably wasn't an issue in their investigation. He had already complained of getting sidetracked and about how the Panamanian cop and the FBI agent, Lina, seemed to have their own agenda and disappeared frequently.

Along with the Internet, Alice made use of her considerable library. She hated to throw out books, especially reference books. Bill Bryson's *A Short History of Nearly Everything* provided one insight on radioactivity. Hans Geiger, the inventor of the Geiger counter, was also known as a Nazi sympathizer who turned in many of his Jewish colleagues. What a creep.

On the Internet she read an essay about nuclear weapons and the former Soviet republics. Then she read about how they might slip one into the U.S.

She knew what she had to do. But first she was going to call Alex.

Duarte and Lina stepped out of the hotel, and the rain hit them immediately. The canopy that they were told had blown away in hurricane Katrina would have kept them dry. He was a little annoyed that Staub had kept them waiting while he made a call.

Duarte turned as Staub stepped through the door. "The café, it is down an alley two blocks."

Duarte noticed the twitch in his left eye was working overtime.

The colonel held out his hand like he was showing them into a ballroom, then started walking at a fast clip. Duarte and Lina fell in just behind him.

Lina took his arm and leaned in like he would help keep her dry, her wet hair already hanging in her face from the rain.

Duarte said, "At least we won't need to shower today."

"Ooh, a joke. I like that." She let loose with her crooked smile.

They followed Colonel Staub into the alley and felt some relief from the rain as the tall buildings seemed to block most of it. He noticed a single car at the far end of the alley, but no one else on either side.

The colonel kept moving fast, increasing the distance between them.

He saw the car pull away from the wall and start down the alley. He moved to the side, but saw the car pick up speed. Something told him they were in trouble.

WILLIAM "IKE" FLOYD FELT CLAMMY IN THE HOT TEXAS AIR outside the room. Standing by the Ryder truck, one of Ike's new friends said, "Looks like the fertilizer bomb used in Oklahoma City."

Ike cringed. He knew the damn Ryder name carried those kinds of connotations. Ike also knew damn well the Ryder logo was too obvious if this idiot could spot it.

Charlie, the oldest of the three, about forty, said, "I heard there was a third guy that walked away from the blast. He's still free. God bless him."

One of the others said, "I heard it, too." He brushed back his dirty brown hair with his hand. "It's a big secret. Not too many people know it, but the truck had two men in it and the other dude helped with the bomb."

Ike looked at the men. "If it's such a secret, how come you know?"

The man looked at him. "Because we're in the Cause. C'mon, brother, you're a member of the National Army of White Americans. You had to hear this shit before.

Ike just stared at him. He had heard it. Too many times.

Charlie said, "I heard he got away scot-free."

Ike just said, "I wouldn't call it exactly scot-free."

Pelly had seen the distance between the two targets and the colonel. He thought he could swing the car in quick, making it look like a hit-and-run. It was one of the options he and Colonel Staub had discussed.

The alley was clear and the colonel had moved to the left side, directly against a wall.

Pelly still had his pistol in his lap, but this seemed like a better solution. He increased the gas, not roaring down the alley but moving fast enough to accomplish his goal. He figured the building walls would help when he struck the targets head-on.

As he closed the distance, the female FBI agent swept her hair out of her face and turned toward him.

It was Lina from the bar.

They were so close he didn't know what to do.

Lina didn't mind walking so close to Alex Duarte. He was the only one out of the three men who hadn't hit on her. In fact, he always appeared to be a gentleman. She could feel his hard bicep that, unlike many men, he never bothered to show off.

The rain had let up, and the building blocked some of it. She didn't mind except for what it was doing to her hair.

She was about to say something to Duarte as she used her hand to push her drooping hair back. Just as she saw a blue car bearing down on them, she felt him start to shove her. She used her weight to pull him with her.

At the last possible second, the vehicle swerved in the narrow alley, clipping the other wall. That combination of their movement and the car turning slightly saved them from certain disaster.

She ended up pinned by Duarte against the brick wall of a building, her body splayed tight to give him room. His eyes tracked the car as it turned the corner with a slight squeal of its tires.

Duarte said, "Wow, that was close."

"Thanks for pushing me."

"Thanks for pulling me. You all right?" He eased back into the alley.

"I'm fine. I felt the tire brush the bottom of my sandal."

"Yeah, I felt it touch my foot."

Lina smiled, noticing Staub rushing back to them. "Are you un-harmed, my friends?"

Duarte nodded. "He drives like he's from Miami."

The colonel looked down the alley where the car had disappeared onto the street. "No, a Miami driver would've hit you."

Lina touched Duarte's arm, leaned in and said, "We should work together more often." She liked his smile.

But saw that Duarte was thinking about the car.

Colonel Lázaro Staub kept his voice calm but knew that Pelly understood his tone.

"Why didn't you shoot them?"

"I thought the car would be easier to explain. I made a split-second decision."

"Then how could you miss them?"

Pelly hesitated, then said, "It was wet. They were quick. I was afraid I had misjudged where you were."

If he didn't depend on the hairy young man so much, he might have pulled out his little Beretta and shot him in the head. But they were also in public. A nice, crowded tourist place called Café du Monde in Jackson Square. He had sipped the coffee and eaten the tiny pieces of fried dough with sugar sprinkled on them as he waited for his assistant. They had done nothing to calm him down. And after the encounter in the alley and the fact that she was soaked, Lina and Duarte had not eaten breakfast with him. Instead they had returned to the hotel.

Now he had to focus. There were problems to solve. Staub wondered if he could leave New Orleans without taking care of Lina Cirillo. Would his ego allow it?

He looked over at the calm Pelly. His face was clear of hair for a change. There appeared to be something about his manner as well.

"Are you still with me on this, Pelly?"

"With respect, *jefe,* I disagree with your plan, because it will disrupt business, but I still work for you."

It wasn't the same as being with him, but it would do. "Our challenge will be to get that idiot William Floyd to complete his tasks."

Pelly just stared at him.

Staub said, "We will leave for Houston this evening."

Pelly said, "What about the ATF agent?"

"He can't stop us, but I hope he doesn't piece it together after the fact." He didn't mention that he intended to deal with Lina Cirillo before they left.

Alex Duarte had taken the few hours of quiet time to walk New Orleans and figure out what he and Félix were going to do next. He didn't know if that near-miss in the alley had been intentional or not. He still didn't know who to tell about Jessup. There was nothing in the papers yet. He knew that in time the killer would expose himself. But did he have time to wait? Had he blown his chance at Jessup's house?

He felt a sour, sick feeling in the pit of his stomach as he thought about the possibilities and silently cursed himself for being so rigid and predictable. These killings were not related to a load of pot. His questions should not have been about a dead informant. There was something much bigger in the works.

He jumped slightly at the sound of his phone.

He flipped it open. "Duarte"

"Alex, it's Alice."

Before she could say anything, he said, "Send that particle reading as soon as you can."

IKE RELAXED SLIGHTLY IN A PLACE CALLED ELLIE'S INTERNET Café, about two miles from the hotel where he had left the three Charlies. He needed to check messages from Mr. Ortíz, but he really wanted to be away from those three morons for an hour or so. He had taken anything of value from the room and had the truck with him, so he didn't think they could cause much damage. Frankly, he was hoping they might steal his pair of jeans and shirts and just leave. That would solve all his problems. He'd just forget he'd ever met them.

Inside the café he ordered a straight coffee and the pastry that most closely resembled something he had eaten before. In this case it looked like a jelly-filled croissant but had the texture of a biscuit and cost six bucks.

The most important thing was, he had his own computer. It was an older Compaq with a grainy fifteen-inch CRT screen, one of those fat, clunky-looking, old models that he didn't think were even made any more. The connection was not that fast either. First, he surfed around the Internet a little, killing time and staying away from his hotel. He checked the local newspaper from Omaha and read all the police-blotter reports. No one he knew had caused any problems since he had left his hometown.

He also browsed the *Chicago Sun–Times.* This was a habit to see if there was ever any mention of his mother or the thing that she had married. He checked the obituaries in the hopes that one day he might read that his mother had finally bought the farm. Apparently, cigarettes and Johnnie Walker Black weren't as bad for you as everyone claimed. No sign of her permanent change of address. He checked under the name that she'd used when she raised him, if that's what you could call it, and under the name she'd taken when she moved off to Chicago with the musician. He occasionally heard that they still lived together. He even wondered if, by some quirk, he had any dark-skinned half brothers or sisters.

He also ran his name in Google and found several mentions, usually in an old newspaper column that quoted him about some rally or event he was involved in as part of the National Army of White Americans. He kept checking and found the one old article from 1995 that mentioned his arrest but left out the fact that it was for Internet child pornography. Now he told people the arrest was for kicking a cop's ass. But that was as big a lie as the rest of his life. His arrest and the subsequent deal with the devil he had made had altered his life more than he ever could have imagined. Maybe for the better, but certainly for the more anonymous. He had done something and known people for which he could never claim credit because of that arrest. No one really noticed it anymore, and it had been wiped from his record.

He finally navigated the old computer to Yahoo and signed in. He opened the unsent message in the "saved" section and read the simple note. "Will be in Houston late tonight. All is ready. Will contact in a.m. O."

Ike swallowed hard, knowing that the time was drawing near to go where his destiny led him. Was that an old song? He didn't know, but got a little nervous thinking about what they had in store.

He knew that it would lead to greater security for the U.S. and that the borders would finally be shut down. The guys he had met from the Minutemen and American border guards wouldn't approve of his methods, but they sure as shit would be happy with the results. They were the ones who had given him the idea of something like this. Thinking about how irate people were becoming about immigration made it easy to say he'd help Mr. Ortíz when President Jessup called.

Ike knew that he'd be a legend among his people and that eventually everyone would know who he was and what he had done. But now he had the very real dilemma of what it would do to him in the immediate future. Sure, Eric Rudolph avoided the FBI for five years, but he'd lived like a hobo. Ike liked his comforts and knew there would be a hell of a lot more people looking for him.

He stared at the screen, thinking about the two paths his future could take.

Colonel Lázaro Staub paused outside Lina Cirillo's hotel door, fantasizing about what he could do to her if they were only back in Panama. He would be under no time limits or have to worry so much about being secret. He had in his room a cargo bag and pack of garbage bags he had purchased in the small shopping plaza a few blocks from the hotel. The bag had plenty of room for a skinny woman like Lina.

The afternoon sun had burned away all the remnants of the earlier storm, and it was really quite warm on his walk back. He was relieved when he made it through the lobby without anyone he knew seeing him.

After he had finished with her now, he'd be back to collect the evidence and then toss it into a convenient canal on their way to Houston. There would be questions but nothing he couldn't deal with from Panama.

He stuck his right hand in his pocket and felt the folded Benchmade knife he had also purchased. It was similar to his favorite back home. When opened, it was more than seven inches long and would terrify the normal person. That was his only question. Should he use it to terrify the FBI agent or was she too quick and strong to give any warning? He'd have to decide as events unfolded.

He knocked on the plain door with his left hand and waited only a short time for the door to open a crack, then all the way.

Lina stood in front of the open door. "What are you doin' here?"

"I wanted to apologize."

"What for?"

"My poor manners the other night."

She gave him a crooked smile. "That's fine."

"I also have some information you should know."

"What's that?"

"May I come in?" He felt his left eye twitch. His right hand tightened on the knife in his pocket.

She stepped aside and allowed him full access to the room.

As he stepped inside, he noted the bed was messy on only one side and her suitcase was on the second bed. This would be sweet. But maybe not too quick. He forced himself to look out the bay window as he heard her shut the door and it automatically locked. A smile crept across his face. And he felt his penis start to stiffen. This was exactly what he needed.

Alex Duarte leaned his head back against the headboard of his bed on the eleventh floor of the Marriott. It was the middle of the afternoon, but the way things were going and after his night in Biloxi, he needed a little rest. He could tell Félix was exhausted as well.

After the car had nearly struck him and Lina in the alley, they'd lost interest in breakfast and never did eat.

He was curious to find out if Alice had been able to get ICE to send the particle reading from the shipping notice. Was it connected to the case?

He thought about calling his pop, too. He was the one person who always seemed to get to the bottom of a problem. During Duarte's last big case, when he'd been looking in one direction, his father had made a simple adjustment to his vantage point. It had made all the difference. His father's counsel had always been important to him. He was surprised to see that as he got older and changed jobs from the U.S. Army to the

U.S. government, he valued his father's opinion more and more. His father may have been an immigrant from Paraguay who had been a plumber for thirty years, but he had insight and knowledge that Duarte didn't think he'd ever acquire. He could reduce complex situations to simple analogies.

As Duarte thought about calling Alice or his father, his cell phone rang. He picked up the Nextel and flipped it open.

"Duarte."

It was a woman's voice he didn't recognize. "Agent Duarte, open your door."

The line went dead.

Duarte looked at the phone and then his bolted door. He popped up from the bed quickly and then leaned toward the small desk and grabbed his SIG-Sauer model P229. He didn't even slip it in the back of his bed-wrinkled khakis. With all that had gone on in this case, he held it in his right hand.

He stepped to the side of the door, weighing the advantages of opening it from one side or the other.

As his left hand reached for the bolt, his right tightened on the Glock. He raised the pistol as he crouched slightly.

His pulse increased, but he kept his head clear as he slowly unbolted the door, then let his hand settle on the handle.

As if it had a mind of its own, his thumb depressed the door latch, and he took a breath before he yanked it open.

43

LINA CIRILLO CRINGED FROM THE CIGARETTE BREATH OF LÁZARO Staub. She had strategically placed a small, round table between them as she sat in a corner of the room.

He had acted a little odd since entering, like he might be about to put the moves on her again. She knew some Latin guys just couldn't accept that a woman wasn't into them. Especially a man like Staub who had power and was not unattractive.

In a way she was flattered he thought she was interested in him and that he thought enough of her to respond. Because of her build and profession, she was often mistaken for a lesbian. Boy, was that an incorrect assessment. She was also a little sensitive about her nose and crooked smile. Both were the result of her repeated attempts to earn a black belt in karate, which she had but only after three broken noses and a jaw injury that made her look like she was out of alignment.

Staub said, "You know, the other night?"

"Yes."

He leaned closer, apparently hoping she would, too. His hands were not in front of him, so she didn't think he was going to try to molest her again.

She leaned in slightly and he said, "I am not used to women refusing my advances."

She smiled weakly. "You're in the big leagues now."

"How very American of you."

"What's that supposed to mean?"

He seemed to flex slightly, but was as startled as she was when there was a knock on the door.

Staub said, "Don't answer it."

"Why not?" She called to the door. "One second."

He seemed to sag back into his chair as she stood up and strode to the door quickly. It was getting a little weird in here.

She opened the door to a sheepish Félix Baez. "Can I come in?"

"Why?"

"So I can apologize for acting like a dick."

She looked him over, noticing the nice long-sleeved shirt and contrite demeanor.

"Join the party," she said, as she stepped out of the doorway so he could see her other guest.

As Félix stepped inside, Staub stood up. "There is plenty of room. I have another commitment. I am sorry. I was just saying my goodbyes. I will be leaving New Orleans soon to return to Panama."

Lina turned and said, "It's been a pleasure to work with you."

Even Félix added, "Yeah, you were a big help." He had to add, "In Panama."

Staub nodded and shook Félix's hand, then turned and gave Lina a kiss on the forehead.

He said, "I'm sure I'll see you again, soon."

Alex Duarte stood next to his hotel door with his pistol raised when he jerked it open. A man dressed in a sport coat and a woman in a business suit stood completely unfazed by Duarte's actions.

Even with the SIG-Sauer trained on them, the very attractive woman, in her late thirties, said, "Are you done?"

Duarte stood straight and lowered the gun slightly.

The woman made a show of slowly reaching into her giant purse and pulling out a black ID case and letting it fall open. "Meg Ruley, FBI."

He looked at the ID and lowered the SIG-Sauer.

The woman continued, "This is Tom McLaughlin with the Department of Energy."

Duarte said, "This is about the particle spectrum, right?"

"You're pretty smart," said the female FBI agent. Then added, "For an ATF agent."

Duarte didn't bite.

The woman said, "May we come inside and talk to you about this?"

"Do I have a choice?"

She just smiled, and that told Duarte everything he needed to know about her. She was a veteran, knew her stuff and didn't waste words when she didn't need to. In short, she was the real deal.

He stepped aside and watched her as she led in the taller man from the Department of Energy. Even in a drab FBI business suit, this woman was attractive. She had neat, brown hair and a body that said she wasn't afraid to work out. The way she moved told Duarte she was confident and that he was about to be thumped by a very competent agent from another Department of Justice agency.

Once they were in the room, the man said, "Those were most unusual readings from the sample." He had a light Southern accent. His glasses obscured heavy lids over brown eyes.

"In what way?"

"It was enriched U-235."

Duarte stared, hoping not to have to admit his ignorance.

The man picked up on it. "Fissionable uranium. Weapons grade."

"A bomb?"

He held up his hands. "Possibly a dirty bomb. We don't believe that a drug smuggler would have the technical capacity to arm and detonate an actual warhead. We still need a lot of info."

"Who is 'we'?"

The man and Agent Ruley from the FBI exchanged glances, and she said, "NEST."

"NEST?"

"Nuclear Emergency Search Team."

He looked back at the man. "And you work for the DOE?"

"And Lawrence Livermore Labs."

"This is serious."

"Could be. We can't take any chances."

Duarte remained silent.

Then the FBI agent, Meg Ruley, said, "It took a little time to track you down through the ICE idiot in the Port of Palm Beach, then your friend, Ms. Brainard."

"Is she okay?"

"Yeah, just in debriefing with our guys in West Palm. They all knew you and said you were okay. I was contacted to find out just what the hell is going on. As I understand it, we have an agent here, too, and someone dropped the ball."

Duarte tried to assess the woman's intent, but, being a seasoned veteran who was also smart, she gave no sign of her intentions.

Then Agent Ruley said, "I know the container had pot in it, but it had something else, too." She looked directly at Duarte. "What was it?"

He said honestly, "I wish I knew."

William "Ike" Floyd had all three of his new assistants out of the hotel room. That was a start. The younger of the three, Chuck, had left a few hours before and was just walking back to the other men standing by the big Ryder rental truck.

Ike said, "We're going to have to go our separate ways."

Charlie said, "Why? I thought we was helping you?"

"Turns out you guys have no skills."

The youngest of them, the one that had just rejoined them, said, "That's bullshit; we got plenty of skills."

"Like what?"

"Didn't you even notice me drive back in that Ford F-150?" He pointed across the parking lot of the Jacinto Arms toward the big, two-door truck with a long bed and full camper top. He added, "I got that so we could sleep in the back if we needed."

"It's set up with beds?"

"Not yet. But I wanted to show you I got skills. I can start any car in the world. As long as someone leaves the door open and a key hidden someplace simple like under the bumper or in the glove compartment, I can start the fucking vehicle." He slapped a high five with his two buddies.

Ike just stared at the scruffy younger man. What the hell was he bragging about? These idiots were really starting to embarrass him. He didn't think he could let Mr. Ortíz even meet them.

Ike just looked at them, hoping they'd take the hint and go to their newly stolen pickup and disappear.

Charlie said, "You been pullin' our chain since you met us."

"How you figure?" Ike didn't like being called a liar.

"You ain't on no big-time mission. You're probably moving some furniture or paper. You're full of shit."

Ike flinched slightly. He didn't like these rednecks thinking they were better than him. It really bothered him that they thought he was lying. He was hesitant to show them the package in the truck, then he thought he knew what would do the trick and also give him a reason to show off to a big dog like President Jessup.

Ike smiled and said, "I'll tell you what."

"What?"

"You know who Forrest Jessup is, right?"

"Oh hell, yeah. He's the dang president of the National Army of White Americans."

"Would you know his voice?"

"Maybe. I'd definitely know a fake from what he says."

Ike smiled wider. "I can call him."

"Bullshit."

"I'll prove it. I need a pay phone."

"Use your cell."

"Nope. Don't want my cell traced to his phone. Can't trace a pay phone."

He spotted one across the street under the front cover of a small convenience store called Santa Anna's Pit Stop. He marched across the street with the three errant racists in line behind him. He could hear Charlie telling his buddies that Ike was full of shit. He'd show them.

He dug his small sheet with phone numbers on it from his wallet. He looked at Charlie and said, "I need a couple more quarters."

Between the three other men, they had nine more quarters, and Ike realized they had been panhandling at some point. They looked less and less like the examples he wanted white people to set.

He dialed the number, then started feeding in quarters like the electronic operator instructed. After three rings he heard an answering machine pick up. "You have reached Forrest Jessup's house. Leave a message." He started to leave his name, then hung up. He had wanted to give the head man an update so he would be proud of the work Ike had done. He also wanted to show these idiots that he really did know Mr. Jessup.

Charlie said, "What about it?"

"Not home."

"That's handy."

Ike nodded. "It doesn't matter. I don't need your help anymore."

Charlie said, "But this big ole Ryder truck is gonna attract a lot of attention. You might need someone to watch it. Because if someone is watching it, they won't fuck with it."

Ike understood the threat. He was even a little surprised this guy could phrase it so well. Then he realized his biggest problem. It was too visible. Everyone knew that a Ryder truck carried the bomb in Oklahoma City. Maybe he did need a lower-profile vehicle.

As he looked across the street, he could just see the top of the camper from the stolen F-150 pickup truck. Ford always advertised that it was the best-selling vehicle in the country. That meant there was a shitload of them around. Not very obvious. He wondered how big the bed of the truck really was, then a plan clicked in his brain.

He looked at the sorry-looking men. "Okay. I'll tell you what. Let's drive out somewhere away from the prying eyes, and I'll show you what's in the truck."

Charlie brightened, his missing teeth reminding Ike of a jack-o'-lantern. "Really?" said the man.

"Yeah, I think I could find a use for you guys. But we won't all fit in the Ryder. Follow me in the F-150." He smiled, but knew they had no idea what had tickled him so much.

ALONE IN HIS HOTEL ROOM, DUARTE STARED AT ALL THE NOTES on the case. He knew they'd be useless now. The FBI agent and her NEST team from the FBI and the Department of Energy would run with this now.

Duarte hadn't argued with the Department of Energy man or Agent Ruley. They were right. He had screwed up. Now they had to scramble to clean up his mess. No one liked to see something like that. He should have recognized that something bigger than a load of pot was in play when his witnesses started dying.

Now Duarte realized that Ortíz, or one of his employees, had used the load as a cover for something else. The theory now was a dirty bomb of some kind. The DOE guy said they had identified the radioactive isotope as U-235, but wasn't willing to tell Duarte anything else.

On the other hand, Duarte had told them everything he knew, including how he had tried to talk to several people but they had all been killed. Nothing the cops didn't already know.

The FBI had asked him about Jessup, who they obviously knew was dead. Duarte answered honestly, saying he didn't know who had killed him. Which was true.

They were looking for someone related to Jessup, and that had to be William Floyd. It all came back to the racist from Omaha.

He looked down at the notes he had made with the initials of everyone involved. He had not shown it to the FBI agent, but he told her the suspicions he harbored.

As he looked at the page, he remembered Félix's comments about William Floyd's initials W.F. standing for "white female" in every police station in the U.S.

Duarte wished he had the resources to continue on the case. With Lina's access to the FBI data banks and to her source, they could continue to search for Floyd. He just wished he had access to her source, Pale Girl.

Then he froze.

Pale Girl. White female. William Floyd. Could it be? Would they use such an obvious code name? Was William Floyd a source for the FBI?

He had to find Lina right now.

Five minutes later, he was surprised to find Félix Baez with Lina in her hotel room. But by the look on their faces, they had been doing nothing too intimate.

When Lina opened the door, her first comment was, "Looks like you've been visited by the new kids on the block, too."

He stepped into the room and sat at the small table with Félix.

Lina said, "You off the case, too?"

Duarte nodded.

"Don't worry. Right now there are teams of FBI and DOE people swarming over the docks and in Lafayette."

"Why aren't you with them?"

"They consider me a fuckup."

"Why? You didn't do anything wrong."

"I lost the source, Pale Girl."

Duarte knew it was time. "We know Pale Girl was driving the package in New Orleans."

Lina looked up at him as she slowly sat on the unmade bed. "And how do we know this?"

"Cal Linley told me he gave it to William Floyd. Then I found the truck in Lafayette."

She held her FBI-neutral expression the whole time.

"And William Floyd is Pale Girl."

Lina was careful. "How do you figure that?"

"Look, Lina, you need to drop this FBI bullshit. If we want to contribute at all, we need to be straight with each other."

"How'd you know Floyd was my source?"

He just smiled. He didn't want to let her think he had just made an educated guess.

Lina said, "What can we contribute? The bureau is all over this."

Félix let out a big enough laugh for both of them. "You're kidding, right? If we depend on the FBI, we could be in a nuclear winter by the weekend."

Duarte nodded. "We can do things unencumbered by administration. Anything we turn up could be a bonus. It doesn't matter who finds Floyd, but someone needs to and fast."

Lina said, "We do have some information we could check. But what do we do with it?"

Duarte smiled. "That's easy. We kick some ass."

William "Ike" Floyd wasn't certain of where he was headed, but on the small access road that started right next to the Jacinto Arms he thought he would end up somewhere that would be private. The simple blacktop asphalt road seemed to go nowhere but also appeared to be quite long with nothing but acres of vacant land on each side. He was proud of himself for coming up with such a good plan and what he would tell Mr. Ortíz about the Ryder truck when he saw him.

Next to him, the oldest Charlie had been rattling on about his life before a cocaine habit had wrecked him. Of course the habit had nothing to do with him. It was disease that had consumed him. He had been a heavy-machine operator in Daytona Beach, Florida, until he smoked some crack one evening and never bothered to go back to his wife and three kids, two of which were probably his.

Charlie said, "I'll tell you what. Something like this can turn your life around. Helping you might be what I need to hold my head up high again."

Ike just nodded.

"I gotta tell ya, Ike. It's mighty impressive that you're doing so well in the National Army at such a young age. What're you? Thirty?"

"Thirty-two."

"What're we helping you with? I mean you can tell us, can't you? Another bomb, like Oklahoma City?"

Ike snorted. "That was minor."

Charlie looked at him and said, "You're crazy."

"That's not what the court psychiatrist said."

"Really, what are we gonna do?" The dirty man stared at Ike, waiting for an honest answer.

Ike returned the stare and gave him an honest answer. "We're going to plant, then detonate, a nuclear weapon."

45

AT THE EDGE OF A WIDE CANAL THAT RAN PARALLEL TO THE ROAD they had driven out, William "Ike" Floyd took his corner of the crate as they hefted it into the back of the stolen F-150 pickup truck. It just fit under the camper top fastened onto the long bed of the truck. Sweat dripped off his nose as he looked up at the three, dirty, huffing men.

"Now what?" asked the youngest of the men, his giant swastika tattoo gleaming with sweat in the bright Texas sunshine. "When can we see this thing?"

The three men all stepped to the same side of the truck in a tight bunch facing Ike.

"C'mon, let's check the van one last time."

The three men followed him to the Ryder van parked in front of the truck. He felt for the small SIG-Sauer pistol under his shirt.

"Get the wood out of there," he said, pointing at the lengths of two-by-fours.

The two younger men hopped up into the truck and grabbed the wood.

Ike hoped that Charlie would follow his friends up into the covered van. It would have made things easier.

He knew who he needed to cap first. He drew the pistol without pretense, trying to stay calm, and fired as soon as it was pointed right at the youngest Charlie's face. The sound in the van from the discharging pistol was thunderous and even stunned the other man inside.

Ike didn't waste any time and pointed the small pistol at the other Charlie as he retreated, this time aiming for his body. He fired once and was shocked to realize he had missed him altogether. He took a second to breathe and then carefully aimed the pistol at the man who was now cowering in the corner of the van.

"Please, Ike, don't."

The plea had no effect on Ike. He squeezed the trigger again, this time striking the man directly in the forehead. He flopped onto the still form of the other man.

Ike turned his attention to the oldest Charlie, who had raced around the side of the van.

Ike didn't mind chasing him because he realized now that killing people gave him a rush. He took one last look at the two bodies in the back of the Ryder truck, then took his first step in search of the terrified man.

Lina said, "If we assume Floyd was in Lafayette with the man who talked to the mechanic, then we have a starting point."

Duarte nodded as he listened.

She wished she had been able to predict William Floyd's disappearance. Lina had met him several times and still talked to the white supremacist by phone once or twice a year as part of her intelligence duties. She knew how important Floyd had been in the past and how the bureau had screwed up by not listening to him. Now it looked like he had once again gotten involved in something big.

Lina said, "You guys know Jessup is dead."

Félix nodded and Duarte said, "I went to talk to him last night, but was too late."

The DEA man jumped up. "You were there last night?" He paused and composed himself. "I thought you said you were going today."

Duarte shrugged. "I couldn't sleep, so I went last night."

Lina knew not to ask any details. She knew the straitlaced ATF man had nothing to do with his death.

Duarte looked at Lina and said, "Can we expect any help from the FBI on our little investigation?"

"Not officially. Meg Ruley is the rising star. If someone thinks we're working opposite her, they won't return my calls."

"What will people at the bureau think happened?"

"Right now, only that there was a radioactive hit in New Orleans. They might even think it was an error. I can see them using this as training or to show off to some senator. No telling. I think if they were really concerned, I'd be in more trouble."

"Could we get the phone tolls?"

"Yeah, sure, except if we tried to get Floyd's. Anything to do with him would be flagged."

Duarte looked at her and said, "How'd he get to be an FBI source?"

Lina wanted to tell him the truth, but her training kicked in and she said, "It's a long story."

Lázaro Staub simmered on the entire drive from New Orleans, through Lafayette on toward Houston. He wanted no record of air travel, and they had time before the physics professor they had hired was ready. This was one of the times he was happy that Pelly spoke so sparingly. He sighed, thinking about how much fun he could've had. He had been so close to running a blade across Lina Cirillo's lovely throat. All he had to do was flip the blade open and make the swipe. The look in her eyes as her life dripped out of her would have been priceless. He had killed only one other woman like that, a prostitute in Colón who had tried to pass information about his operation on to the authorities.

Unfortunately for her, *he* was the authority to whom she had tried to pass on the information. He had done it in the office of the National Police only because he loved the idea of this woman thinking she was doing her civic duty and having her throat slashed at the desk of the officer in charge.

That had turned into a tricky business, with too many rumors flying. Pelly had been with him then and had gotten rid of the body. Along with a good-sized rug that was in the office at the time. Staub let out the rumor that Pelly had killed a girl who had called him a monkey. Not only was it completely plausible, but it enhanced his enforcer's reputation, not that the hairy young man's reputation needed any enhancement.

Staub glanced over at Pelly. He had seemed down since he had missed the ATF agent and Lina in the car earlier in the day. He had not shaved obsessively like he usually did, and now he looked like something out of a cheap horror movie with his thick, curling black hair working its way up his cheeks almost to his eyes and down his neck to his chest.

Staub said, "You know, Pelly."

"Yes, boss?"

"I may have been hard on you about missing Duarte. It was rainy, and he is quick."

Pelly kept driving silently.

"You are a big help to me."

"Thank you, boss. But . . ."

"Go ahead, Pelly."

"Are you sure we should go ahead with this? I mean with the whole plan."

"I know you worry that there is no bottom line to this, Pelly. By picking this target we get some satisfaction, and William Floyd and his group will get all the blame. You'll see. In a year, business will be better than ever, and the Americans will be looking under every rock for terrorists."

Pelly nodded. "Maybe I see some value in it, boss."

Staub patted him on the shoulder. In time, everyone did what he told them to.

William "Ike" Floyd hesitated by the front of the Ryder truck. He had made sure the two men in the back were dead, and he was proud of his marksmanship. He felt like a badass now. He thought he'd catch the older Charlie hustling down the canal or back out the access road that led to the highway near his hotel, but he'd been wrong. Ten minutes of searching the area proved that the low brush was a lot thicker than he had originally thought and now he had a missing man on his hands. A missing witness.

He had run out after him, but was surprised to find no trace, not even a trail of the scruffy old racist.

He weighed the value of searching for him right now and leaving a truck with two bodies on the side of the road, or disposing of the truck and then having to dispose of the third man later.

He spit and said, "Shit," as he walked to the rear of the Ryder rental and pulled down the rear door.

He had already thrown an old piece of string with a washer tied to it to see how deep the water was. He had plenty of room.

He jumped in the cab and started the truck, working it parallel to the water. He turned the wheel, threw the truck in low gear, revved the engine and then took his foot off the break as he flopped out onto the sandy edge of the access road.

The truck slid off the edge and turned sideways as it hit the water and floated away from the shore.

Ike smiled, thinking it couldn't have gone into the water better. Then his smile faded as he realized it was still floating. The big box on the rear was a well-sealed, giant flotation device.

He watched as the truck lolled around in the dark, slightly smelly water. There was no current or flow to the canal. The water around the bright yellow truck bubbled, and it tilted one way, then the other, but didn't sink.

Ike started to panic, wondering what he could do to fix this. The bomb was safely tucked into the Ford pickup, and he was ready to drive off to find the missing man, but he couldn't leave this mess to attract the attention of the first plane or helicopter that wandered by. Not to mention whatever vehicles traveled the isolated access road.

Then the truck shifted and belched. The cab pointed further down and then started to sink. Slowly, like a crippled ocean liner at first, then in a great glop of escaping air, it disappeared underwater.

Ike relaxed a little. That left one problem to solve. Ike pulled out his pistol and headed back to the Ford to start his search for Charlie.

ALEX DUARTE SAT IN LINA'S PLAIN HOTEL ROOM ALONE WITH
the FBI agent. Félix had left complaining of aches and pains as well as a
lack of sleep. The DEA agent's edginess had become more apparent
every hour.

Duarte looked at Lina and said, "I'm surprised Staub left so quickly."

Lina shrugged. "I was surprised he stayed so long. He really didn't add
anything here in the U.S. But who can tell with a guy like him?"

"I thought you knew him pretty well."

"Why?"

"You seemed pretty, um, friendly with him."

She stared at him, the color rising in her face.

"You know what I mean." Duarte hoped that acted as a catchall apology.

"You and Félix kill me. You can't see past your stupid dope deal."

Now she had Duarte's attention.

"The colonel had a few questionable contacts, so I acted friendly to
him to see if he'd talk. I stopped short of being physically friendly and
seemed to turn him off. There's a lot law enforcement guys like you
never get. This is called 'intelligence,' and I was trying to gather it."

If she was trying to make Duarte feel like an incompetent, immature jerk, she'd succeeded.

She didn't let up. "Didn't you and Félix notice he disappeared for a few days? Did you wonder where he went?" She looked up at the ceiling and said, "Jeez."

Duarte said, "Well, I . . . you know . . ."

"You guys are too interested in roughing people up and the rest of that police bullshit that you missed something close to you. There's a lot to intell, and that guy had something going on. It may have been a personal thing. Maybe a kinky one, but I don't know."

"He's that weird?"

"I definitely got a funky vibe from him."

"You don't think he was involved in any of the deaths, do you?"

"No way to tell."

Duarte looked off in space and said, "Wish I had some DNA to send to Alice to compare with our sample."

"Like what?"

"Anything, I guess. A hair or even an old cigarette butt with his saliva on the end."

Lina looked out onto her balcony. "We might be able to work something out."

Ike drove the pickup slowly along the access road the way they had come, hoping to catch a glimpse of the fleeing man. It had been two hours since he'd lost him, enough time to have made it back to the highway, but Ike thought he would've seen him by now.

He felt like he was on some big-game safari in Africa, hunting the dreaded white-trash moron. He smiled, thinking about his cool as he'd fired at the two men he had sent to the bottom of the canal. Sure, they were two unarmed men in a confined space, but it was still something Ike wouldn't have thought he could've done just a few months ago.

Now he had to find this man to avoid possible trouble with the

Houston cops. He had heard not to fuck with Houston cops, and he didn't intend to ignore that advice.

His eyes scanned the acres of low brush on either side of the road. The problem was that the smelly, decaying racist could've just laid down and taken a nap, and Ike wouldn't find him. He now understood why they used so many men to search for escaped prisoners.

He stopped the pickup occasionally and walked out into the open fields, hoping to scare Charlie out of hiding, but had no luck. Finally, after two hours of searching, Ike decided to head back to the hotel, clean out his stuff and wait for Mr. Ortíz in case Charlie made it to the tough Houston cops and told them what had happened.

As he drove up the road and approached the highway, he could just make out the main building of his hotel. The sun was dipping in the west, and long shadows were cast over the area behind the hotel. He blinked his eyes when he thought he saw a figure just off the road about two hundred yards from the hotel.

It was a man, walking unsteadily, his shirt dark with sweat from his back and underarms. Ike smiled. It was Charlie. The older man apparently could walk pretty fast.

Ike smiled as he rolled down the window and idled up next to the exhausted man.

Charlie was so tired he barely looked over, and when he did, he showed no signs of surprise or fear. All he said was "Why?"

Ike pointed the pistol out the window with his left hand, point-blank at Charlie's weathered face. "Because now I can." He pulled the trigger once, hoping that if anyone at the hotel heard it they'd write it off to a backfire or part of a distant storm. He left Charlie where he lay just off the road. Who would ever notice an old drifter dead on the side of a little-used access road?

Alex Duarte looked at Lina as she studied what had been faxed to them from Lina's FBI office. On the small, round table they had notes, some computer phone tolls that Lina had gotten really fast through a contact with a phone company and a LexisNexis address profile on Cal Linley and Forrest Jessup. They hadn't dared ask for any information on William Floyd because they hadn't wanted to draw any attention to their efforts.

Duarte stretched his arms and looked up at the ceiling. When he finished, he looked at Lina. She had been telling him about the FBI and William Floyd.

"He's considered a domestic terrorist because of some past connections. When we first heard about him making contact with a known drug smuggler, we figured he was using the pot to finance something they were doing. Whatever he's up to, it's not at our direction."

"What would he be financing?"

"That's why they sent me instead of using a local agent. I'm supposed to find out what he's doing. He's on his own now. We need to rein him back in."

"Were you ever going to tell us your agenda?"

"No."

He looked at her.

"I wasn't authorized. You had no need to know."

Duarte nodded.

"I was only following orders." She gave him one of her crooked smiles, looking like a Picasso masterpiece.

"That line didn't work for the Nazis."

"The FBI is not the Gestapo either."

He went back to looking over the phone calls to and from Forrest Jessup's house. "These aren't normal toll records."

She smiled, "I used a different source to get them."

"What kind of source?"

"The NSA."

Duarte tried to keep the shock off his face. "Is that legal?"

"Do you care?"

He shrugged and went back to the records. "Here, look." He pushed the sheet of paper toward Lina. "He got one call." He looked closer. "Jesus, that was today? How'd they get these?"

She just smiled.

Duarte continued. "He got one call. It originated from Houston. See the eight-three-two area code."

Lina nodded. "So."

"Cal Linley thought his package had something to do with the oil business. Jessup used to be in the oil business and lived in Houston."

"Could be a coincidence."

"We need to start taking some chances. This may be a viable lead."

He pulled out his cell phone and dialed the number. After four rings, a man answered. "Hello?"

"Hey," said Duarte. "Where is this phone? I got a call from it."

"In the Santa Anna's Pit Stop off Brylan Street."

"In what town?"

"Jacinto City, Texas."

"Near Houston?"

"Yep."

"Thanks," Duarte said as he hung up.

He looked at a small map on the back of an advertisement booklet. It showed the Gulf Coast and East Texas. "If I were on my way to Houston, I'd go through Lafayette."

"Based on one call, you think he's in Houston?"

"It's where the information points."

"It's a stretch."

"You think they drove to Lafayette, then back to New Orleans?"

"I didn't say that."

Duarte said, "But what would be in Houston?"

Lina said, "A lot of Middle Easterners."

"That the FBI paranoia coming out?"

"No, it's just that there's not much else to Houston that might relate to a dirty bomb."

Duarte stared at the map as he considered their options.

47

ALEX DUARTE WOKE UP IN HIS NEW ORLEANS HOTEL ROOM CON-
fused and tired. He had dreamed of Agent Ruley and the case. In the
short hours he had slept, Ruley had come to him in some kind of uniform, in her business suit and in a bikini, and each time she had said the
same thing. "You fucked up. Now it's time for the first team to take the
field." In real life, she had been the model of professionalism and quiet
competence. He wished she had the confidence in him to let him work
with her, but he knew he was essentially on his own. He had made a
mess of things. He did not deserve to work with the team now trying to
find out what was on the *Flame of Panama* and where it had gone.

He sat up in bed and saw it was seven on the nose. He tried to clear
his head and decide on his next move. Then his Nextel rang.

"Duarte."

"Good morning, sunshine."

He could picture Alice Brainard's smiling, pretty face behind the voice.

"Good morning."

"Sounds like you had a rough night. Did the NEST people get up
with you?"

"Oh, we spoke."

"They were really nice to me."

"That's a shocker. How many dinner invitations did you get?"

She laughed, then said, "Two."

Duarte sat up in bed and said, "What are you doing now?"

"Just looking through newspapers and breaking news online."

"Anything on this mess?"

"Nope, not a word."

"That's something, then." He thought about it and said, "Can you look in the Lafayette paper?"

"What for?"

"I don't know. I'm just looking for something that might point us in the right direction. Anything on murders, racists, Nazis. Anything at all."

After a few seconds, she said, "Here's an article on a set of three murders in Lafayette. A U-Haul worker and a young couple."

"I knew about them."

"Let me take a look in some of the other regional papers."

Duarte heard her hum to herself while she scanned some pages.

"Here's a dead man found outside of Houston. They call it breaking news, and the cops are still on the scene. "

"Anything unusual?"

"The body was that of Charles Kilner of Daytona Beach. Wanted in Florida for possession of crack. What do you think?"

Duarte considered it. "Don't know. That's the first time I've heard his name." But it still sat in Duarte's brain. He went on to say, "I know you got the one blood sample. I'm sorry, it's just happening so fast I can't keep up with everything."

"So you're still working on the case?"

"Not as far as the Department of Justice is concerned, but we're still poking around."

"Who's 'we'?"

"Félix, Lina and I."

"Anything else I can help with?"

"You've already done enough." He paused, then added, "I do have a cigarette butt for a DNA sample."

"Send it on." She chuckled at her intentionally tired tone.

He said, "Alice, I can't tell you how much I appreciate the help. When I get home, I intend to spend a lot of time showing you how great I think you are."

There was another silence, then Alice asked, "When are you coming home?"

"As soon as I can. I promise."

He had never meant something as much in his life.

William "Ike" Floyd had all of his belongings together and was all set to meet Mr. Ortíz later that evening at a warehouse in Houston. Mr. Ortíz had e-mailed him that everything was in order. Ike wrote back that he had no problems. He smiled a little writing that because he *had* had some problems but solved them himself. Three problems that had been eliminated, and no one would ever know.

He walked into the Jacinto Arms' small front office. The same, tired-looking young woman who had sat there the last two days never even set down her *People* magazine. Her big, brown eyes just gazed up at him.

Ike smiled. "Just need to settle up."

She leaned up on the stool and tapped a few keys of her computer. "That'll be one seventy-seven fifty, Mr. Johnson." Her eyes stayed on the keyboard of the computer.

Ike dug out some money and laid down a hundred and eighty bucks. "You know where this address is?" He showed her the warehouse address Mr. Ortíz had given him.

She squinted at his handwriting on the small notepad. She hit a few keys on her computer and then typed in the address.

After half a minute, Ike heard a printer working hard. Then the girl silently pulled out a Mapquest map to the warehouse.

Ike smiled and started to thank her when he noticed a police car turn down the access road next to the hotel. He stepped over to the big window and saw several cars and one set of police lights down the road near where he had left Charlie.

"What's going on?" he asked the doe-eyed girl.

She shrugged. "Cops found a body."

"When?"

"Last night. You didn't hear the sirens?"

"No. I was out like a light."

"They already had a photo of the dead guy. Asked me if he was registered here."

"Was he?" Ike didn't think she had seen him with the Charlies.

"Nope. Only you and two families from Illinois. Cops talked to them. They talk to you?"

He shook his head, then said, "Thanks for the map."

The woman said, "You give back the Ryder truck?"

Ike nodded and said, "Yeah, all set. Have a good day." He walked out of the small office smiling, knowing that once he left here, there was no way to trace him. Nothing could stop him from his mission now.

Alex Duarte had spent forty minutes on the phone trying to track down a Houston ATF agent who knew about the murder Alice had told him about.

Now he had on a young man with a slight Spanish accent who had graduated from the ATF academy in Glynco, Georgia, a few months earlier.

The new agent explained all he knew about the body the cops had found with a bullet in his head.

The agent said, "Yeah, the cops think he had been hitchhiking, and a trucker or someone tossed him out of the vehicle, then shot him. Oh yeah, and he's got a Klan tattoo on his arm."

Duarte said, "Was the body found anywhere near a place called Santa Anna's Pit Stop?" He heard the agent ask someone else in the room.

"Yeah. Someone says it's across the street near an old motel." There was a pause and then, "How'd you know that?"

Duarte considered this, then said, "I've got some more checking to do, but I'll call you back tomorrow. Then I'll give you everything."

He hung up without waiting for an answer.

He was on to something.

Pelly felt his mouth drop open when they entered the cavernous warehouse in an industrial section of Houston. It felt like a giant aircraft hangar. The sheer space inside the metal walls and roof was mind-boggling. The stacks of crates and even full cargo containers were almost as impressive.

What surprised Pelly most was the fact that this giant industrial complex was owned by the Balast Corporation, which was a subsidiary of the Central Trust of the Americas, which was wholly owned by an unnamed individual whom Pelly knew to be Mr. Ortíz. Or, more accurately, his boss, Lázaro Staub.

Staub nudged him as someone hustled off to find the manager. "Not bad, eh, Pelly?"

"When did this happen?"

"We bought it three years ago as a transshipment point for goods going into and out of Central and South America."

"I never knew."

"No need to. This is completely legitimate. We never send loads here."

"But we'll use it for a nuclear bomb?"

Staub chuckled. "You worry too much. It'll only be here long enough for Dr. Tuznia to arm it. Then the professor will be paid, and he'll go back to whatever low-paid college job he has."

"What are we paying him with?"

"Cash."

"You have that much cash with you?"

"Of course not. I had it shipped here."

Pelly saw a heavyset middle-aged man hustle down the steps of a glass office in the corner of the giant hangar. Even though the whole facility was air-conditioned, Pelly could see this piglike man sweating as he bolted toward them.

He wheezed. "Mr. Ortíz. It's an honor to have you visit."

The man had the Texas twang Pelly had heard in the movies.

The colonel said, "Thank you indeed, Mr. Duplantis. I hope you were told I might be utilizing the warehouse this evening for an hour or so."

"Yes sir. We slow way down after five, so it's no problem."

Pelly caught the man's eyes darting to him and noticed the startled look on his face. Pelly didn't care. He was still upset over meeting, then losing, Lina and then finding out she was the FBI agent Colonel Staub had been working with all along.

Pelly ran his hand over his cheeks, and even he was a little surprised how hairy they had become. He gave the warehouse manager a slight snarl and smiled to himself when he saw the man flinch.

There was nothing to do now but wait for the Ukrainian nuclear scientist Dr. Tuznia. And for William Floyd.

48

IT WAS MIDAFTERNOON, AND ALEX DUARTE HAD PUSHED THE
tiny Cobalt he had rented to its limit of about seventy-five miles per
hour. It was the last car in the Hertz office at their hotel in New Orleans.
Now, Duarte, Lina Cirillo and Félix Baez were already past Lafayette,
well on the way to Houston.

Lina, in the passenger seat, said, "I gotta say that when you called me
this morning I never thought I'd be on my way to Houston this afternoon. I'll say one thing for you, you are decisive."

From the backseat, Félix Baez chimed in. "I still think this whole
thing sounds thin. The radioactive cargo. The lead. Our trip. I don't see
how this will help us find out who killed Gastlin." He sat amid a half-
empty case of Beck's beer.

Duarte didn't like that his partner had started drinking as soon as they
left at nine in the morning. He said, "I told you, I did some checking
with the Houston ATF. The phone call to Jessup's house from Jacinto
City near Houston is only a few hundred yards from where the body of
the Klan guy was found last night. It's too much of a coincidence."
Duarte didn't want Félix to think they had forgotten about his murdered

informant. "Besides, this might tie into Gastlin's death. If we're really trying to help find that cargo, then this is the right move. New Orleans is covered by the NEST team. They wouldn't be following up on something like this."

That answer seemed to satisfy Félix.

Duarte kept his foot pressed to the floor as the small engine whined and they moved closer to Houston.

Félix said, "Still wish we could've found a flight."

Lina shot back, "You wouldn't have been able to drink this much on a plane."

Duarte calmed them both down by adding, "If none of us are supposed to be on this case, it's best that there is no record of where we travel right now."

Thanks to the wonders of computer-generated maps, they found the crime scene a few minutes after exiting the interstate highway. A lone patrolman sat in his cruiser keeping the scene secure until a final search could be made.

The sun was low, but still provided enough light to see the area.

Duarte identified himself and asked a few questions. The patrolman only knew that someone walking his dogs had found the body and that it had been dead only a short while when it was found. No one had heard anything or seen anything.

Then they found the pay phone in front of the little store named Santa Anna's Pit Stop. It appeared to be little used.

As Duarte surveyed the area from the phone, he turned to Lina, who was doing the same thing. "The only thing I see worthwhile is the hotel."

Lina said, "The cops already checked it."

"But they didn't have a photo of who they were looking for."

Lina said, "Good point. Let's go."

They let Félix snooze in the backseat as they parked in front of the little office of the Jacinto Arms. The young woman on duty looked as happy to see Duarte and Lina as she would to see masked robbers.

"Sixty-five a night is the best I can do." She said it with no emotion, almost like a computer.

Duarte flashed his identification. "Just have a few questions."

"Already talked to the cops. Don't know nothin'."

Duarte held up the driver's license photo of William Floyd and set it on the small counter. "Was this guy a guest here?"

Her big brown eyes slowly tracked down to the photo, and then she actually seemed interested for a moment as she studied the photo. "Yeah, he was here."

"Can I see his registration?"

She fumbled with a few cards next to her computer and handed Duarte one.

He looked it over, but all it said was "Bill Johnson, New York."

Duarte said, "You get anything else from him? What he was driving? Any information could help."

She nodded and typed in a few keys. "He was drivin' a Ryder truck but said he was done with it. I didn't see what he left in." She handed a sheet of paper from the printer to Duarte. "But he asked for directions here. It was still in my Mapquest on the computer. No one else needed directions."

Duarte stared at not only the address where Floyd was headed but a concise map, too. Man, was modern police work getting easier.

Pelly and Staub had eaten a good meal at a chain sports bar a few miles from the warehouse. It was the first restaurant Pelly had seen in the area. Now they were sitting in a small office by one of the doors to the warehouse, waiting for both William Floyd and a professor from a nearby university whom the colonel had somehow heard would arm his nuclear weapon for a crateful of cash.

Pelly hadn't looked in the sealed crate yet, but knew the footlocker-size box did indeed have a lot of cash in it.

The manager, Mr. Duplantis, had been told to leave, and the colonel had been shown how to set the alarm. In the bright fluorescent light of the office, Pelly wondered if Colonel Staub ever worried about the moral consequences of his acts.

Pelly justified his own actions one of two ways: business reasons or teaching someone a lesson about making fun of him and his condition. But a nuclear weapon set off in the U.S.? That was going to kill a lot of people no matter where they sent it. He mulled over the prospect as he sat in silence with Colonel Staub.

After more than an hour, the bell for the front door rang. Pelly looked up at the colonel, who nodded for him to answer it.

Pelly walked past the big bay door that allowed trucks into the facility and went to the small door marked PUBLIC/ADMINISTRATIVE. He opened the hollow metal door, then froze for a second. This wasn't who he had expected.

Alice Brainard had gotten Scott Mahovich working right away on the samples that Alex had sent her. She had a growing sense of the importance of this case.

No one was saying that a nuclear weapon had come from the cargo ship, but they weren't taking any chances. No one at the sheriff's office had asked her about the FBI interview. She had just continued her work. But all she could think about was Alex Duarte and his safety.

Scott, the DNA scientist, popped into her office. "I'm working on these samples you gave me, but in light of the interest by the FBI, I'm going to have to report what I've been working on."

She cut her eyes up from the clothing she was searching for fibers. She was past the point of leading this guy on. She was not in a cute workout leotard. She didn't have on makeup or have her hair in anything but a ponytail.

She leveled her stare and said, "You will work those samples up, keep your mouth shut and stop bothering me."

"Or what?"

"Or I'll get up, march over to you and you'll have to tell all your deputy buddies how a girl kicked your ass."

He hesitated.

She stood up quickly, scooting the chair out from behind her.

He held up his hands. "Okay, okay. But when will it end? Am I going to just keep doing samples for your boyfriend?"

"Yes, until he doesn't need our help anymore." She went back to work, ignoring the tall, gangly man. She thought, That felt kinda good.

Pelly heard the colonel call out, "Who is it?"

Pelly smiled, knowing this was not what his employer expected either. He stood aside so the guest could enter. "Please, Dr. Tuznia, come in."

The forty-year-old woman did not look like a nuclear scientist. She was very well-built with dark hair that ran across her pretty face. If it weren't for her Slavic cheekbones, she would have looked Hispanic.

Her hips swayed in a very unprofessorlike way in her midlength skirt. Her large breasts jigged slightly as she walked. Pelly didn't even mind the fascinated look she gave him. As she stepped through the door, she ran a confident hand across his overgrown face and winked.

"That is impressive," she said, her accent sounding like a Russian spy in a cartoon. "Hypertrichosis?"

Pelly nodded.

"I like it." Her long straight nose was the perfect highlight to her high cheeks and white teeth.

Pelly didn't want to miss the look on the colonel's face as she walked into sight. This was the spitting image of every woman he had ever ordered whipped. She even looked like the secretary the colonel had beaten for using the phone for personal calls.

Staub stood inside the office, smiling at first, then, failing to hide his surprise, said, "Who the hell is this?"

The professor stepped into the office and offered her hand. "Marise Tuznia."

Staub took it, his mouth still agape. He didn't give his name.

"I thought Dr. Tuznia was a man."

"He was. That was my father. I am also a Ph.D. in physics. I could call my brother. But he is a doctor of dentistry."

Staub stood speechless.

Pelly enjoyed every second of it.

The professor said, "Now, Mr. Ortíz, do you have my money?"

Staub nodded. He stepped over to the crate he had had brought up to the office, popped opened a big folding knife and cut the seal around the top. Then he pried off the top of the crate.

Even Pelly had to catch his breath at the sight of the U.S. currency stacked inside the box.

The good-looking professor stooped down to the crate and ran her hand over a couple of rows of cash.

Staub said, "Do you wish to count it?"

She gazed down at the fifty-dollar bills and shook her head. "Even if you are off by a million or two, I'm still rich." She stood and said, "Where is the device?"

"On its way."

The professor looked at Pelly and smiled. "What could we do with the free time?"

Pelly smiled until he saw the look on his employer's face.

49

ALEX DUARTE NAVIGATED THE STREETS OF HOUSTON CAREFULLY
as they looked for the entrance to the industrial park that housed the
address about which the hotel clerk had said William Floyd had asked. It
was almost dark now, and traffic had quieted to the occasional big rig
tearing out on a late delivery.

They knew Floyd was no longer using a Ryder truck, but had no idea
what he was driving. What concerned Duarte most was, if they were done
with the truck, what had happened to whatever they were transporting?

"Wish I could've talked to Forrest Jessup. I think he would've known
what was going on and clued us in."

From the backseat, Félix mumbled, "This guy Floyd is the key. He'll
tell us if Ortíz killed Gastlin."

Duarte thought about that as he shot a look to Lina, who was giving
him a glare back. Had Félix lost track of what they were doing?

The DEA man said, "Lina knows this guy, and she hasn't given us shit.
That's the fucking FBI for you."

Lina turned to face him. "What's that mean?"

"You probably already know about this asshole, Ortíz."

"No one knows who he is. I only know Floyd, and I guarantee he didn't do anything in Panama."

"Why don't you tell us everything you know about Floyd, then?"

"Because he's a source, and some of it's not for release."

"We're not fucking reporters. What's that mean, 'not for release'? Does that mean it's classified?" His speech was slurred.

"Yeah, pretty much."

"You said you guys got him on a child pornography beef. What sort of information could he give that would get him out of that? I'd never make a deal with a child molester." Félix folded his arms like he had just had the last word.

Duarte was concerned about his friend's demeanor and insistence on focusing on a single murder when the possibility of some kind of dirty bomb was a very real threat.

Lina said, "Let's just say he knew some very dangerous people."

"When?" asked Félix.

"The mid-nineties."

"And you still keep track of him?"

"He's involved in the whole white-power scene. He knows militiamen, Klan guys, Nazis. His latest group of friends are the border-protection people. They've been preaching to him about the need to secure our borders before something catastrophic happens."

Félix said, "Not all terrorism comes from other countries. Look at Oklahoma City."

Duarte looked over at Lina, who was silent and obviously tired of this conversation.

Félix threw down another beer, settled into the backseat and started snoring almost immediately.

Staub steamed at the behavior of this Ukrainian whore who apparently had one, overpriced skill. He sent Pelly to help her drive her Audi in through the big bay door into the central receiving area. Pelly then had to retrieve a huge case out of the new car's trunk.

Staub said, "Nice car on a college professor's salary."

She looked up from watching Pelly set down the heavy case and said, "Expecting this windfall from you, I took out a loan."

"Do you care what we do with the device?"

"I will be relocating, so I do not care. I believe your cash will ensure a very nice life for me anywhere I choose. And I promise I never willingly chose Houston."

She turned to her case and patted Pelly on the back. "Thank you so much, Pelly." She smiled and leaned in close. Her breasts pressed against the young man's back.

Staub couldn't believe someone would show this kind of disrespect to him. Ignore him and slobber over Pelly. He felt the blood rush to his face as he couldn't escape the image of his father and María.

He wouldn't let that happen again. Not with this arrogant bitch.

He worked to control his voice. "Pelly."

"Yes, boss?"

"Why don't you start cruising the area looking for our friend Mr. Floyd?"

"You don't think he can find the place?"

"I'll be surprised if he can find Houston."

"Yeah, sure, boss." Pelly smiled and nodded to the female professor as she started to set up some tools and supplies.

William "Ike" Floyd had trouble reading the street signs in this dark and dirty part of town. The lights all seemed to be in front of the big warehouses and nowhere near the street signs. He had a map from the slow girl at the Jacinto Arms, but it didn't seem to be helping him as he puttered up and down streets looking for the specific address.

The Ford pickup truck drove smoothly and attracted a lot less attention than the big rental truck.

It was just late enough that he couldn't find anyone to ask directions of either.

Finally he got a glimpse of the sign that looked like his street. He turned and slowed immediately when he saw the length of it and the number of giant warehouses lining both sides of the extra-wide road.

In the first parking lot, a small car sat under one of the parking lot's streetlights. A man stood outside the driver's door, looking down the street, too.

Ike pulled into the lot, hoping the man might have a better idea of where the address might be.

Ike rolled his window down as he approach the tall, fit-looking man with dark hair who was wearing a light-colored windbreaker.

"Excuse me," said Ike.

The man stepped closer to him and then seemed to stare for a moment.

Ike was startled when the man reached in the open window and grabbed him by the shoulder with a grip that stunned him.

The man said, "Get out of the car, William."

Colonel Lázaro Staub silently watched as Professor Tuznia carefully laid out tools from the large case she had retrieved from her Audi. The suitcaselike box opened out into trays, and she looked like she was preparing for surgery. He watched her slightly large bottom as it swayed, and then occasionally, when she turned, he'd catch a glimpse of her ample breasts. She reminded him of María Ortíz from his childhood more than any woman in Panama he had ever beaten. She hummed some unfamiliar tune as she stopped to wipe down a mirrorlike device.

Staub used his most impressive voice in his best English. "And what would a physicist use that for?" He smiled and stepped toward her.

She didn't even turn around to face him. "You would not understand."

Staub felt his left eye twitch. Who the hell did she think she was?

Then the professor stood straight and faced him. "Where did Pelly go?"

"Don't worry where he went. I am the one who hired you."

"And he is the one with nice legs and that wild, furry face." She smiled and placed one of her small hands over her chest.

Staub did not like the implication. Was this whore already thinking of cheating on him? He felt that familiar rage start to build in him. It didn't matter if he was not in Panama. He still had power. The power to cripple the U.S. She shouldn't speak to him like that. He looked at her more closely. How could a professional dress like that? The low-cut top, her muscled calves showing from under her skirt. His eye shifted into overdrive. He pulled out a cigarette and started to light it.

The professor didn't turn around, but, as if she had eyes in the back of her head, said, "Do not smoke."

He froze and stared at her shapely back. "I own this entire complex. You do not presume to tell me what to do."

"I'll tell you not to smoke while I am working, or you can find someone else." She stood and turned, leveling her dark, oval eyes at him. "Someone else familiar enough with these things to arm your weapon?"

He remained quiet and leaned back against the outside of the office, the unlighted cigarette still in his mouth. He glared at the professor, who had gone back to her precious tools. He picked up a thick yardstick that was lying against the wall where he was leaning. He flipped it between his hands, the whole time focusing his anger on the busy woman in front of him. He stood up and started to pace, occasionally coming close to the professor, the entire time imagining what it would be like to put the bitch in her place. Then, without even realizing it, as he walked past her, he swung the yardstick and broke it over her backside.

She flinched and stood up, spinning as she did. "You struck me."

He stared at her, the broken yardstick in his hands.

She said, "Are you crazy?" She just looked at him. "You are. You're insane."

Before he could control it, he felt himself take a step and his hands start to move on their own. "You think I'm crazy." He had his hands around her throat before she could react. He dropped his right hand and grasped the top of her blouse and yanked. The cotton top ripped off, revealing a tight black bra and plenty of breast. He hooked a finger in the front of the bra and pulled violently, popping the clasp and pulling it mostly off her shoulder.

She stood defiantly, no fear in her eyes. What had she been through before coming to the land of the free?

His right hand joined his left around her throat. He slowly applied the pressure as he ignored her slaps and clawing. Then, as her oxygen was cut off, little by little he saw fear start to spread onto her face. He enjoyed the look so much, he forgot how vitally he needed her special talents.

50

DUARTE USED HIS NATURAL SPEED AND DECISIVENESS TO REACH
William Floyd before he could react. The ATF agent didn't even bother
to draw his pistol. He had his right hand through the open window of
the pickup truck and on Floyd's shoulder before Floyd could clearly see
who it was assaulting him. With a quick squeeze on the truck's door and
the right pressure on his shoulder, Duarte had "Ike" Floyd on the
ground and immediately bitching about the treatment.

He just hoped Ike was the guy with the answers. As he patted him
down roughly while holding his shoulder and pinning the larger man to
the ground, he found a SIG-Sauer .380 tucked in the prone man's waistband. He tilted him and yanked out the pistol.

"We got a lot to talk about."

"Who the hell are you?"

Lina Cirillo had hardly noticed the pickup truck that pulled alongside their little rental Cobalt before Alex Duarte had sprung from
the shoebox of a car and yanked the driver out of the truck. Félix Baez

never stirred from his deep sleep in the backseat of the small car. She jumped out without waking him.

Now she had her pistol in her hand and rounded the far side of the truck to see Duarte holding down a larger man. As she got closer, her stomach tightened as she realized the man on the ground was William "Ike" Floyd.

Lina came to a stop in front of them and said, "How'd you subdue him so quickly?"

Duarte looked up. "He surprised me; I just reacted." He eased his hold on the prone man and then helped him to a sitting position. "Now we find out what's going on."

She saw the recognition in Floyd's face as he looked up at her. His eyes opened wide as she thought about her options.

Duarte said, "Okay, tell us what you brought out of New Orleans."

Ike looked up at Lina. "Why? The FBI never listened to me before."

Lina heard his bitterness and thought that it might even be justified.

Duarte was more confused. "What's that mean?"

Lina cut in. "Don't worry about it."

Duarte twisted his head to glare at her. "You're still going to keep your source and his information from us? After all we've done?"

"It's not that simple. We . . ." She stopped when she saw Duarte cock his head and stop paying any attention to her at all. Lina said, "What is it?"

"We're not alone."

"Félix is probably awake."

Duarte was clear in his tone. "No, it's someone else."

Pelly saw the cars stopped under the light in another warehouse's parking lot. His police training and instinct told him to be very careful and not let anyone see his car. There were no other vehicles in the neighborhood this time of night. He pulled the Impala off the road into the small lot of a business wedged in between two large warehouse complexes.

Even from a distance he could see someone move quickly to pull a man from a pickup truck. He left his car, checked his little Beretta and darted closer to the parked cars. Finding cover in the darkness and shrubs, he easily covered the distance between his car and the truck.

He settled near a bush where he could clearly see the two men who were now on the ground.

One was holding the other down.

Then Pelly saw the woman, and it only took a second for him to realize it was Lina, the FBI agent who had seen him clean-shaven. He looked at the men more closely, and then saw the man being subdued was Ike Floyd. What happened to the Ryder rental truck? Whose pickup truck was that?

He lowered his head and started to move to a better position to decide if he had to take action. He scurried along a low line of planted shrubs away from the two parked vehicles to approach at a different angle. He crept closer now, using the cars to cover his approach. The downside was that he lost sight of the people at the cars, too.

Alongside the Cobalt, he started to reach for his Beretta as he peeked around the corner of the car toward the big pickup truck.

The first thing he saw was the barrel of a Glock right in front of his face. And heard a man say, "Don't move."

ALEX DUARTE HAD SENSED THE FIGURE MOVING CLOSER TO THE car and then took a guess at which end of the vehicle the intruder would try to use for cover. It was the same thing he would've done. He had his Glock out and waiting as a shadow-covered face came into view.

Duarte said, "Don't move." Not a shout, just a simple command.

In a blur, he saw a movement, and, before he could react, felt the gun fly from his hand and heard it chatter on the ground.

In an instant, he saw the flash of a pistol and, using his own considerable speed, swatted it from the man's hand. He felt a fist as he instinctively bobbed his head and fended off the blow with his right hand. Duarte rolled to one side, and his attacker moved in the opposite direction so they could assess one another.

Then, as he focused on the man's face for the first time and the light from the streetlight fell on him, Duarte simply said, "You."

The man, equally astonished, said, "You."

The hairy first mate of the *Flame of Panama* recognized Duarte, too.

Duarte let a small smile spread across his face. He'd been waiting to meet this guy.

The man said, "What's so funny?" He had a noticeable Spanish accent. Duarte said, "You'll find out."

"Or maybe you'll be surprised." The hairy man moved to his left, alert and ready for action. "I like your moves. You're quick and precise."

"You're pretty quick yourself."

"I work at it."

Duarte smiled a little more. "Me, too." Then, as the man stood, Duarte saw the first front kick blast toward him. He blocked it hard and followed up with a round kick to the man's ribs. He took most of the blow but managed a hard elbow into Duarte as he threw the kick.

They tumbled toward each other and then over a low row of shrubs, each managing to throw a punch or kick along the way until they were well in front of the parked truck, both men panting and battered a little.

Duarte realized he was in a fight with the first guy that was as well trained and in as good a shape as himself. He'd always liked the advantage, and now knew what it was like to face someone who prepared for fights as hard as he did. This was not a Bruce Willis movie. This was a good old-fashioned street fight.

Duarte hoped the fight might wake up Félix in the parked Cobalt. At least he might distract this guy long enough for Duarte to regain the advantage. Lina was busy with Floyd.

They moved from side to side, and then the hairy man backed up, a little at a time, the whole way feinting with punches and kicks. Duarte didn't realize what he had been planning until it was too late. The first mate had backed to his pistol, which had come to rest way back in this part of the parking lot, twenty feet from their first encounter.

Duarte tried to spring onto the man, but the latter was far too quick, reaching down and covering Duarte with the small handgun.

The hairy man took a second to catch his breath and said, "Sorry, I wish we had time to finish this. You're the biggest challenge I've ever faced."

Duarte kept his eyes on the man, looking for a weakness or opening. The man had retreated just far enough to ensure his ability to hold Duarte at bay. He obviously knew what he was doing, and now Duarte wondered how he could've let this killer gain the advantage. All he knew was that this guy wouldn't hesitate to kill him or Lina.

William "Ike" Floyd was scared and shaking as the FBI chick, Lina, leaned on him with that autopistol of hers screwed into his right ear. She didn't seem nervous, and he had no idea what they had planned for him.

Lina leaned in close to him and said, "Who's out there?"

"Don't know. Probably Pelly," he panted.

"Who?" The name had a ring to it.

"Pelly. He works for Mr. Ortíz." His voice cracked as he spoke.

That caught all of her attention. "Ortíz is here?"

"I think so. I haven't seen him yet."

Lina shifted her weight and moved away from him slightly. Then she said, "Sorry, Ike, I can't have you blabbing about things."

He sensed a tension in her hand and blurted out, "You can't just kill me, you're an FBI agent."

"I have to kill you *because* I'm an FBI agent."

"I won't tell, I promise. I've never told anyone."

The FBI agent seemed to tense, and Ike knew what was coming. He involuntarily squeezed his eyes shut and hoped he wouldn't pee in his jeans as he waited for the imminent blast from the pistol.

Duarte walked well in front of the first mate and didn't even bother to raise his hands. The guy already knew what to expect from Duarte and was pretty fast himself. He still hoped Félix would enter the fray and wondered what Lina would do when she saw them. The first mate marched him directly toward Lina and William Floyd, and he could just make out their forms as he moved forward.

Then Duarte stopped as he saw Lina and realized she had her gun to Floyd's head. He was lying on his side with his eyes squeezed closed, and Lina looked ready to execute him. At first he thought it might be an interrogation tactic, but then he realized she intended to pull the trigger.

Behind him, in an amazingly calm voice, the first mate said, "Don't do it."

Lina's head snapped up, and she hesitated about where to point her pistol.

The first mate said, "Shoot him, Lina, and I'll shoot your friend here."

Duarte was startled. How did this guy know Lina's name?

Lina looked at them and slowly lowered her pistol. Duarte felt a shove from behind and moved forward in a daze of confusion.

He sat across from Lina as the first mate, whose name was Pelly, had instructed. Duarte's head hurt from all the questions he had. He looked over at William Floyd, who seemed to cower next to Lina. She kept the gun to his temple in an effort to discourage Pelly from shooting Duarte.

Lina had just explained her brief meeting with Pelly in a bar.

Pelly rubbed his furry face and said to Lina, "You saw me clean-shaven. Quite the difference, no?"

Her dark eyes stared at the simian-like man.

Duarte said, "Lina, don't give up your gun. I've seen this guy's work. He's not gonna let us go."

Pelly gave him an odd look. "What work have you seen of mine?"

"The U-Haul mechanic."

"Oh, yeah, that was me."

"The young couple in Lafayette."

Pelly tilted his head. "That was my friend Ike's work."

William Floyd kept looking at the asphalt, apparently not too proud of shooting the young people. Ike mumbled. "What's it matter now? Yeah, I did it." His eyes occasionally darting to the gun barrel near his head.

Duarte continued. "Cal Linley in New Orleans, and I almost had you at Forrest Jessup's house in Mississippi."

Pelly shook his head. "I had nothing to do with those men. I don't even know who they are."

Ike's head snapped up. "Cal and President Jessup are dead?"

Duarte had always had some problems reading people. It just wasn't one of his strengths. But Pelly had admitted to some killings. Duarte didn't get the sense that either of these two were lying about other murders.

Duarte looked at Ike and asked, "What did you guys bring in?"

"What do I have to bargain with if I tell you?"

Duarte didn't know why he might want to bargain. He tried to look like he was focusing on Ike, but his eyes scanned down to his own pistol tucked in Pelly's belt. The first mate squatted just far enough away. He knew his tactics.

Duarte thought he saw a slight nod from Pelly, then Ike threw his weight toward Lina, knocking her off balance.

Duarte started to move, but felt the barrel of the Beretta against his neck.

Across from him, Ike now had the advantage, as he used his much greater size to wrench the gun away from Lina. He backed away, holding up the small automatic.

He looked at Duarte and said, "Guess I don't need to bargain now. We brought in a nuclear weapon."

ALEX DUARTE SHIFTED HIS WEIGHT, TRYING TO KEEP LINA FROM cutting off the blood flow to his legs in case he had the chance to act. Pelly had used Duarte's handcuffs to secure his arms around Lina in a bear hug in the bench seat of the F-150 pickup truck, tucked between William "Ike" Floyd and Pelly, who kept his Beretta in his hand.

They had managed to leave the area without waking Félix. His captors never even realized he was in the car. Duarte wanted to keep his DEA friend out of this now. He would've just been another hostage. Duarte figured that maybe Félix was just too drunk to wake up. In any event, no one noticed the sleeping DEA man.

What really concerned him now was the idea that the entire dope deal had been a cover to smuggle in a nuclear weapon and he had fallen for it every step of the way. The real questions he had now focused on Ike's relationship to the FBI and who had killed Cal Linley and Forrest Jessup.

Duarte said, "So, Lina, you two met in a bar?"

Pelly snorted.

Lina turned her head to the hairy man. "I didn't peg you as a killer in that little disco."

"Nor did I guess your occupation." He cut his eyes to Duarte to make sure he was secure and not trying some diversion. That impressed Duarte. This guy was sharp.

Then Pelly said, "Lina, why were you about to shoot my friend Ike back there?"

William "Ike" Floyd said, "I'll tell you why."

Duarte could feel Lina tense on his lap.

Pelly said, "Please, Ike, tell us." He looked like he was enjoying this.

Ike said, "Because the FBI doesn't want people to know I'm the third man at Oklahoma City."

Duarte had heard the theory that a third man—besides Timothy McVeigh and Terry Nichols—who worked for the FBI had walked away from the bombing, but it was always espoused by some gun nut or militia creep. Occasionally a cop would believe it, too, but Duarte had always dismissed it as a fantasy of the fringe groups.

Ike continued, "I told them about the plot. They had me by the short hairs, and I did my job. I told them what was happening, and no one believed me until it was too late." He sounded like he might cry he was so upset. "I couldn't tell my friends I was involved, because then the FBI woulda called me a . . ."

Duarte finished his sentence. "A child molester."

Ike snapped his head toward the ATF agent. "Yeah, exactly."

It made too much sense to be a lie, and Lina's silence confirmed it for Duarte.

Duarte leaned forward slightly and said to the FBI agent, "You were never sent to help us. You were sent to keep him quiet."

She remained silent.

Duarte felt like an idiot.

Ike felt some sort of release to finally say out loud what he had done. Sure, the FBI knew it, but they had scared him into silence years before. He never realized how serious they were until this bitch, Lina, was about to kill him to keep him quiet.

He had been mesmerized by the news following the blast when the news anchors had blabbed on and on about John Doe #2. After Timothy McVeigh had been arrested by an Oklahoma state trooper, everyone had seemed to focus on that numbskull. No one ever asked how smart he was. Sure, he was crazy, as crazy as anyone Ike had ever met, but he was a dumb-ass. So was his buddy Terry Nichols. Once those two were fingered, no one asked if anyone else was involved, and "John Doe #2," Ike, had faded from the public consciousness.

Over the years, so had the bombing. After 9/11, no one seemed to care about Oklahoma City. Middle Easterners were all anyone talked about.

Now, years after he had anguished about working with the FBI, he had said it out loud: He was John Doe #2.

But that didn't mean he was sold on Mr. Ortíz's crazy-assed idea.

Pelly liked hearing other people's secrets come out. He had no idea that Ike had such an interesting history. The whole story sounded like one of Colonel Staub's elaborate plans.

As they approached the big warehouse, Pelly said to Ike, "You did well getting such a low-profile truck."

Ike just nodded.

Once the truck stopped, Pelly slipped out and orchestrated the two federal agents' exit from the high vehicle. He allowed Lina to slip out of the embrace, leaving Duarte handcuffed in front. He nodded toward the door, and everyone started shuffling that way.

As they entered the large area where the professor's vehicle was parked inside by the small glass office, Pelly stopped and stared. He couldn't believe it. In front of him stood Colonel Staub standing over the still, naked body of Professor Tuznia. She was draped over her case of tools, her large breasts hanging to one side as her head lolled down toward the floor. Her dark eyes were still wide open.

Colonel Staub looked up at Pelly and his captive, but said only, "Make no comment. I have already arranged for an alternative."

"So fast?" asked Pelly.

"Money can do wonders." He cut his eyes to Duarte and Lina. "And we can deal with these two at the same time." He smiled at their expressions. "Yes, my young friends. Nothing is ever as it appears." He walked toward them. "I could ask how you found us, but it does not matter now." He winked at Lina.

Lina mumbled, "Asshole."

Colonel Staub stepped closer, standing next to the small office. "I should have a little extra time to deal with you, Lina." He looked at Pelly. "Where is the third member of your little group? The DEA man."

Pelly answered, "I didn't see him. These two had Ike in a parking lot down the road."

Suddenly, the glass to the office shattered, at the same time the thunder of a gunshot echoed through the giant metal structure.

Pelly ducked, drew his Beretta and scanned the large storage area. There were several doors an assailant could've entered. He raised his pistol, seeking a target.

He glanced at his prisoners and was shocked to see that Duarte had managed to vanish in that second of distraction. Lina still stood, shocked, next to Colonel Staub.

The colonel looked at Pelly and said, "Take the bomb somewhere safe. You know what to do. Make it quick."

Pelly fired two shots as he moved. He grabbed Ike's arm and dragged him toward the door, too. He heard return fire, but thought it was directed more toward the colonel.

In a matter of seconds, he and Ike had the truck with the bomb and were headed down the street.

53

ONCE ALEX DUARTE HEARD THE FIRST SHOT, HE ACTED WITHOUT hesitation, ducking slightly and running first to the side, as Pelly focused his attention toward the shooter, then back into the rows of stacked merchandise. The tall shelves allowed him to disappear in a matter of seconds.

He heard a few more shots and some return fire as he turned down one row toward the sound of the shots. He knew it was Félix Baez. No one could've slept through that racket back at the truck. He'd really used his head, following the pickup truck back to the warehouse.

"Félix," shouted Duarte.

"Here," came one quick response, but it was enough, and Duarte found his friend.

Félix crouched behind a shelf. "I was hoping Lina would make a break, too. Now we gotta get her back." He turned and fumbled with his DEA identification, where, like all good cops, he had an extra hand-cuff key secured. He had Duarte free quickly.

Félix said, "The hairy guy and Floyd just ducked out the front door."

Duarte peeked down the aisle and saw Staub with a gun to Lina's head.

Félix said again, "Let's get Lina."

Duarte shook his head. It hurt to say it, but he did. "We need the other two."

"No way they're more important than Lina."

"They have a nuclear weapon in that truck."

Félix just stared at him and said, "The back door is this way." They both scurried toward it, then barreled out the door and into the Cobalt.

As Duarte started the car, Félix said, "We need backup."

Duarte said, "He took my cell. Where's yours?" He stomped on the gas, just seeing the taillight of the truck as it took a corner a few blocks away. The little car bounced and rattled over a curb and onto the street.

Félix said, "My phone is lost in this mess in the backseat."

Duarte could hear him sift through old newspapers and food wrappers as he searched for his Nextel.

Félix called out over his shoulder as he looked in the back, "Who was the dead, naked woman?"

"My guess is she could activate the bomb." He bumped over railroad tracks, still having the truck in sight. They tried to close but the little whining engine couldn't do it. They stayed in sight several more minutes as the truck weaved in and out of the light traffic, leading them farther and farther from the warehouse and Lina. Duarte's stomach hurt just thinking of her back there with Staub. But they had to find the truck.

"Staub killed Gastlin, didn't he?"

"Yeah."

Félix was silent as he sat forward without his phone, simmering. Duarte could see his face change color as the DEA man thought about the Panamanian police colonel.

They automatically fell into a grid search, hoping to catch a glimpse of the truck or at least see a cop he could hail for help.

Duarte turned his head to his friend and said calmly, "Félix, look for your phone again. We need to get help." He hoped it might distract the DEA man as well as help them as their situation grew more desperate.

Then Duarte saw Pelly's plan in his head. He slammed on the brakes, throwing the unprepared Félix hard into the dash.

Félix cursed then said, "What? What is it?"

Duarte started to back up the small car to turn it around and said, "Staub said he had a replacement for the dead woman. A replacement to arm the weapon. This was a trick. They're going back to the warehouse."

Pelly had no idea why the colonel would kill the pretty Ukrainian scientist other than her looks. It was done, so it no longer mattered. He had worked for the colonel so long that he knew what the man thought in certain situations. He knew his job was to draw Duarte and his partner away from the warehouse so that he could bring the bomb back and have the new scientist arm it. He had even had to slow down a couple of times so the little Cobalt driven by Duarte would catch up enough to keep him interested. Then, when he had him near the other side of the city, Pelly lost him for good and returned, using a good, direct route he had memorized on his trek away from the warehouse.

The entire ride back, Ike seemed like a different man. Quiet and nervous, he only looked up occasionally. He seemed disturbed by Lina and her actions.

Pelly gained respect for her. Not only was she beautiful, she was willing to take drastic steps as part of her duties. She was great. He wondered if he would ever get to see her again when all this unpleasantness was finished.

Staub raised the garage door as soon as Pelly drove the truck back into the lot. He spun it around and backed into the bay next to poor Professor Tuznia's Audi. He popped out of the pickup and felt some relief when he saw Lina, unharmed and tied to a chair next to the office door. A boney, balding, nervous man was next to her, smoking a cigarette. Obviously the new professor.

As Pelly walked behind the Audi, he noticed the trunk lid was open and the naked body of Professor Tuznia lay curled in the clean, empty trunk. The colonel had not even bothered to close her eyes. Pelly took a second and pushed down her eyelids.

Colonel Staub said, "Quickly, Pelly, take Ike and uncrate the front of the weapon. We have little time to waste."

The skeletal, balding man paced back and forth in front of the office, then changed his direction and headed toward them near the truck.

With Ike's massive shoulders and arms, they easily slid the crate back onto the tailgate. Pelly used a crowbar from a nearby shelf to pry open the wooden face of the crate.

The colonel joined them as the bald man reached in and swept away some packing straw. He had apparently already discussed with the scientist what was needed and shown him the cash.

The man worked amazingly fast, fastening wires and then splicing in his own plug. The plug fit into the back of a cell phone. The man taped the phone next to the open space on the bomb where the wires came out.

The man looked up at Staub. "When you want to detonate, call number of phone."

Pelly thought the man sounded German, with his sharp sounds and Ws changed to Vs.

Staub looked at a small sheet of paper. "I have the number."

The bald man said, "On the fourth ring, it will answer automatically. Press the numbers one, two, three, four, and that will trigger the mechanism. It will then initiate the first reaction that will then start the fissionable material."

Staub smiled. "How big will the blast be?"

"This is a warhead that would've been launched by a Soviet SS-18 missile. Modified, of course. Should be very good explosion. The tamper material is U-235. This surrounds the core. It should yield ten full kilotons. Enough."

The man didn't look remorseful or proud to Pelly. He was just another guy trying to make a buck off his skills.

"And this phone will detonate it anywhere?"

"Anywhere Nextel has service, so not too many places, but it should work if it has a signal."

"Excellent," said Staub as he motioned for Pelly and Ike to help shove the whole crate back into the truck. Then Staub looked at Ike and said, "Start driving."

The wide man said, "Now?"

"Of course now."

"Where?"

The colonel looked at him like he was an idiot. "Nellis Air Force Base, Nevada."

"Where in the hell is that?"

He handed him an envelope. "Here is a map, and a number to call when the bomb is in position."

"Why there?"

"It is the perfect target. Symbolic, military and devastating."

Ike moaned, "It'll take me more than a day just to drive there."

"We have time. I will not call the number until you say the truck is in position and you are a safe distance away."

Ike just stared at the colonel and swallowed hard.

The colonel raised his voice. "No delays. Get started, now."

Pelly and Colonel Staub watched as Ike shuffled over to the pickup truck, closed the tailgate on the open bomb, crawled into the driver's seat and slowly pulled the truck out as Staub used a remote to open the big door. Pelly could tell Ike was a beaten man.

Pelly waved to his American comrade.

Ike gave him a dispirited nod back.

The colonel said, "Good luck, Ike. You will be a hero in the new America."

Ike didn't look thrilled with his potential status as hero. He backed into the lot and paused. Then, after about thirty seconds he pulled onto the street and headed toward downtown Houston.

Staub turned back toward the office. He called over his shoulder, "Thank you, Professor. Here is your cash." He gestured toward the crate now at the door of the office.

The bald man said, "I will count."

"As you wish." Staub placed his phone and a few things from his pocket on a shelf outside the office, then turned toward Lina, who had been following the tall colonel with her eyes every time he moved.

Pelly felt a twinge of anxiety the way the colonel looked at Lina and said, "Now to tie up loose ends."

Duarte felt sure they had been gone too long on their wild-goose chase when he found the street to the warehouse again. As he came down the street, he saw a vehicle, then said, "Unbelievable. It's the truck."

Félix said, "You gotta leave me off. I'll get Lina."

Duarte didn't answer.

"I can call in help from the office phone. C'mon, just slow down. I'll jump."

Duarte nodded, watching the truck turn the first corner. He slowed the small Chevy Cobalt as Félix opened his door and sprang out onto the street. He wasn't graceful as he lost his balance and tumbled toward the curb, but Duarte relaxed a little when he looked in the rearview mirror and saw his friend struggle to his feet and start loping toward the warehouse.

After turning the corner, Duarte saw the truck moving at a reasonable speed and punched the gas to close the distance. He had no gun, so he knew he'd have to ram the truck to disable it. He was prepared to do anything and sacrifice anything to keep a nuclear weapon that he had allowed into the country from being detonated.

PELLY WATCHED AS THE BALD PROFESSOR QUICKLY COUNTED the stacks of cash in the box. He may have been a physicist, but he wouldn't finish hand-counting the crate full of cash until early morning. He'd have to count a sample then get moving. Pelly wouldn't mind sending the bald man on his way as broke as when he arrived. That was cash that could be used to expand the business. Business that would probably suffer after the colonel made the call to the trigger phone.

The bald man looked up at Pelly, apparently noticing his face for the first time. He flinched and said, "I need help getting this to my car."

It was an order, not a request. Pelly said, "It'll cost you a million bucks."

The professor stared at him.

"That's only about ten of the stacks of hundreds. You can afford it."

"I could hire a real monkey for a lot less." The man had no humor in his voice, but it didn't matter. The comment was all Pelly needed.

He turned toward the man, who had foolishly gone back to counting his cash. He shifted his Beretta for a fast draw, although right now he didn't plan to use it.

As he took a step toward the man, he said, "You think that's funny, Adolf?"

Duarte even took his foot off the gas as he came closer to the truck. Whoever was driving didn't seem to be paying any attention at all and didn't know there was a car coming up behind him. Duarte backed off as he saw a main road coming up in the distance. Traffic would give him better cover and maybe a chance to get some help.

The little Cobalt dropped back and its engine lost the constant whine that Duarte was becoming accustomed to.

The truck came to a stop at the intersection and lingered. Duarte eased up behind the truck and caught a glimpse of William "Ike" Floyd in the driver's seat. His hangdog expression and blank stare explained why he had not moved, even though there was no oncoming traffic.

Duarte made some quick calculations as to his chances of jumping out of his car and grabbing Floyd before he drove off. But he waited, wondering why Floyd was hesitating.

He had to work on the assumption that the bomb was functional and that it was still in the back of the pickup truck with the small camper top.

He considered his options as the truck slowly pulled onto the larger road.

Pelly stepped closer to the professor hunched over the box of cash. Before he threw the first punch, he knew what would hurt the man the most.

Pelly said, "Hey, look at me."

The man turned his head to look up at the standing Pelly.

Pelly drew the pistol, placed it on the man's forehead, pulled back the hammer and said, "Get out. Right now."

"But my money."

"Will do you no good in hell." Pelly tensed his finger, and the man sprang to his feet and darted toward the outside door. A smile crept across his face as he stepped out of the office and back into the warehouse.

Then Pelly heard the colonel's voice rise. He turned to see his boss leaning in toward the bound Lina and cursing at the FBI agent. He bent in close to her and placed a hand on her forearm, squeezing and speaking into her ear.

Pelly said, "Hey, boss, we need to go."

The colonel didn't turn to look at him, but said, "Not yet, Pelly. I have to teach this whore a lesson."

Pelly had heard Colonel Staub make similar comments over the years, always to disastrous effects on the women he was speaking to. Pelly felt his stomach tighten as he tried to determine what, exactly, he was feeling. Was this remorse? His hand slipped onto the handle of the Beretta and said again, "We have to go, boss."

Staub ignored him, still focusing on Lina. He whipped out the small automatic pistol he had in his belt and swung it in a wide arc, striking Lina in the temple. Her head lolled to the other side as the colonel lined up for his follow-through.

Pelly shouted, "Wait."

It was just loud enough for the colonel to look up.

He looked as shocked as Pelly felt. Somehow, without conscious thought, Pelly had drawn his gun and had it pointed at his boss.

The light traffic on the four-lane street made keeping the big F-150 pickup truck in sight easy.

Duarte kept one car in between them as he became more anxious about stopping William Floyd before he managed to get to an interstate. He had pulled alongside the truck twice. The driver's window was open and Floyd looked like he was extremely preoccupied, running his hand over his face and then hanging his head out the window slightly, trying to get air.

Duarte considered this and decided to use it to his advantage and act.

The stoplight ahead of them changed to yellow. There was a Buick in front of Floyd's truck and no one on the side. This was his chance.

The light turned red, and traffic on the cross street started to move forward. There was nowhere for the pickup to go. Duarte stopped the little Cobalt slightly behind the big truck, then, without any hesitation, hopped out of the small car, darted to the side of the truck and moved up toward the driver's door silently. It was a tactic he and other cops had used before but always with a gun drawn. This was too big to risk Floyd getting away. Even if he did shoot Duarte, it would attract police attention. Anything to get the word out.

He grabbed the outside door handle with his left hand and yanked, feeling the door swing wide immediately.

No other drivers even noticed the quick action.

He heard Floyd say, "What the hell?"

But that was all he got out before Duarte swung a right elbow hard into the big racist's face. Blood spouted from his crushed nose and split lip as Duarte stepped up on a running board and kicked him hard to the other side of the wide truck cab. Duarte threw an extra kick into the big man's head to daze him, but it bounced hard off the opposite door, and he slid off the bench seat onto the floorboard. Maybe it was a gratuitous strike.

Félix Baez was shaky from jumping out of Duarte's car. He knew the ATF man was serious about catching the truck but had thought he'd slow down a little more. He had stood up immediately and started moving toward the giant storage complex. He slipped in through the door he had pried open earlier. As soon as he was inside, he knew exactly where to head and what to do.

He had his pistol in his hand and ducked a little as he scurried toward the bright overhead lights in front of the glass office he had shot up earlier.

His right knee throbbed from his fall and tumble. His arm still hurt from his mishap.

As he came up the aisle, he saw the slender, fit-looking, hairy first mate. There was something else familiar about him that was obscured in the hair that seemed to coat his entire upper body. As he stopped to survey the area, it hit him. That was the Panamanian security officer who'd checked his identification the first time he met Colonel Staub.

Félix was exposed and couldn't see as well as he wanted from this position. He backed away and started climbing the shelves so he would have the high ground to fight from. He negotiated several large boxes on his way up, then crawled through some toasters on pallets to end up at the front of the shelf and overlooking the whole office area.

He saw the hairy guy looking toward Staub, who was standing next to Lina. The FBI agent's head hung to one side.

That son of a bitch had to pay. Even though the hairy guy had a pistol in his hand, Félix lined up his shot on Staub. He had to make sure Lina was safe before he could turn his attention to the hairy guy.

Félix drew a deep breath and checked the scene once more. The hairy guy seemed to be covering Lina, too, but was too far away from her and had Staub between him and Lina. Félix sighted in on Staub and slowly let out his breath.

55

COLONEL LÁZARO STAUB WAS AT A LOSS. HE SAW HIS LONGTIME assistant, Pelly, pointing a Beretta at him, but he couldn't believe it. Had he gone mad?

Next to him, Lina shook her head to clear it, then she, too, was transfixed by Pelly and the barrel of the small pistol.

Staub said, "Pelly, have you lost your mind?" He let his eyes move off of Pelly and saw the crate of cash near the office but saw no sign of the new Ukrainian physicist.

"Where is the scientist?"

"I sent him on his way."

"Is this a money issue, Pelly?"

"A business issue. This whole plan makes no sense from a business perspective." He looked at the FBI agent and said, "I want Lina released, too."

The bound FBI agent said, "Thanks, Pelly."

Staub felt his heart skip a beat. "I get the feeling you knew each other before today."

Pelly just smiled, the fur wrinkling around his mouth.

Staub cut his eyes to his phone on the shelf next to the office window. Was it time to make the call? He didn't think William Floyd had driven far enough away. He had planned to blow the bomb shortly, in hopes of taking out Duarte and anyone else who could identify them. He had given up Nellis Air Force Base as a target. All Staub needed to do was get into Mexico, and from there he could assume the identity of Wilfredo López of Argentina, living quietly off his fortune, content in the knowledge that he had had the final laugh about the U.S. invasion of Panama. He preferred his primary plan of continuing his career with the national police in Panama, but he could live with his backup plan.

Now his concern was Pelly and his ability with a pistol.

"What do you want, Pelly?"

"Release Lina and let me take the cash. We'll call it even."

As Staub considered the offer, secretly proud that his protégé had enough intelligence to think about the cash, he jumped at the sound of several gunshots in close succession.

Staub felt the impact of the bullets in his chest, like a fist, causing him to lose his grip on the small pistol as he fell backward. Somewhere in his head he heard it clink onto the cement floor. It sounded like it echoed.

From the floor he could see that Pelly had not fired. His assistant spun and started to open up at an unseen assailant high up in the shelving, popping off three quick rounds.

Staub heard his wheezing breath and knew the wounds were serious. He fought to keep consciousness and stave off shock.

Where was his phone? He still needed to arm the warhead.

Alex Duarte didn't care if he had killed William Floyd. He ignored the man slumped on the floor of the truck and immediately hit the gas and pulled the Ford truck into the corner of an empty parking lot to some kind of furniture store.

He reached down and found the little SIG-Sauer in Floyd's waistband and pulled it out, tucking it in his own belt.

He checked Floyd's pulse, which was steady, although blood from several lacerations pooled on the floor of the truck.

Duarte jumped out of the truck and raced to the rear. He popped open the tailgate and tried to slide out the open crate but realized it was too heavy. Instead he crawled up into the covered bed of the truck.

He ran his hand up the front of the metal cylinder in the crate, wiping packing straw away as he moved. Near the top of the open crate, he found several wires and a cell phone attached to it. He knew immediately that this was the triggering system. The question was whether they had installed an antitampering device. If this were really a nuclear weapon and they had spent such a large amount for transportation and arming, he doubted they would have overlooked something as simple as a method of keeping someone from disarming the bomb.

He swept away the straw from the small cell phone attached to the device. He could clearly see the open hatch in the bomb and the connection to the phone. He wondered when Staub planned to detonate the bomb.

He backed out of the truck bed, bounded back to the cab and tugged the limp form of William Floyd onto the ground. He dragged him back to the tailgate, ignoring the couple of street people who had taken notice and started to stare at him and the truck.

He sat William Floyd up and checked his eyes. He appeared conscious but dazed. Duarte patted him on the face, not sure exactly what to do. He shouted, "William Floyd, wake up. Wake up." Slapping him a little harder.

The man mumbled something unintelligible, then said, "What? What?"

"What was your target?"

Floyd's eyes settled on Duarte's face. "Nevada. Nellis Air Force Base."

"How does it detonate?"

"Mr. Ortíz has to call. Once he calls and sets the code, it starts the chain reaction."

Duarte looked at him. "Do you really think he was going to let you drive all the way to Nevada?"

Floyd just stared at him.

Then Duarte felt a chill as he heard the phone on the warhead ring.

PELLY TWISTED HIS BODY AT THE SOUND OF THE FIRST SHOT. HE
raised his pistol to acquire the target and saw the muzzle flash up high in
the shelves. He adjusted his sights, saw the figure of a man crouched on
the top shelf and fired three times. The man on the shelves continued to
shoot at Colonel Staub as Pelly sent two more rounds his way.

The man tilted, then tumbled off the top shelf, slamming onto the
cement floor.

Pelly, using his training, continued to scan the area for other threats,
then spun on his heels to check on the colonel's condition. His employer
lay motionless on the floor.

He moved quickly to Lina.

"Are you unharmed?"

She was panting. "Yeah. Who did you shoot?" She couldn't see from
her seated position.

Pelly took another quick glance at the still form of Colonel Staub,
then rushed across the open loading area, past the Audi with Professor
Tuznia's body in the trunk, to the front of the shelves where the gunman
had fallen. He stepped around the shelves, then nudged the body with

his foot. After a second, he crouched and turned the battered head faceup. The DEA agent, Félix Baez, was dead from two gunshots to the chest and a fractured skull from the fall. He also had a days-old bullet wound to his right arm where his sleeve had been torn. Pelly touched the hole in the side of his forearm, wondering where the wound had come from.

He hustled back to Lina. "I am afraid it was your friend Félix."

"You killed him?"

"I did not know who it was, but it doesn't matter. He was going to try and kill me. At least he stopped the colonel."

Lina craned her neck to see the fallen Panamanian cop and druglord.

Pelly looked over, too, and thought his boss might still be breathing, but by the position of the bullet wounds and the blood staining his shirt it didn't matter. He looked at Lina and said, "You'll be found soon."

"What about the bomb?"

"Ike does not have the phone number. It is harmless." He stood up and backed toward the office. "I'm sorry to leave you like this, but I doubt you'd give me a head start otherwise." He leaned down and muscled-up the crate of cash. "If I call you later, would you come help me spend this?"

Lina gave him a look without one of her crooked smiles. "Sure, just give me the address where I can find you."

"A cop to the end. I appreciate that. Perhaps I'll call you in a few months and at least see if you've changed your mind."

She looked over to where Félix had fallen off the shelf. "I can guarantee it would be a waste of your time."

"Goodbye" was all he said, as he turned and quickly made his way to the Chevy Impala, thinking of how he would leave the U.S. He strained under the weight of his crate and knew, however he left, it would be in style.

Colonel Lázaro Staub could hear Pelly's voice, but the words didn't come in clearly in his mind. He lay on the floor of his giant warehouse, wheezing lightly as he tried to maintain consciousness. Now the only thing that mattered was calling the bomb. Even if William Floyd was on the next block, it made no difference. Staub knew he was as good as dead. Even if he survived the gunshot wounds, he would be imprisoned in the U.S. for the rest of his life. He might even get stuck in the same federal facility as Manuel Noriega. That would be ironic. At least by detonating the bomb, he would be exacting the revenge he had lived for.

He tried to sit up, but pain shot through him like a lightning bolt.

"Mierda," he mumbled to himself as he relaxed and wheezed to catch his breath. He turned his head and focused on the glass of the office. He didn't see Pelly, and assumed whoever had shot him was either dead or had fled. Pelly had returned fire immediately and was deadly accurate with his firearms.

His vision seemed to come back into focus as he saw the short set of shelves next to the office. He knew his cell phone was on the third shelf. Revenge was only about fifteen feet away.

Rolling onto his side, then face down, he struggled to his hands and knees. Somehow it was easier to breath from this position. He started to crawl toward the shelf. From his peripheral vision he saw Lina still tied in the chair. She was speaking to him, but he couldn't understand what she was saying. He thought it was gurgling until he realized it was his own gurgling he heard.

His shoulder hurt and his breath came in shorter gasps as he crawled toward his phone, but now he had only one goal: detonate the bomb. He would wipe out the city of Houston. In the bargain he would catch the clever but treacherous Pelly as well as Lina.

After what seemed like an hour, he found himself at the base of the shelving unit. He used his hands to start to lift himself upright. Pulling his feet beneath him, he could stand under his own strength. Breathing was much easier, too.

His hand shook as he reached for the phone.

Now he heard Lina. She was pleading. "Don't do it, Lázaro. Think about the children in the area. Please don't."

He ignored her as his shaking hand picked up the phone. He reached into his pants pocket to recover the phone number provided by the Ukrainian. His vision was blurry, but he could still read the number. His thumb mashed button after button on the small Nextel phone. He double-checked the number before he hit the "send" button.

All was in order. He glanced around the warehouse and saw only Lina in the chair and a body near the main storage shelves. He didn't even care who it was. All evidence of their struggle would be swept clean in a few seconds.

He took a second to consider his life, feeling it leak out of him as he stood with the phone. He said a short prayer, asking God for strength. Now he understood what a Muslim suicide bomber might feel like, defending his country's honor.

Staub hit "send" and put the phone to his ear. He heard one ring. Then another. His heart continued to beat, but he felt it fading. Would he even live to feel the heat of the blast?

The third ring tone came through, and he checked the paper for the code to press in: 1-2-3-4. Now his clouded mind remembered. Then, as he was about to remove the phone from his ear to enter the code, he heard a voice.

"Hello."

He was stunned. "Who is this?" His voice was weak, but he still conveyed his outrage. Had he dialed the wrong number?

The voice said, "This is Alex Duarte of the ATF. How are you, Colonel Staub?"

"Duarte! How did you . . ." Staub would have continued, but he felt his consciousness start to slip as he lost his grip on the shelf and headed for the cement floor like a brick.

He had failed.

57

ALEX DUARTE LISTENED ON THE PHONE HE HAD YANKED OFF THE
nuclear weapon. He could tell the line was open by the sound of the
other phone falling on the ground and what he took to be a few seconds
of heavy breathing or wheezing, but now there was just silence.

Then, away from the phone, he heard Lina shout, "Alex, it's clear
here. I think Staub is dead."

He tried to shout back but knew the tiny phone speaker wouldn't
broadcast his words clearly. He knew he had to get back to her.

Duarte loaded the cowed William Floyd into the cab of the truck and
drove as carefully and defensively as he ever had back toward the warehouse. He felt confident he had disarmed the weapon, but he was going
to have plenty of professionals looking it over in the next hours. The
warehouse sounded safe now, and it provided some cover for the truck.

At the warehouse he shoved William Floyd in front of him and
immediately saw Lina, apparently unharmed, still tied to a chair. He
ran to her and saw Colonel Staub's body near the office and the small

phone on the floor near his hand. The colonel's pistol lay on the ground near Lina. He snatched it up, then started to untie Lina. "Where is Pelly?"

"Gone," she paused and said, "Félix is dead."

"Where? How?"

"He and Pelly shot it out. He's over there." She nodded toward the main shelves.

"Where'd Pelly go?"

"Don't know. He left with a crate of cash."

He finished untying her. "Call for the cavalry, then keep an eye on your Pale Girl," Duarte said, pointing at William Floyd, sitting sullenly on the concrete floor.

He spun and raced to the body of Félix Baez. Before he reached his friend, he could tell he was dead from several major wounds. Duarte checked his pulse still. As he did, he noticed the wound on his arm. The long-sleeved shirt Félix had been wearing covered it. Now the sleeve was ripped, and the wound just below the elbow was exposed. It was a gunshot that had passed through his forearm. Immediately, it occurred to Duarte how he had been wounded. It made everything fall into place.

Félix had killed Cal Linley and Forrest Jessup. Duarte should have figured it out by how the DEA man had taken his informant's death. He had seen the signs when Félix lost control at the Ryder manager in Lafayette. His obsession had gotten the best of him. His questioning had gotten out of hand. Way out of hand. On the night that Duarte had tried to see Forrest Jessup, he had fired at the man's killer. Félix had taken the bullet in the arm and kept running.

To be certain, Duarte used a box cutter on the lowest shelf to cut a small clump of hair from Félix.

As he walked back to Lina and Floyd at the office, he took an envelope from the manager's desk and saved the hair.

He sat down on a plastic chair as if he had lost all energy in his body.

The pickup truck with the weapon was just outside, and the men involved were largely neutralized. This was not his normal day at work. This would be something to tell his father.

THE SCENE AT THE WAREHOUSE HAD REMAINED ALMOST UNDIS-
turbed after more than four hours. Alex Duarte had settled into the
manager's chair inside the office, answering any questions the local
homicide detectives or FBI agents had. Although the FBI agents spoke
mostly to Lina.

The Houston bomb techs did a lot of staring at the weapon after
carefully removing it from the crate, but they were professionals and
admitted they had never even seen a nuclear warhead. They wanted
nothing to do with it.

Duarte had noticed several of the cops make quick phone calls to their
homes insisting that their spouses take the children and start driving.
One burly young man ended the conversation with a loud "Now!"

They had removed Félix and Staub, maybe because they looked like
there might be a chance to revive them. There wasn't. Duarte wondered
how he would handle his friend's involvement in two unsolved homicides. That was for later.

No one had touched the body of the naked female physicist in the
trunk of the Audi. They had photographed her and sketched that part

of the crime scene, but she had apparently looked dead enough and spooked the paramedics that they were waiting for the medical examiner's team, which was tied up on another death in a different part of the city.

William "Ike" Floyd had been sequestered by local FBI agents as soon as they arrived. He sat in a chair surrounded by young, clean-cut agents in the far corner of the warehouse. Lina supervised to ensure no one talked to him and he didn't say anything.

At the open bay door, several Suburbans pulled up, and there was some commotion. By this time, Duarte was too tired to care who was arriving but could tell it was a boss.

Out of the newly arrived crowd he saw Meg Ruley emerge. Even though it was early in the morning and she would've been traveling most the night to get here from New Orleans, she looked like a recruiting poster for the federal government. Tall, attractive, professional, with the perfect combination of business suit and hairstyle. Now she wore an FBI badge clipped to her belt, with a small automatic pistol just behind it. That was an old trick to ensure the local cops knew you were also a cop and not just some administrator here to screw things up.

Duarte could tell by the way she took command and sent one of her Department of Energy representatives over to the bomb that she was not about to screw anything up. He doubted she ever had.

She saw him through the glass and waved like they were old friends. She motioned him out.

As he reached the door, he heard one of the DOE scientists near the trunk of the Audi say, "That's Marise Tuznia."

Meg stopped her march toward Duarte and said to the man. "And she is?"

"Ukrainian physicist. I thought she taught at Rice or somewhere out here."

Duarte remembered the young man in Omaha who said the plan involved "U-cranes."

Meg said, "They must have killed her after she armed the bomb."

Duarte said, "No." Meg and the DOE man stared at him. "Staub killed her before she could do it. Lina saw the man who worked on the warhead."

Meg nodded. "Thanks. That'll help." She walked closer to him, placing a hand around his waist like they were on a stroll.

She said, "I heard that you may be privy to several things that need to be held in the strictest secrecy."

Duarte remained silent.

Meg said, "We'll worry about that later." She looked around the busy open bay. "You did a fine job here. And I don't just mean for an ATF agent. I mean you did a bang-up job and averted a major catastrophe."

He just stared at her.

"I mean it. You did a good job."

"You, too."

"Yeah, but I expect the FBI to do a good job."

"Glad someone does."

She kept her smile, used to dealing with all sorts. He wondered at her exact position in the FBI, because this woman was a boss even if she didn't broadcast it. She looked like a pretty good boss, too.

She handed Duarte an envelope.

"What's this?"

"Just a note."

"A note?"

She smiled, revealing perfect teeth that could have been a predator's if she wanted them to be. "It's a letter saying you are not allowed to speak about this case or the sources used in this case, mainly William Floyd, for any reason."

"You can do that?"

She caressed his face. "You are so cute." She lowered her hand and looked at him, losing all sense of good humor. "I wouldn't want to see that cute face behind bars for violating the terms of that letter." She turned and nodded to Lina, who had been standing close by. She started walking toward them. As Meg walked away, she called out to Duarte, "I'll be in touch. We'll have a drink."

Duarte was impressed with how the woman had carried out her duty even if he didn't agree with the duty itself.

Lina stopped next to him and said, "I am so sorry about Félix."

Duarte nodded.

She kissed his cheek and gave him a quick hug. "Sorry about this whole mess."

He just watched as Lina followed Meg to a waiting FBI Suburban.

In the time since he had first taken a Jeep across the open border into Mexico, then chartered a plane to Argentina, where he had acquired new identification and established a residence, Pelly had tried to adjust to his role as a man of leisure.

He had had time to shave properly, establish several bank accounts in Argentina, Switzerland and Spain.

Now he sat in a small office of a doctor on the southern coast of Spain in a town called Gijón, where he was about to start a form of electrolysis that this doctor claimed would eliminate the need for Pelly to shave.

He had undergone similar treatments in the past, all with little or no effect other than causing the lying doctors to meet a painful end. He thought those days were behind him until he had looked this young doctor in the face and realized that if he had traveled this far for a treatment that this man guaranteed would stop his hair growth and it didn't work, he would kill this man as well. Perhaps right here in his little office in this small tourist town.

Pelly leaned back in the chair, amused by the man's Catalán accent. He sounded a little like Yosemite Sam from the cartoons he had watched as a child. He closed his eyes to relax and thought of Lina. The same thoughts he had had for some time. If he were not more wolflike than manlike, if he had a comfortable estate in Europe and South America, would she consider coming to him? He could dream. He wasn't so foolish to think she could be trusted, but he could dream.

He jumped as the small needle touched his hairy cheek. This had better work, for this doctor's sake.

Alex Duarte sat in the chair in front of Alice Brainard's desk. Having been home almost a week, he had not seen her as much as he wanted. His bosses as well as the DEA had questions, but the Department of Justice had handled most of it, explaining that Duarte was under a court order not to speak of the incident.

Alice, like the helpful champ she was, had run all the DNA tests Duarte had asked her to.

Now she looked serious, her easy smile absent. "I have the results on everything."

Duarte nodded. "I'm listening."

"The sample from the cigarette matched the blood under Gastlin's fingernail."

Duarte let out his breath. "So it was definitely Staub."

"And the hair matched the blood sample you sent me."

Duarte caught himself. He knew that Alice might suspect that the samples came from Félix and that the blood he took from Forrest Jessup's house the night he was murdered meant that in their brief scuffle Duarte had shot his friend in the arm. He didn't want to confirm Alice's suspicions. Félix was being honored as the great DEA agent that he was. Duarte didn't want anything to tarnish that. He had taken the murder of his informant so hard that it had broken him. Gastlin's death had been a burn zone on his soul. But it didn't change the fact that he had given his life to save others.

Duarte finally said, "How hard would it be to just trash all the results?"

"Like they never existed?"

"Yeah. Can you do that?"

"If I beat up on the DNA scientist who developed the samples, yeah, I could forget you ever gave them to me."

He smiled as he found himself leaning across the desk and kissing Alice on the lips. That was a first for him on duty.

That night he waited a few minutes later than usual before arriving for dinner. His brother was already in the main house and he walked around to the front door. As he opened it, he heard his ma say, "Alex, is that you, sweetheart?"

"Yes, Ma."

"Why are you using the front door?"

"I brought a guest. Is that okay, Ma?"

His mother stepped into the formal living room, which had never once been used, and looked out toward the door. She stopped as the smile washed over her face.

Duarte said, "Ma, this is Alice."

His mother started to reach out her hand then took an extra step and embraced the bright blond forensic scientist.

Alice returned the hug.

Duarte heard his father coming down the stairs. Before he even was in sight, he said, "Alex, did you do good work today?"

Duarte didn't hesitate. "Yes, sir. I did good work today."